PAPERBACK

a novel

Russ Barnes

Xynobooks, LLC

To all those who've suffered my writing...

Take risks! You've got to jump off cliffs and build your wings on the way down.

ROBERT BLOCH

FOREWORD

This book is actually a novelization of a screenplay written in the early 2000s. The original screenplay was a too-clever-by-half response to my criticism of a then-popular turn in films. While I liked M. Night Shyamalan's films, I was not impressed with his reliance on gimmick reveals to further his plots.

I decided to write a screenplay that wasn't necessarily a spoof of that emerging genre, but an attempt at a subtle commentary on it. Judging by the screenplay's tepid response from industry decision-makers, I wasn't very successful.

In writing the story out as a novel, I was struck by the flaws in the screenplay. I believe a much more satisfying and interesting story has emerged as a result of my corrections. However, the screenplay remains fascinating as a study in contrasts.

If you'd like to receive a copy of the original screenplay, email readers@xynobooks.com, reference this book's title in the subject line, and the good people there will send you a copy, free of charge.

CHAPTER ONE

Dani pulled the cart as fast as she could. Its wire basket was over-heavy loaded to the very brim. It squeaked and squealed under the weight of two full bags of groceries.

Every time she crossed over a crack or depression in the sidewalk, the poor thing nearly turned on its side. Steering it was a feat of concentration and strength. But Dani managed. Barely.

Already dipping below the office buildings and towers of downtown Chicago, the disappearing sun was quickly being replaced by a gray pallor that crossed the sky clear to the lake. Autumn leaves, blowing in the late afternoon breeze, scraped along the cold concrete and asphalt streets.

The leaves crunched under her feet and the cart's wheels.

Her right arm ached, and she switched pulling arms. She wasn't used to the extra weight.

Stretching her free shoulder for relief from the dull throbbing, Dani also pulled her wind-tangled blond hair out of her face. Her mitten snagged and plucked a few strands of hair out with a pinch.

She mumbled, "Ouch." But it was lost in the noise of the city.

A cold gust caught her beanie, but she seized it with her free hand and pulled it snugly on her head. She bundled up under her thick cardigan and drew her scarf up over her mouth. She pined for the beat up old truck she failed to have taken to the farmer's market.

Winter was on its way.

The red light at the intersection was a short but welcome respite from her burden. Dani caught her breath and flexed her cramping fingers. Her bus stop was across the street, and, there, she could take a proper rest, because buses in Chicago were notoriously late. It promised to be a mixed blessing as the rapidly setting sun chilled the already cold air.

She would have preferred taking the El, but the bus was the more direct way home.

"Sweetheart, take some aspirin when you get a chance. It's the only miracle drug that I know. If it can keep these old bones moving..." the elderly woman standing next to Dani said. She and her little terrier were both bundled like they were prepared to sled the Iditarod.

Dani smiled.

"Thanks. It's this cart. It's just... too full. I really need to learn my lesson. But I never do." Planning for the day, Dani knew she would be buying some of the heavier items offered at the market, just not so many of them. It was her intention to celebrate in style even if she and Shannon really couldn't afford it.

"Take your time with it, honey." The old woman returned Dani's smile.

Dani could not help but study the furrows in the old woman's face.

What had happened in this woman's life that had been etched all over her once-pretty face? Dani wondered what would be written across her face in 40 years.

The traffic light turned green and the walk signal flashed on the opposite side of the street.

The previous corners she crossed had proven tricky, so Dani gingerly guided the cart down the ribbed incline onto the street.

For an instant, the warning sighs of her fellow pedestrians didn't register with Dani. The sighs certainly weren't for her.

"Look out!" the old woman cried. Dani felt several pairs of

hands pull at her. A car flashed by in a streak. Her eyes locked onto the dark silhouette of the driver. He was but a blur, too.

A blast of wind sent her hair into tangles, and fortunately, she fell back into the outstretched arms of some teenaged boys who happened to be walking home from school.

After assuring the concerned citizens at the cross walk that she was whole and healthy, though a little shook up, Dani allowed one of the kids to pull her cart to the bus stop. He insisted, and she thought it was sweet.

Yes, they probably saved her life, but Dani was relieved that none of her protectors except the boy had headed for the same bus stop. Their concern was appreciated, but after the third time being asked how she was, it felt intrusive. When the boy left, she was happy to be alone with her groceries.

Street lamps flickered on as the last of the blue sky darkened. The lights placed in the bus stop awning buzzed to life, and the nearby churning waters of the Great Lake sent one last chilling breeze down the streets..

A fluttering caught Dani's attention. Pigeons would sometimes roost in the awnings. She decided to ignore the bird hoping it would leave her in peace and poop-free. But another gust of wind caused more rustling. Not from the awning, it was coming from under the bench. Slightly fearful of what she might find, she bent over to look.

It was not a dingy, dappled gray bird. It was a well-worn, coverless old paperback book. When the wind caught its pages, it sent them back and forth in a flurry.

Dani stared at it. She hadn't seen one of those—a book that is—in as long as she could remember. All her reading was done on screens and tablets these days.

Another burst of breeze caught the tattered book's pages, and they flitted crisply. It didn't sound much like a bird once she could see what it was.

It was refuse. It clearly belonged in the trash can at the end of the bench, but it would stay where it was. She did not want to get her hands dirty with the detritus that surely covered it from its life on the streets.

Dani pulled herself upright and looked down the street for any signs of the coming bus.

The wind gusted. The pages fluttered again like a song whose faint lyrics stuck in her mind, replaying over and over. It annoyed her.

"Fine," she muttered to herself. She pulled off a mitten—at least it would stay clean—and plucked up the paperback by the edges of a few pages then tossed it into the nearby waste basket.

With her hand unmittened, she reached into her bag. Feeling around for a few seconds, she found a wet-nap. She used it to wipe her fingers clean before she touched her cell phone.

Dani checked the time. *Damn it. Where is this bus?* she thought. If it wasn't there now, it would be another 30 minutes or longer. That was the Chicago mass transit way.

With the temperature dropping minute by minute as the sky grew darker and darker, there was no chance of her food spoiling. But the cold was getting to her. Though she had been prepared with her sweater and mittens, Dani planned on being back at home before sundown.

"Brrr."

Her arms wrapped across her chest, she drew her head down into her chest.

You could play that word game on the phone. She shook her head. No.

She stared at the bricks of the shuttered hardware store across the street. Its name was still written across the building. The lightness of the bricks, once protected from the elements by the sign, betrayed its past with the outlines of the old store name.

She yawned and caught sight of the book out of the corner of her eye. On top of the other trash, the pages of the book waved to and fro in the breeze.

Still singing to her.

Dani was overcome with sorrow. It sat there waiting to be

carted away and buried in the earth for all eternity. She smiled. It was a silly guilt that she had, but she gave in and rescued the ancient paperback from its terrible fate.

She fought another yawn as she pressed the bent pages back into shape. Turning it over in her hands, it was easy to see that the cover was long-ago torn off. There was a little bit of the spine still attached to the binding glue. She could tell that the cover was once yellow in color. There was no title page, author description, copyright page. Only torn edges and fringes remained.

She flipped through the pages looking for a title or name at the top of the pages. She found only page numbers.

How weird, she thought.

Shrugging, Dani opened to Chapter 1.

She read:

...The artist had mastered painting at an early age. Colors. Shapes. Figures. All were mysteries bestowed meaning by his brush. A prodigy. The giver of sight to the blind masses. But his talent was never more apparent than when he took up hammer and chisel. He had a god's gift. A gift that tortured him, and those who bore the brunt of this torture were the ones he should have loved. Loved with a delicate touch only an artist, like himself, possessed. Loved the most above all. Suffering the moods of inky coal and temper of red-hot flame, they continued to love him despite him. Especially his fiancé, who saw in him her everything...

CHAPTER TWO

Shannon stunk. His arms were aching. He was drenched in his own sweat. The fine powder had turned to mud on his skin. White chips flecked throughout his mop of black hair, across his bare chest and over his safety glasses. A mess, he had stripped to his boxers, so he would not soil any more of his clothes.

He didn't want to add to Dani's work.

The sunlight that lit his studio during the day was gone. Dim blue light, from the LED street lamp outside, streamed in from the large window that stretched nearly the length of the room. Shannon preferred the old orange halogen lamps, but the city was busy replacing them with the weaker LED lights. Their dim light made him feel like he was losing his eyesight, but when he stared straight at them, they were surprisingly painful to look at.

"Lights," he barked.

Instantaneously, the room was brilliant with glare of the klieg lights he had installed.

He noticed pieces of rock were scattered everywhere. On their coffee table. In their small kitchen. Plastered over their couch.

Dani was going to kill him when she saw the mess.

It was a ritual they went through every time he started on a new sculpture. She would be pissed that the powder made it into their bed. He would shrug. It was what he did. She got over it—if only until the next sculpture.

Shannon looked for the time on the microwave readout. Dani

had been gone for hours. He knew he didn't have enough time to clean up before she came through their door. But if he made the attempt—if she saw him sweeping up—it might assuage her.

Nah, he thought. She would just find something to nag him about.

Besides, the rock called to him. Taunted him. The granite had been little changed by his month long effort.

He raised his chisel and hammer. *Alright, bastard, you are mine.* Shannon flung at it with all his might. His worries disappeared like smoke. His ears were filled with the clink of metal and the crack of rock.

A dark shape filled his head. It was amorphous. With each strike of his hammer and chisel, it undulated, pulsated, shifted its shape.

This was what he was to sculpt.

The dark, unformed mass was becoming a man. *But who?*

No one had contracted him to create a likeness. This rock was all his, and he didn't know any man who deserved to be set in stone who wasn't already set in stone somewhere.

With every blow of his hammer, it was becoming.

He searched his mind, but it lacked a face.

CHAPTER THREE

The bus rocked back and forth. The motion would have lulled her into a nap, but the metal frame amplified each pothole with a harsh squeak, and shook her awake. The Chicago streets were one giant pothole, the way the bus rattled.

Dani held the book in her hands. She had continued to read it. The coverless tome captured her attention.

"Superior. Next stop," the bus driver called out. Dani snapped back to the world, and she closed the dingy brown pages.

More tired than she thought, Dani yawned, stretched and tried to limber herself up. Her body ached, though.

With her stop fast approaching, she would have to move quickly once the doors opened. This driver, Dani knew, was notorious for stranding pedestrians blocks beyond their stops. She said as loud as she could without yelling, "Driver, next stop, please."

Dani wedged the book between two stuffed bags of groceries in her wire basket.

Again, Dani yawned.

Stop it. You're making yourself tired.

She stretched her arms wide. A familiar passenger, a little boy from the neighborhood, ducked under her arms as he moved towards the rear exit doors.

"Sorry," she said hoping for a smile in return.

"No worries," he said rubbing his sweaty hands over his jeans. He propped himself against the metal post near the double doors, his attention back on a smart phone. His little—almost elegant—black fingers danced across its face.

Dani wheeled her cart next to him, swaying with the slowing bus. She leaned over the boy to get a better vantage of the street outside. Too absorbed to protest that Dani's hair was dangling on his phone, he pressed himself against the rail.

The brakes screeched, and the bus shuddered to a halt. Dani grabbed hold of her cart. Already top-heavy, it was in danger of tipping, again.

"Good night and be careful," she said to the boy as the doors opened.

He absently walked down the steps to the sidewalk. "You, too." She followed him out.

Dani had a smile again for the boy, but he was already a ways down the street.

"Thanks, driver" she said as she pulled the cart down the steps and onto sidewalk.

" 'Night," she heard him say. The rear doors shut behind her.

A whoosh signaled the brakes releasing. The bus creaked forward slowly picking up momentum.

It left a wake of exhaust that momentarily bathed her in warmth and the vague scent of burned natural gas.

She waved away the cloud, but her mittened hand did little to clear the air. She choked down a cough, watching the bus move slowly into shadows of the street. For a moment, and barely a moment, Dani caught the sight of something very strange in the rear window of the receding bus. It was a man or rather the head of a man unnaturally attached to a neck above a suit and tie.

This head was faceless. Where eyes would have been, the eyelids were fused. Where nostrils should be, there was only a flat surface. Where a mouth might have smiled, there were thin lines of lips fused together. She thought she could see jaws and teeth moving underneath the thin, pink skin.

A wave of fear shot up her spine from her loins. She wanted to run, even scream.

Her racing mind rationalized what she had seen as a trick of the light perhaps some weird reflection. But as the bus disappeared into the darkness, the fleshy skull still watched her. Watched without eyes.

Dani was left all alone.

She closed her eyes and slowed her breathing. She willed it, the image—wishing it a figment of her overactive imagination—away. When it was vanquished, she let her eyes open again.

Almost directly across the street from her, Dani could see the second story lights of her and her husband's loft burning. They were on the top floor of the converted 1950s office building. *Shannon must still be working to have all of them still turned on. I wonder what he would think. Probably nothing good. He wouldn't believe me. And he'd be right to think it was nothing. Just my imagination.*

Dani let it go. She let it go like she let the things she hated about her marriage go.

Shannon had a way of making her feel as if she were the most stupid woman on earth, albeit one he found highly desirable in bed.

She was making it work, though.

That was what the stuffed, heavy cart was about. What this meal was about. They would celebrate his triumphs together as if she had anything to do with them.

She knew she had—even if he said otherwise. She did everything for him. When they didn't have any money from his work, they had the money she earned from her part-time job at the dry-cleaners. When he was hungry, she fed him. When he was dirty, she cleaned him. When he was aroused, she sated him.

Dani nodded to herself. She was absolutely right. If it wasn't for her, none of his creations would see the light of day. But living only for him was wasting her away.

And giving you hallucinations, girl.

"Faceless man," Dani said to no one and chuckled.

Checking for traffic—there was none—Dani pulled the cart

across the street to her front door.

CHAPTER FOUR

T he clank of Shannon's chisel on stone resonated off the cold concrete walls, and greeted Dani as she opened the door.

"Shan? Shannon? I'm home," Dani called out into the loft. She let the door shut behind her but it bumped her cart. She caught the cart before it was crushed into the door frame.

Dani sighed, relieved she stopped an impending disaster. She collected herself and tugged the cart's handle, leading it down the makeshift hallway they had created with the backs of two enormous book shelves abutted next to each other length-wise. On the wall opposite, Shannon's early water colors were neatly arrayed at eye level under spotlights that almost blinded her when crossing them at the right angle.

"You won't believe what I was able to get. They're really trying to sell out their excess produce. Anyways, I'll put it on as fast as I can. You must be starving."

Shannon's clanks were all she received in reply.

Emerging into the loft, Dani made way for the kitchen area of the great open room. It was a haphazard collection of what was supposed to be a kitchen—like much of the loft had been assembled, but it worked.

In the middle of the room, his back to her, her husband beat away at the latest slab of rock. She learned the hard way never to break his concentration. If he hadn't replied by now, he wouldn't. Shannon had never hit her, but he was quick to anger and downright mean when he wanted to be. She was not timid, either, but her young husband could scare her. His temper needed release from time to time. She tried not to be the catalyst for that and blamed it on him being an artist.

Dani stripped out of her cold weather clothing, and threw them atop an empty kitchen table chair. She wrenched free the grocery bags from their wire prison, placing them on the counter top. The old novel, once wedged between the bags, fell to the bottom of the cart. She had wrapped it in a plastic bag. She grabbed it from the bottom before collapsing the cart's frame.

Unwrapping it from the bag, Dani held the book between a thumb and index finger touching as little of it as possible. It looked dirtier than it had at the bus stop and in the bus.

How am I going to read it like this?

Dani tossed it at her small desk in the corner of the kitchen area. She missed, and it thunked off the window and fell onto the hardwood floor. She might douse it with disinfectant later. "Ick."

She washed her hands, and noticed flakes of stone were everywhere. She grabbed wet paper towels and wiped off the counters. When he was sculpting, the powder rained over everything. It was nothing new to her, but no less annoying.

"I'll have dinner on the table in 45 minutes. You think you'll be ready?" she called out again risking Shannon's wrath.

With no answer, Dani emptied the contents of the grocery bags into the refrigerator and cupboards. Simultaneously, she threw pots and pans onto the stove.

"We have to be at the Cornerstone by 9:30. They expect us on time, this time!"

Her only answer was the ringing of the hammer and smash of stone.

Dani looked towards the center of the room. For a moment, it looked as if Shannon and the rock were one connected shape. His hammer was a blur. But he and the rock were inseparable,.

It took a moment before she noticed he was naked save for

a mask and goggles. Like everything else in the loft, he was covered, from head to toe, in a thin white dust.

Thankfully, he remembered to drape their sofa and television in muslin and hang plastic sheets from the tops of the two, huge book cases. The plastic was protecting Shannon's early, small sculptures that were displayed there. She hated dusting them. He wouldn't, so she had to, and that he had covered them was a small blessing that would save them an argument.

"If we were early, it would be the first time," she said watching a drop of sweat break the white cake on his skin in a long, winding line down his spine.

Shannon stopped beating against the rock. He pulled the white surgical mask from his mouth and onto his neck. Standing straight, he relaxed his arms letting the hammer and chisel hang at his sides. Raising an arm, he popped the goggles up onto his forehead with his bicep. He caught a whiff of his armpit and recoiled.

Dani laughed softly. *That's what you get,* she thought.

"Is that right?" Shannon mocked his wife and locked eyes with her. He dropped the hammer and chisel onto the muslin-covered futon. He moved into the kitchen. Cornering Dani against the refrigerator, a grin lifted the corners of his mouth. She pressed against the cool metal of the appliance trying to avoid his touch and the mess that came with it. She bit her lip. He smelled worse than expected—like a dusty, sweat-covered teenaged boy.

"I asked you a question," he whispered in her ear, so close that she could feel his warm, musky breath on her skin.

"Just don't touch me, filthy pig," she pleaded while trying to make herself small.

He blocked Dani's potential escape holding both arms out with hands pressed on the refrigerator. His arms were muscular from years of pounding on solid rock. There was no way she could even think about moving them, but, being honest with herself, she really didn't want to. This was the most attention he had paid her in weeks.

"Who do you think you are?" he asked brushing his cheek against hers.

"Who else could I be?" she replied.

His blue-green eyes bored into her brown eyes.

Shannon leaned over leaving Dani with no more wiggle room at all. Inch by inch, he lowered his mouth into hers. She cringed as his powdered, sweaty chest pressed onto her. She pushed at him, but Dani did not take her lips from his.

"Shannon! You're disgusting! It's like wrestling in the mud!" Dani said after pulling her mouth free.

Her face was frosted white.

"You tracked dust all over the place. Look at the mess!"

"I've got dust all over. I mean all over. You want to find out exactly where?"

"Not right now. I have to make our dinner, so we can get ready. We have a date tonight. We need to eat right now."

"Great. I'm starved."

He gently pushed her away from the refrigerator, reached in and grabbed a carton of orange juice. Rebuffed, he switched off.

"Shannon, that's a new—" Before she could finish, the juice was nearly gone, and what hadn't made it into his mouth dribbled down his chest. The mud turned a gooey brown.

"That hit the spot. I'm going to check this invitation of yours. Make sure you got the time right." Shannon walked to Dani's desk.

"If you get that dust—"

"—What dust? Where?" he smiled.

Her pad in his hands, he flipped through electronic pages until he found what he wanted.

"Well, damn. You're right. This sure doesn't leave us with any extra time, wifey-dear."

Dani rolled her eyes and banged around pots and pans. Her hands became as much of a blur as his had been, and all at once, she was fast at work putting their vermicelli to boil and whipping up their cream sauce.

"Do you mind taking a shower now? We have a little time to

spare. Please?"

"What the heck is this, Dani?"

Shannon found the old book flung onto the floor.

"A book."

"Duh. I know it's a book. I'm not a total imbecile. I thought we did all our reading on the pad? Besides, this thing's a tiny disaster area." He dipped his nose towards it, and immediately recoiled. "It smells like pee. Please, tell me you didn't pull it out of a toilet."

"Shower, please."

She shooed him towards the far corner of the loft and their only bathroom. He didn't budge. The old paperback held him fast. Shannon flipped through the pages.

"No cover. No title page. But hey! We do have page numbers. Why would you bring this home? Aren't I enough for you? What can this coverless trash offer you that I can't?"

"It's very good... What I had a chance to read, at least," she said almost embarrassed.

Dani emptied the boiled-soft vermicelli over a strainer. Dodging past her, Shannon grabbed a beer from the refrigerator.

"Let me be the judge of this. I'm the artist around here."

"A very broke artist if we don't make it to the Cornerstone on time," Dani chided.

"Hush, woman. The maestro is summoning the words..."

Shannon crossed into the living area ignoring his unfinished stone. He pulled the muslin drape off the sofa and wrapped it around his shoulders. He caught her watching. With a muslin cape, he became a silent film star—all eyes and over-exaggerated expression.

Shannon's large eyes lowered to the pages of the tattered tome. Clearing his throat and thrusting forward in time to the talkies, he began his performance.

"...He stood at the edge of the crowd. Looking for his

wife. Scanning. Desperate to find her. The only one who could possibly understand and understand him."

Shannon looked up from the book. Dani stirred the cream sauce. She wanted him to continue.

"Keep reading. I like it."

He started again. This time, he eschewed the overacting. He, too, was interested. Shannon was genuinely surprised

" *'Where is she?' His voice a whisper, quaked. Had she left? Embarrassed by him? He knew he was capable of inflicting great pain. Mostly through indifference. Tonight, had she witnessed the worst indifference of all?"*

"What?" Dani asked.

"Hmmm."

"What? Don't stop, Shannon."

She plated up their pasta.

"It is good. But, I gotta shower."

"Keep reading. I told you it was good. Shower later," Dani smiled.

CHAPTER FIVE

Dani watched as her husband flipped the pages in one hand and forked food into his mouth with the other. Her food, however, she kept pushing across the plate in wider and wider circles. She should have been nervous about running late for the reception. Instead, she thought about canceling their plans because of the book.

Because of the book.

She was jealous that he was reading it instead of her.

"How do you like it?" she asked breaking the silence.

She stabbed at a piece of pasta and ate it, out of sheer habit. It irked her that he just ignored her.

"Hello? I'm over here! I asked you a question, Shan."

"Shhh."

He flicked his clean plate into the center of the small table towards her.

"Shhh?"

Dani's temper was rising.

"Hush now, honey. This's the good part."

Sarcasm dripped off her lips, "So, while you're enjoying that 'nasty, ratty old collection of toilet paper scraps,' I'll get right on these dirty dishes."

"That'd be wonderful, babe." This time, he didn't even raise his nose from the book. "It was good, too. The food, that is."

She rose from the table, grabbed both of their plates and moved to the sink. At the sink, Dani scrubbed furiously. Anger building insider her, she absently scalded her hand in the hot water. It was all she could take. Whatever was left of her pleasant demeanor, she dropped entirely.

"The book? The food? Shannon, you're such an ass. Ahhh!"

He lifted his head.

"What's wrong now?"

"Nothing. Nothing at all."

She made short work of the remaining dishes and threw them, carelessly, into the drying rack.

"You need to get dressed."

"Is my little lady mad, because I'm reading her book?" Shannon got up from the table. He dropped the book on the table near their sofa.

Dani ignored him, giving him a taste of his own medicine.

Sidling up behind her, he put his arms around her. His hands folded over her belly. He pressed his groin against her backside.

"Does she need some special attention?"

Breaking his grip, Dani flipped around and faced him.

"Whenever you do this, I just—"

"—Sweetheart, look at me. Look at me." He pulled her face to his. "None of those girls—none of them—meant a thing to me. Who am I with right this moment?"

Tears welled in the corners of her eyes.

"Don't shut me out. Please..."

"Who's my only girl? You. Dani's my only girl. You're my wife."

"We have to get ready to go," Dani said blankly.

" 'Dani? Darling? Light of my life?' Are you going to talk to me, or order me?" Shannon broke out of his best Jack Nicholson impersonation. "Do that Shelley Duvall impression that I love so much."

"I want my book back," she pouted.

"It's mine. I like it," he said.

"Just give my book back. Read it after I'm done. It's a chick book, okay?"

Shannon furrowed his brows.

"What's that supposed to mean?"

"It speaks to me," she stiffened as she said it.

"It speaks to me, too. Must mean I'm a chick." Shannon grabbed the book up off the table. "Here."

He put the book in Dani's hands and closed them around it. "There. All yours, my love."

He pulled Dani into a kiss. She let him for a moment.

"Stop it! Stop it, Shannon. We don't have time." Dani giggled.

"It's usually, 'Don't stop! Don't stop!' Let's do it. A quickie? I need it, and we both know you need it. In the shower. We'll kill two birds with one stone. Then you can scrub my back."

She rolled her eyes. "It's always about you."

"I'll scrub your back!" He dropped his arms, faux defeated. "No, Dani, this is for you."

Shannon pulled her hand to his manhood.

CHAPTER SIX

They'd pulled all the muslin down from their furniture before Shannon went to shower alone. She begged him to get ready while she cleaned up the mess, but he insisted on helping. Now, she probably wouldn't have time to bathe, herself, thanks to him.

Dani curled on the sofa reading the book's yellowed pages,. But every next minute, she nervously checked the time before finally accepting the fact that he'd be ready when he was ready. There was no hurrying him, so she settled in to read.

But Dani could not stop waiting for Shannon.

She had always been somewhat of a tomboy. Playing with and besting her brothers, taming them. It was this man, with a pent-up energy and an immutable, sorrowful anger, like the granite he shaped that she needed to tame, now.

Despite everything, her love of Shannon seemed boundless. Friends, family, even strangers marveled at her limitless stream of affection—all of which—all—flowed towards the socially awkward young man she had met in college. She would say to friends that it was his discomfort among people —that he acted like a wounded, trapped wolf—which drew her to him.

In the years that they had been together, the young woman could never curb his worst habits. He tamed her.

"Dani. Dani!" Shannon's voice awoke her from her thoughts. "Come here for a sec!"

She gathered herself and put the paperback on the end table.

"What's wrong?"

"I can't hear you, babe. Come here." The heavy rush of water from the shower muted his voice.

She walked across the loft leaving blank footsteps in the white powder Shannon had failed to sweep up, and she refused to do. A negative image. On the areas of the cold, gray concrete floor that were clean, she left white positive prints. It was a beautiful mess.

Dani caught the time on their antique, art deco clock. They were going to be very late, and Shannon had no one to blame but himself.

The bathroom door was open, and steam rushed out. Dani, her arms folded, leaned on the jamb.

"We're already way behind schedule."

"Babe, please, I need you to wash the middle of my back. I can't reach it. It feels covered with powder."

His naked body was a blur through the misted glass walls of their shower. She couldn't see his problem area.

"Shannon, c'mon," she whined.

"I know we need to go. Help me out."

"Argh! You're pissing me off."

She slid the shower door open.

"You know tough words turn me on."

He stood before her, naked, the water flowing down his chest.

"I know a lot of other more useful four-letter words—Give me the soap, please."

Saying nothing, he took her hand and pulled her under the water, clothes and all. Their lips found each other. Shannon pulled her wet clothes off. Any protest Dani had left evaporated like steam from the shower. He held her for a long time letting the hot water blanket them.

She gave in, and they loved each other.

CHAPTER SEVEN

Lined with parked cars on both sides, the narrow, lakefront street had barely enough space for a single car to pass. Yet, the parade of taxis and limos managed to snake along.

Further up the street, all traffic stopped in a mass of disembarking people.

Dani held Shannon's hand.

They walked towards that coagulation of people, the Cornerstone building, at the end of a mixed brownstone neighborhood.

Dani looked beyond the honking yellow cabs and the bustle of people to the lake in the distance. A bright orange harvest moon hung over the rippling water, and it seemed to her to be perfectly framed between by the trees and buildings lining the street.

"Would you look at that moon," Shannon said.

He stopped in the middle of the street.

Dani tugged at his arm, but to no avail. He stood like a stone marveling at the moon.

"I noticed. It's beautiful. But Shannon," she said, "no stopping, or we're going to be late!"

"Who cares? They'll wait. They always do. Besides, look at that jewel on the water. I wish I could make something as magnificent!"

She pulled again. He moved, this time, but not because of her, but because of the angry taxi driver swearing at him in some

Eastern European tongue.

He clenched his jaw.

"Ahhh," she tried to deflect his attention away from the yelling, "ignore it. Don't get mad. This is your night, and we need you at your best. It's what keeps us fed. Remember? Let's go, Shan."

She could see Shannon's ire rising, and she stopped tugging at him, and, instead, turned and flipped the taxi driver off. If she hadn't, Dani was sure that he would have erupted and beaten the man bloody. His temper was that bad.

The driver sped off, but was immediately stopped behind the throngs.

Shannon pulled her into his arms and lifted her onto the sidewalk.

"My tough girl... No butterflies tonight, I confess, but I'd rather be home reading my book. Curled up with you. With the light of that moon bathing us from those big windows. Naked. Us, not the moon. Though, technically, it is naked."

He drew her up until their lips met. Well-dressed, high-society patrons of the arts flowed around them annoyed at their public display of affection. It so inconvenienced them.

Lost in his embrace, Dani heard their titters:

"That's the artist and his latest. He's always got some new girl."

She let their gossip go. His lips and searching tongue won her and doused any anger at their jealousy.

He let her down with a nibble on her ear.

"Lots of diamonds and pearls in that crowd. We might be in the money tonight. Still, that book. There's something about it. And you."

She swallowed her smile, but he could see it in the corners of her mouth.

"Really?" she asked. "Me? Or the book. It *really* better be me."

"Yeah, really. Time for a shortcut."

They weren't going to make it through the crowd if they stayed on that particular path.

Shannon pulled her into the small alley between the brick buildings. The orange lights of the alley cast them in sepia tones. They made their way to the rear loading dock for the gallery. It was a short distance away but lined with trash bins and detritus.

"The book or me?" she asked pressing her luck.

He smiled as he knocked on the smallest of the roll-up doors of the receiving bay.

"And?" she asked again.

With the sun almost fully set, the October chill that blew through the alley bit into them both.

"Don't make me choose." A wry smile thinned his lips and narrowed his eyes. "I love you both."

"Stop it, you tease."

"You know me better than that, Dani. I'm no tease." He reached for her ass.

Dani sighed. "Later, Shan. Later. We have to be here tonight for this."

A loud continuous clacking startled them. The sliding door rolled up revealing one of the gallery assistants: a thin, young college student wearing skinny jeans and an emo pompadour. He stood in the empty loading dock holding the door's chain.

"Thanks, Trevor. I really want to make a grand entrance this time. The front door just won't do. Billy will understand."

Trevor was not amused.

Dani and Shannon passed into the building, and the kid let go of the chain. The door dropped with a clunk, clunk, clunk and a thud.

"How about running out and getting me a coffee, Trevor? Dani, you want one?"

Trevor rolled his eyes and walked past them into the gallery proper.

Dance music had just now begun playing and echoed in to them from the main floor.

"Shoo, shoo, little art college wannabe."

Dani smacked Shannon in the arm.

"Be nice to him, Shan. If we didn't have his help—"

"—Little punk. I've been paying whatever it is his salary's been for the last two years. He could show a little respect."

Dani kissed him. It shut him up, and the rise in his pants signaled to Dani that she had successfully distracted him.

"Ahhh. Sorry. You know how I get. Glad-handing turns my stomach," Shannon said.

Raising a finger to his lips, Dani silenced his complaint.

"I love you."

"I needed that." He smiled and let her lead him into the main gallery. "How about I carry you inside?"

"Don't you dare."

CHAPTER EIGHT

That old and cowardly and familiar thing crawled up from the dark, black pit in the back of his mind. It was cold and envious, born from being a talent raised in poverty. It was a thing that he tried to hide and shove back down, but these people, with their greedy eyes and ravenous mouths always seemed to set Shannon's beast afire.

Clichés, every single one of them, Shannon thought as he scanned the crowd.

These were the haughty rich of Chicago and New York dressed in their finest, and yet they milled about in the dark, industrial gallery as stupidly as cattle. These were the people who did worse than spit on him when he was younger. They ignored him.

Now, they recognized him, his true genius.

But, still, he remembered their slights, and it took everything for him to try to swallow them back down into the darker regions of his mind.

These guests wandered about robotically. They were, to a one, smiling, joking and admiring his sculptures, his paintings and his photographs, but did they understand them?

To the credit of the gallery staff, all of his exhibits were placed with an artistry worthy of their intrinsic value, some even suspended, like magic, from wires in the ceiling.

The over-dressed, bovine attendees marveled at them.

"Where do you think Billy put the bar this time?" he asked Dani. He needed vodka, straight.

Dani looked at him accusatorily. It made his stomach churn worse.

"Don't you want to mingle first?" she asked pulling him into her.

A sourness crossed his face, and he coldly broke her embrace. "I need a drink."

Dani tried to hold onto him. She feared one of his angry outbursts.

"We'll grab wine. Talk to a few buyers. It'll be nice. I promise. Sell a few pieces first. Don't talk to them drunk. Please, Shannon."

"I hate these people," he said.

His voice was almost loud enough to hear over the booming techno music. Dani nervously looked at the people nearby for any sign that they heard him. Luckily, they hadn't.

"I know. I know, Shan. But they pay the bills. Be gentle with them."

"They're bloodsuckers. They'd roast me on a spit and eat me if they could."

"No, they love you. They love your work. Don't you see? Look at them. Really look."

"They never cared for me."

"That's over. You're a success now. Their success"

Shannon shoved her away, hard enough to knock her into one of his suspended paintings, and stormed off. Dani, her face ashen, smiled apologetically to the few who had noticed.

She hoped he would be able to maintain control, but it was always the same. The kisses and flirtation were always confident—until they walked into the show. Then, he became Mr. Hyde.

A hand lightly tapped her shoulder. She caught her breath and spun around.

"Well, hello there, Dani, my love."

"Oh, Billy," she started breathing again.

Billy smiled sipping his lemon drop martini. He wore a cardigan with a bright, cyan ascot, decorated with geometric patterns, exploding from the "v" of the sweater. His vintage horn-rimmed glasses made him look like an older Buddy Holly, but the rouge on his cheeks betrayed him and made him look more like a Victorian dandy.

"I see the star of the show's making himself right at home." Billy's lisp became more pronounced after a few drinks. "Honey, next time he pushes you like that, push him back and call the cops."

"Well..." she couldn't find the words. "Sorry, we're late. We couldn't find a cab—"

"—Quite all right. Sales of dear maestro's art seem to do better without him insulting our idle rich guests anyway. I just can't seem to think of why. Do you think we'll get a repeat performance of last fall?"

"We won't." Dani bit her bottom lip not wanting to over-promise.

"I hope we— I mean, I hope we do, minus the police. You know that old trope, 'There's no such thing as bad press?' Well, your husband proved that right. The media coverage did wonders for his value. Enough to more than offset my liability premiums. Next time, though, he gets to fight with my insurance company instead of the boys in blue."

No matter how much he protested for her benefit, Dani knew Billy was Shannon's most reliable supplier for loose women and drugs.

"You're very lucky that I—"

"—No, Billy. You're lucky that you have Shannon. He's made your gallery and you very famous." Dani turned and walked away from Billy and towards a familiar face.

"Mrs. Ashby! It's so very good to see you again. Shannon and I are delighted!"

Rolling his eyes, Billy sipped his drink and waved at Shannon, who was roaming across the room.

Shannon, returning the smile half-heartedly, waved back at his manager.

What the hell is he smiling about? Shannon thought. He turned around to face the bar and pointed at his empty tumbler.

"Another one, please."

The bartender, an older, balding man with a British accent, said, "Right you are, sir."

"Double it. No triple it. Otherwise, I won't make it through the night."

"Triple it is."

The man filled Shannon's glass.

"Just what the doctor ordered."

He raised the glass to his lips and swigged like a thirsty man at a desert oasis. It burned going down, but Shannon wanted it to.

"If I'm not mistaken, sir, this's your night."

"I prefer to think of every night as mine."

"Ah, of course. However, I meant that this show is in your honor. Yes? You are the artist?"

The bartender's deep blue eyes were young behind the aged face. Shannon captured them with a mental photograph and stored them. He would paint them tonight when he returned to the loft.

"Yeah. All this shit's mine."

Shannon chuckled and motioned towards his freshly empty tumbler. The bartender filled it again with a triple shot.

"I'm pleased to be in the company of such a talent. Even one who might not think of himself in those terms. I find it my privilege to work in many galleries and see the best art in the world. Mr. McClarty, I don't see any—uh—shit—hanging in this gallery. If you'll pardon the expression?"

"Pardon? I own it. I see shit all around me. The art and otherwise."

Shannon swept his free arm wide.

"I'm only qualified to speak about art, sir."

The bartender smiled, but his attention focused elsewhere.

"What may I help you with, my good lady?"

A young woman, about an inch taller than Shannon, writhed against the bar. Her burning, wet eyes were red, matching the color of the lipstick on her pursed lips.

Shannon nodded to her.

She ignored him and stared at the bartender.

"I didn't think I'd ever see you at one of my shows."

The artist motioned at his glass. The bartender automatically obliged.

"I'm sorry, do I know you?" she asked.

Shannon smiled.

"Oh, sorry. Not yet."

The woman held out her hand.

"I'm Asia. My date's supposed to get me a drink, but I don't know where he went. I will allow you to get me one."

"Why, thank you, Asia," Shannon turned back to the bartender, "The lady would like a cranberry sour."

"Yes, sir."

"Shannon McClarty."

She took his hand. He caressed her's for a time, before dropping several more dollars in the bartender's tip jar.

"Boyfriend, huh? I didn't know you were dating."

"You aren't in my gossip circle, Shannon."

"Which one is he? You've got me curious," Shannon said leaning with his back to the bar.

Asia grabbed her drink and turned to scan the gallery. She pointed.

"There."

"Looks a little fey if you ask me."

"I'm not asking. Believe me, he's not. Are you jealous?"

Shannon drooped back over the bar.

"Not really."

"I don't believe you."

His studying eyes tightened into slits. He swished the last of his drink in his mouth and swallowed. She was beautiful. A work of art that he would love to count among his own.

CHAPTER NINE

They had her head spinning. The white-haired dowager Mrs. Ashby grabbed Dani and led her to the clucking hens who were the older woman's best friends. The bouffant-styled ladies were gathered under Shannon's largest painting at the show.

"I think his latest work is absolutely breathtaking. For instance —" Ashby spread her arms wide before the painting, "—the lines and angles are the most extraordinary I've seen since... Since oh, you know who. What did you think when you first saw it? It's stunning. Simply stunning."

"I... I... I don't quite remember," Dani said.

She tried to think of her first impression, but the fact was that Shannon never showed her his completed work until it actually made it to the gallery, so her first impression was often right in that moment.

"So vivid. So full of life," one of the women clucked.

"I agree." Dani nodded.

Mrs. Ashby and her mother were so alike, Dani wondered whether they would have gotten on as friends. *They probably would scratch each other's eyes out, but maybe I'll play matchmaker one day*, she thought.

Mrs. Ashby continued, "Yes! So vivid. So full of life! A vibrancy!"

"I think it would look lovely above your fireplace at the Telluride chalet. Your photos of it are quite beautiful. This would be a great compliment," Dani said.

She didn't want to hard sell, but this was an opportunity too good to pass up.

"Dani, darling, you are good. Very good. I'm glad my little pep talk has sunk in since the last showing."

Dani smiled, and the rest of the women tittered happily.

"Good counsel is good counsel, Mrs. Ashby. I take it where I can get it."

"Do call me, Betty, Dani. We're all on a first name basis. It does make the exchange of money all that more pleasant." The older woman reflexively clutched her pearls and looked about the gallery. Her face hardened in frustration. "Where is that husband of yours?"

"Mrs.—Betty, I don't remember where I left him."

"Let's you and I go find him."

Mrs. Ashby grabbed Dani's hand and pulled her through the crowd. The other attendees, well aware of just who Ashby was, granted them immediate right of way.

"I must tell that little, mincing Billy to lower this damned music. Must it always be that pounding beat? It reminds me of chemotherapy! Listen to me, my dear Dani, even though you'll soon have the money to do it, never buy $30,000 shoes. They are not worth it."

Ashby pulled off her high-heels and flung them behind the nearest bar. She was still commandingly tall, as tall as Dani in her heels.

They finally stumbled upon Billy who was busy flirting with the very young catering waiters.

"I brought you a present, Billy," Dani said as politely as she could through the pounding speaker nearby.

"Oh, Mrs. Ashby! I didn't realize you were here! So glad to see you!"

Ashby dragged the both of them away from the music and into the foyer near the coat-check. Several late arrivals were handing over their coats, and Ashby shooed them into the gallery.

Turning to Billy, she said, "Knock off the glad-handing, Billy. I asked you last time to keep the music pleasant. Not this incessant migraine-inducing beat."

He rolled his eyes in surprise. "Mrs. Ashby! I didn't know you had such a broad musical knowledge."

Dani tried to hide her smile, but the two "queens" were evenly matched in cattiness and made for a few easy chuckles.

Clearly annoyed at Billy's intransigence, Mrs. Ashby continued, "Having two prep school sons, you learn a few unexpected things. Now, knock off the sycophantic drivel. Dani's already doing your job. She's on the verge of selling a centerpiece for at least six figures—"

"—You're buying?" Billy nearly dropped his martini glass.

"You are?" Dani echoed him, her eyebrows raised.

"Of course, I am. Don't act so surprised, Dani. I have a new decorating season to begin. Now, the key is that my girlfriends will naturally want to keep up."

"We were looking for Shan, Billy. He should be thanking Mrs. Ash—Betty—right now," Dani said.

"You know, I haven't seen him in a while. He was hanging out at the bar last I saw. But that was half an hour ago. I'm his gallery manager not his babysitter."

"Find him. I need his advice on color schemes. I won't have my pieces lost in a sea of bad taste." Mrs. Ashby recovered her aplomb and beckoned for champagne from a passing waiter. "Billy, find him, please."

He tsked and marched away, head held high. He hated to be an errand boy.

"I'll make it quick," he said over his shoulder.

Ashby added before he was out of earshot, "My God, to think that man would dare squeal with the amount of commission he's about to pocket. Once we move you and Shannon to Manhattan, we can rethink the arrangement if his attitude fails to improve."

CHAPTER TEN

E *rrand boy? Is that what I've become?* he thought.
Billy whispered under his breath, though he knew no one could hear him with the music blasting, "Selfish prick. Where the hell are you? That old bag wants to spend big money on you, and you're nowhere to be found."

He downed the remainder of his lastest martini and smacked the glass down on a passing silver tray. Billy nearly shattered the glass which would have sent the poor waiter's burden crashing to the floor.

He was so mad, insulted, really.

He hated being ordered around in his own gallery. He wanted to push through the crowd and knock them on their silk-covered asses. Instead, Billy slid through their number like a fish swimming through a forest of sargasso.

A hunter.

Billy had last seen Shannon at the bar, but as he approached it, Shannon was nowhere to be seen.

"Would you like another, sir? What was it? Appletini?" the bartender asked with his prim Brit accent, a bar shaker pumping in his hands.

"Later, Jeeves. I'm looking for McClarty. Have you seen him?"

The bartender opened his mouth, but stopped, swallowing his words, considering.

"Out with it. I don't have time," Billy said.

"He went up the stairs to the offices." The bartender put

another martini glass on the bar and poured. "He wasn't alone."

He hated this part of being Shannon's manager more than any other thing.

"Oh, hell."

The gallery owner stiffened his spine and pulled his jacket straight. He started for the stairs that were in the rear of the room.

The bartender called out, "Sir, you forgot your glass."

"Keep it cold. I'll need it."

It took him little time to ascend to the top of the stairs. Below him, the attendees moved amongst the spotlighted art. The women's diamonds glinted in the light.

His office, a conference room and a storage closet were on this level of the gallery. Both his office and the conference room were dark, but their doors were open. They had no occupants. That left the closet. Its door was closed. He tiptoed toward it. Even with the blaring music, the closer he got, the louder the occupants of the closet became, as he suspected.

Billy pressed his ear against the door, and he heard, "You still like that? You like that? I bet you do. Better than your boyfriend."

It was Shannon, all right.

Moans of pleasure answered Shannon.

Billy froze, poised to knock. Then, he noticed someone behind him. He turned.

"I'm sorry. The party's downstairs. This area's off limits."

He smiled but was unsure if he could be seen.

The man stepped towards Billy. He was a knot of tension, and every move he made seemed to wind him tighter.

"Sounds like the real show's up here."

Billy panicked. He spread himself out over the door.

"I think you may be mistaken!"

The moaning stopped. They must've heard Billy's frantic voice above the music.

Billy could see the handsome young man more clearly now. His fists were clenched, and the muscles of his jaws were flexing. Out of the corner of his eyes, Billy could see the gallery crowd looking up at them.

"He comes out with my girlfriend, and I will fuck him up."

Billy stammered, "Go downstairs, please. You aren't meant to be in the private areas!"

"Fuck you."

The storage closet door cracked open, and Asia peeked out. Her makeup smeared, her hair tangled, she saw her boyfriend and pulled the door, but her boyfriend easily threw Billy to the floor and grabbed the door before she could close it.

Asia screamed, "Stop it! Stop it!"

"Hey!"

Shannon threw open the door. He threw a wide right that connected with the boyfriend's temple. The young man stumbled backward. He regained his footing and threw several jabs at Shannon's chest.

"No, damn it! Stop!" Asia hissed, trying to get between them, but Billy pulled her away.

The boyfriend grabbed Shannon's arm and twisted him against the second floor railing. Shannon pulled away as the young man tried to throw several more punches. Shannon landed a good gut shot that sent the young man teetering at the edge of the stairs.

A fearful buzz rose in the crowd even above the loud music.

The boyfriend grabbed for the rail, lost his balance, and then careened down the steps thudding on each one.

"No!" Asia cried.

Billy still held her.

"Oh, my God."

Shannon reached out much too late.

As if on cue, the music abruptly stopped. Whispers of "call the cops" flitted around the gallery.

Asia sprung away from Billy and rushed past Shannon down the steps. She tried to help her boyfriend up, but he pushed her away as he stood.

Several men and one woman from the crowd, presumably doctors given the class of the attendees, attempted to keep him on the floor. He would have none of it.

"Baby, baby! Let me help you. He means nothing to me!"

Asia followed her boyfriend. He pushed through the crowd ignoring her pleas.

The crowd turned its attention upward to Shannon and Billy. The collective gaze burned on the artist's face. He knew he was growing red.

He tried to look away, but his eyes found Dani in the sea of faces. She looked more disappointed than he had ever seen. The heiress, Bettina Ashby, standing next to her, shook her head in disgust.

Dani lowered her face. Ashby grabbed her and moved toward the gallery exits in consensus with the crowd.

The shame Shannon felt kept him from calling out to Dani, but he could not keep his eyes from her. That was when he noticed. The man walking behind Dani—following her—was somehow wrong.

Wearing a plain black suit, black tie and white shirt, he could have been anybody. He wasn't out of place. He wasn't in place. *What the hell?*

Then, he knew. The man who was almost touching his wife had no face. His bald head had no hair and no ears. He was a blur of pink flesh.

"Dani!" he called out, but she was gone, out the door, and with her, so was the faceless man.

Shannon turned to Billy.

"Did you see that?"

"Of course I saw it, you son of a bitch. Look what you've done. For your sake, I hope the police don't show, because I don't have any money to bail you out."

"Billy! The man right next to Dani. Did you see him?"

"Schmuck, go home. I'll pick up the pieces tomorrow."

Billy slammed the door of his office in his face.

Shannon bolted down the stairs after Dani.

CHAPTER ELEVEN

Her arms were crossed against the bitterly cold air blowing off the lake. The dark of night had lowered the temperature from the chilliness of the evening. But her arms could, just as easily, have been crossed against the pounding humiliation she suffered moments before by the actions of her husband.

She touched her temple in reflex. It was something she did whenever she and Shannon fought. There was still a bump where her skull had cracked underneath her scalp.

Dani and Shannon's relationship had always been fraught with pain for her. The worst of it had been that time; the only time Shannon had hit her. It was an open-handed slap. Her eye blackened, and the socket fractured.

Immediately, Shannon regretted it. He tried to comfort her, but the damage had been done.

To save herself the embarrassment of a police report, Dani eschewed a trip to the emergency room. In those days, they lived next to a nurse practitioner who was kind enough and discrete enough—after thoroughly vetting Dani's story and Shannon's contrition—to treat her eye and check for signs of concussion.

Days had passed before Dani spoke a word to him. It was months before she let him touch her again. To his credit, he took every amount of punishment on bended knee. The mistress, whom he was seeing at the time, and who had sparked the fight which resulted in Dani's injury, was dropped, and his dalliances were curtailed.

Why? she asked herself. *After everything,* why *am I still with him?*

Tonight, she reckoned, *was the last straw.*

She couldn't go back. The physical pain, she could endure. But every act of adultery, without even considering the very public act he perpetrated this night, broke her heart.

"Dani! Dani!" She heard him call, but she kept walking away. "Dani, please! I'm sorry!"

"Leave her alone, you fool," Mrs. Ashby said to Shannon sternly.

The grand dame stopped him on the sidewalk outside the gallery.

"You've done enough damage. The only reason I'm considering buying any of your work is because of that girl. If she were me, you'd find yourself neutered and homeless after tonight."

At the intersection, Dani looked over her shoulder. Shannon was shrinking away from Ashby who easily slipped into her limousine and slammed the door shut in his face.

Shannon raised his head and caught her looking. He ran towards her.

"Dani!"

"Miss, it looks like you need a ride."

Dani was surprised to find a cab waiting for her at the corner. The cabbie, who had a kind face that reminded her of her grandfather, propped open the passenger side door of his cab and smiled.

She got in, and it sped off.

Dani, through the rear window, watched Shannon reach the corner only to see him fade away in the red taillights.

CHAPTER TWELVE

Slumped over with his hands on his knees, Shannon choked on his breath. He hadn't run so fast since high school gym class, and that was too long ago.

Lifting himself upright, steam plumes rose from his mouth.

The sweat generated from his run was now, itself, running cold down his back.

To add to his misery, the bitter air off the lake was freezing him. His overcoat was back in the gallery. He didn't feel like walking back to face Billy. Without a coat of some kind, the night air would not be pleasant.

He checked his hind pocket. His wallet was there. It would take $20 to catch a cab home. He flipped through the bills. He had enough.

I must be hallucinating. Too much sex drive can do that. He pushed visions of the faceless man out of his mind.

It was stupid.

Silly.

"What the fuck did you do, dumb-ass?" Shannon asked himself out loud.

He pulled the bills out and slid his wallet back where it belonged.

"Couldn't keep it in your pants! Just once! Christ!"

He looked up and down North Broadway. Traffic was curiously light, and there were no cabs in sight.

She must have cursed me. Shit, he thought.

He walked south towards Belmont where he would cut over west and catch the El at Sheffield. Shannon hated the train, but it would take him almost to his doorstep. He was a big enough guy that most of the criminal element that used Chicago's transit system would leave him alone.

Shannon stuffed his hands in his pockets and held his arms rigid against his sides. Moving briskly down the sidewalk, he looked cartoonish but began to warm up some.

He noticed a group of homeless men gathering across the street at the Treasure Island grocery store. The store was holding one of its charity drive giveaways in the parking lot.

He crossed the street deciding to indulge some nostalgia.

As a young artist new to the city, this Treasure Island, and its philanthropic customers, was one of the first places he sought help in a hard, hard world. He worked there as a bagger then cashier for a year, so he could put a foundation down to allow him to go to college.

Before attending the School of the Art Institute of Chicago, Shannon lived his entire life in Beardstown, Illinois. Dominated by a meat-packing plant, Beardstown had a single street that led right to the plant doors. His dad, when he deigned to be a father, worked there. Shannon, himself, worked there as teenager and then as an unhappy young man. What he loved about Chicago most was that it didn't smell anything like boiling entrails, blood and manure, though it did smell like shit in some quarters.

In the corner of the Treasure Island parking lot furthest from the store, men, dirtied and roughened by life on the streets, gathered around blue, plastic barrels filled with assorted clothes, shoes and other necessities for life on the streets. At the end of the line of barrels, a buffet of coffee, clam chowder and sandwiches was laid out.

The food smelled great.

"You look like you could use a coat," one of the homeless men said. He handed Shannon a tattered, old overcoat. It had a few holes, but otherwise looked warm.

"Thanks."

He took the coat and slipped it on. It smelled musty and moldy, but the instant, covering warmth was welcomed.

"No prob. Wasn't really mine. But I'll take the thanks anyway. Nice to get someone who'll talk to me... Your lip's bleeding, by the way." The man strung his sentences together, manically.

"Wha–Oh," Shannon felt his lip. He examined the blood on the tips of his fingers when he pulled them away. "Guess you're right. Hmmm."

"Gonna make it hard to eat some chowder."

Shannon smiled, but it sent a pinch up his lip. "Oww. I'll make do."

He half-heartedly sorted through the remaining barrels before moving to the food, his real target. The coat-giver shadowed him much to Shannon's dismay.

At the buffet, they both grabbed hot apple cider and a bowl of steaming chowder.

"There's room at the end of those tables. I'll kick those two out. They just sittin' there. They been long finished. Don't need to be sittin' "

Coat-giver was as good as his word sending the stragglers packing. Shannon looked for another alternative, but with no space available, he had to sit with the man if he wanted to eat now.

"What you doing out in this cold without no coat anyway?" coat-giver asked.

The white chowder had splattered across the man's beard.

"I lost it," Shannon answered between dollops of the delicious creamy broth. "Had a little trouble this evening."

"I got trouble every evening. You know, I heard a lot about you."

A year ago, Shannon would have been surprised by anyone knowing his name, much less a homeless stranger. But since his first showing with Billy had become an international affair, that this man knew who he was didn't faze him.

"You aren't the only one, my man. One little indiscretion, and I make the front pages. It sucks. It really does."

" 'Specially when you got a guy like that talking about you."
Coat-giver chuckled and pointed towards the farthest table.

"Hmm," Shannon mumbled, his mouth full.

He lazily followed the point of the man's finger.

"He's been askin' about you all day. Made me look out for you. He wants to talk to you. Real funny dude. He missing his face." Coat-giver snorted and beat the table as if he'd let loose with the greatest punch line of all time.

It was the second time that evening fear shot right up his spine. Since glancing that faceless visage at the party, Shannon dismissed the whole thing as a trick of the light. Now, seeing the man sitting under the orange glow of a lamp, in his black overcoat and his gloved fingers crossed, and absolutely no discernible features on his head—even hair, there was no dismissing him.

He was real.

And waiting.

"He wants to talk. You better head on over. Can't explain how he can do it without lips, but you can hear him just the same. Go on now. He ain't lookin' to hurt you… yet," coat-giver said followed by his biggest smile.

Shannon rose to his feet. His face, now stony, hid his fear and panic. They churned underneath his silence. He cleared his throat and stepped away from of the picnic-style table.

The artist studied the faceless man.

He has to have a face. You can't see anything, because that light's too bright. He's bald, yes. But faceless, no. Don't be stupid. You've got to be hallucinating, Shannon.

Feigning a step towards the table where the man sat, motionless, Shannon instead bolted!

He ran past his coat-giving friend and out of the parking lot. When he was near the old church behind the grocery store, Shannon could still hear coat-giver's howling laughter.

CHAPTER THIRTEEN

Wiping tears from her eyes, Dani took a quick inventory of the clothes arrayed on the bed. It was a week's worth, and it was all she could carry with only one large suitcase to her name.

Her mother would welcome her with open arms. Dani knew it. All she had to do was call.

But she steeled herself. She was not yet prepared to admit defeat, and worse yet, of stupidity to her mother, who, having suffered through three philandering husbands of her own, did not offer her daughter much in the way of a shoulder to cry on. Be that as it was, Carol Strauss was always a safe harbor in rough seas to her daughter. It came with a price, but it was safety.

No more threats. This was it. Dani wanted separation.

Book the flight. Then, call Mom, she thought.

Dani shut each dresser drawer except the top. On her tiptoes, she pulled back the right rear corner of the top drawer. The wood there was split ever so slightly, and when she discovered the defect, she instantly knew what she could use it for. Between her index and middle finger, she expertly freed the only credit card she had solely in her name. It was her rainy day fund.

Shannon had made sure that it rained that night.

A few swipes on her tablet, and Dani picked the earliest flight out of Midway to Orlando.

As if on cue, the front door of their loft slammed open. She heard Shannon bolt inside.

"Dani! Dani, baby! I have to tell you something. I saw something incredible tonight. Unbelievable really."

She rose from the bed, tossing the tablet onto a pillow. She grabbed the empty suitcase and snapped it open. Dani tossed her pile of clothes into it.

Rounding the partition that separated their bedroom from the rest of the loft, Shannon stopped. "What... What are you doing?"

She ignored him.

"Come on, babe."

He moved to her with his arms open. He tried to embrace her. Dani shrugged him off with a simple, "Don't."

"Honey, you can't be mad."

"Honey someone else. Honey that bitch you were fucking in front of the whole riverfront."

Shannon smiled, pleadingly.

"I thought we had an understanding."

"You thought wrong."

She pressed against the suitcase, and it snapped shut.

"As long as it wasn't in your face, you were good with it. Right?"

Dani stopped and stared at him, her face curled with disbelief.

"Can you hear what you're saying? Do you know how stupid you sound?"

He moved to her again.

"You know how I am. I can't help myself."

"I was stupid to ever marry you."

"Don't say that, Dani. I love you."

"Is that so?"

She lifted the full suitcase up off the bed.

"Yes. With all my heart."

His arms were still open, hoping for her to rush into them.

"But you don't, Shannon. You only love yourself."

"No, I promise."

He knew he had lost the battle.

"Your word is no good with me anymore. I'm sorry. I wasted

your time.

Dani pushed past him and set the suitcase down in the loft proper.

"Dani, what can I do?"

"You've already done everything. Do me a favor. Sleep on the sofa. My flight leaves in the morning. I can't bear to look at you, much less for you to touch me."

"Please!" he cried out like a little boy. "Don't leave me! Don't leave me alone."

CHAPTER FOURTEEN

The pounding didn't stop until 3 a.m. The clang and ping of the hammer and chisel still echoed in Dani's head. She had wanted to run out of the bedroom and scream at the top of her lungs at Shannon. She didn't, because she thought he probably wanted her to—that he would have taken it as a victory.

He wasn't winning any more fights as far as she was concerned. There were to be no more fights at all.

Her flight to Florida that morning would be freedom.

Maybe not, she thought remembering that her mother was not exactly the easiest person to live with.

Dani would be staying with her mother for the first time since graduating college. As a six-year-old, Dani chose to live with her father after a nasty divorce. Carol never really forgave her daughter, even when Bill Strauss died in a car accident that left Dani in her care less than a year later.

Dani pulled the comforter tightly around her body. The bed was especially cold without Shannon beside her.

It fell on her.

The sorrow.

She didn't want to cry. Only moments ago, her anger had made her strong, but that was fleeting. The tears came anyway.

With her face held into her pillows, Dani hoped that Shannon could not hear her sobbing.

White powder covered his nearly naked body from head to toe. Streaks of powder mud, from his sweat, flowed down his body like melting candle wax.

Shannon didn't give a shit that he stunk. He was mad. Not at Dani.

At himself.

Pushing the hammer and chisel off the sofa, he sank into its soft cushions and pulled the quilt that usually covered it over him. He was still warm from working, but the open space of the loft was cold, and the cold had started to attack.

He reached for the lamp above his head, but stopped before twisting it off. He wasn't all that tired. The gallery fight and the faceless man had left him amped, and the paperback, waiting underneath the end table, invited him.

It nearly fell apart when he picked it up, pages dropping from the binding. He scooped them up and carefully put them back into place.

Shannon found his bookmark. His dog-ear was a fresh compared to the brown paper and weather stains.

He began to read.

The words transported Shannon a world away.

CHAPTER FIFTEEN

Sunshine crept slowly into the loft. Their building faced east, and the large glass windows, which were covered—to little dampening effect—with sheer white drapes, let the warm, orange light stream in. During the summer, it got very hot, but in the fall and winter, the sunlight was welcome. It cut through the cold air as it now did this morning.

Shannon was still wide awake.

Reading.

Nearly halfway through its brittle pages, he pulled another dog-ear before carefully folding the paperback closed.

As he stood, he pulled the quilt over his body. The stone dust still caked on his body billowed into the cold air. He waved his hand to clear it, but it was too much. Some of the dust was caught in his inhale.

Shannon choked back a cough by clearing his throat. He stifled the noise. He didn't want to warn Dani of his coming.

At the door of their bedroom, he watched his wife sleep.

Alone.

Though the comforter covered Dani nearly to her cheeks, he could see that her arms were extended into the depression where his body normally lay. Her golden hair was tangled across the pillows, and her face was as beautiful as ever and serene in sleep.

Shannon remembered the first time he had seen her this way. They had spent three weeks dating without so much as a good night's kiss–but not without lack of trying on his part. He knew that she was wary of becoming attached to an "artist" with no real job prospects.

Yet, he persisted.

She was pretty, but he had bedded women whose faces and bodies sold magazines. Dani's attraction was more than skin deep. Their dates felt like going home. There was a relaxation that he had never felt with any other person. Whatever it was that he was missing, she had it, and there was the tantalizing promise that she would give it to him.

On their last date, the date that led to his proposal of marriage, his latest work had been turned down for a small new artists' exhibition in New York City. He had almost called her to tell her the date was off, but he didn't feel like drowning his sorrows by himself. She could see the disappointment in his eyes immediately. She said nothing and still held his hand. She may never have let his hand go that night–through dinner and a movie that he didn't have enough money to pay for. He asked her to marry him as he walked her back to her brownstone.

Dani never answered with her voice, but she did with her lips. They made love for the first time then, and he held her in his arms the entire night as she slept.

His wife was still that woman.

Slowly, he slid onto the bed.

"Dani," he whispered. "Dani, honey. Wake up…"

She yawned and pulled the pillow over her eyes.

"Go away."

"Come on, Dani. This's important."

"Go away." Though still groggy, her voice had force behind it.

"No. I need to tell you."

Dani threw the pillow off her face.

"Tell me what? I'm tired of fake apologies."

"I'm not apologizing. It's about the book."

Shannon threw the quilt onto the floor and slipped under the comforter with Dani. She pulled away.

"You want to talk about a book? Get away from me."

"No."

He edged closer to her until her only options were to fall or get out of bed.

"The book you found. It's—"

"To hell with some stupid book! I'm going to get on a plane this morning, and once I'm in Florida, I'm shopping for a divorce attorney."

"Yeah." He ignored her threat.

"What is wrong with you, Shannon?"

"Absolutely nothing. I couldn't sleep, so I read. I'm halfway through it. I can't... I can't explain it."

"Start talking sense before I call the cops and file for a restraining order."

He held the tattered book near her.

"Get that nasty thing away from me and out of this bed!"

"This book. This book is about us. About me."

"For God's sake. Fine... I'll play. What are you talking about?"

Dani pushed Shannon away.

"Ugh. What are we doing?"

"Dani, are you listening? It's literally about you and me."

"Do you mind if I use this for my divorce filing? You're certifiable."

She rose.

"Wait, Dani! Listen. Listen to this—"

Shannon scoured the pages finally finding his bookmark.

Dani harrumphed but did not leave the bed. She waited.

"Listen, Dani. For me. Listen..."

Shannon began to read.

" 'He stood at the edge of the crowd, looking for his wife. Scanning. Desperate to find her. The only one who could possibly understand. 'Where is she?' his voice, a whisper, quaked. Had she left? Embarrassed by him yet again? He knew he was capable of inflicting great pain, and had done so. Mostly through indifference. Tonight, had she witnessed the worst indifference of all? Her love for him

*could not bear more infidelity especially one so public.
One where he was so celebrated...'*

"Doesn't that ring a bell?"

"So, the main character's a louse just like you? The book got that right."

Dani got out of bed and moved to the dresser.

"No, wait!" Shannon reached out for her. "How far did you get in the book? Didn't you read about how I was a child prodigy? I mean, this is me!"

Pulling on her jeans, Dani shook her head.

"It's not about you. It couldn't be. It's fiction. It's a novel!"

"No, babe, there are specifics."

Dani folded her arms against her chest.

"Does your ego know any bounds?"

She shook her head looking at him with disgust. Finally, she moved with purpose. Dani pulled her shoes, then shirt on.

"What about the descriptions of your love for me? About how we've been together through everything."

"If I ever needed proof of just how self-absorbed you are, I have it now... Will you listen to yourself? You sound ridiculous," she said.

"How can you say that? You loved this book!"

"I barely read a page of it before you took it from me. That book is just a book. It is a ratty old paperback. It is not about me, my life or you. It is the product of a mind that neither one of us know or have known."

Shannon jumped from the bed and moved to Dani.

"Do you think I'm imagining this?"

"I think you imagine a lot of things, Shannon. Including how much I love you."

"You think this is some ploy to keep you from leaving?"

"You'd have to do much better than this. My flight leaves in two hours. I'm calling a cab, and I am getting the hell out of here."

"No! Let me take you. At least, let me do that. Please..."

There were tears in his eyes, and Dani, as hardened as her heart had become, could not resist that.

CHAPTER SIXTEEN

Only the rattles of Shannon's old Ford pickup and the rush of air around the old truck kept the awkwardness in the cabin from being completely silent. Traffic was light on the highway toward Midway Airport, and Shannon was not pleased that they were making better time than he had anticipated. Dani's flight was an hour and a half away, but he desperately wanted the intermediate time to convince her to stay.

Shannon fished out the old paperback from the crease in the ripped up old bench seat where he had jammed it.

"Read it aloud from page 135. I marked it."

He pressed the book against her folded hands with one hand still on the wheel. She refused to take it from him.

"Mind the road, Shannon," she said.

"C'mon, read it."

She plucked the book from his hands and put it in her lap. She did not open it.

He snickered, "Are you going to read it?"

"No. Get me to the airport on time and in one piece, please. Maybe I'll take it with me on the plane."

"Whoa. That book stays with me."

"Finder's keeper's."

"Look, I only want to see if it has us driving to the airport. Page 135, Dani."

"Are we on this again? It's a novel, not a travelogue."

Shannon reached over and tried to grab at the book, but Dani held it from him. The truck veered as he, leaning and reaching, pulled the steering wheel inward. Cars in the adjacent lanes honked and sped past but avoided any collision.

"Pay attention, Shannon! Drive! You can't read it right now!"

"Then you do it. Please. It's all I'm asking."

Dani sighed. "I should be at the airport by now... Okay."

Relenting, she flitted through the pages. Several flew out, but she gathered them up and put them back in place. At page 135, where Shannon's dog-ear waited, she started to read silently. A moment later and she bit her lip.

"Huh."

Shannon, every next second, looked from the road, studying to see if his wife had found what he wanted her to find. Dani continued to slowly scan the pages.

"What?"

"Nothing," she said.

"It's gotta be something. Enough to keep you from giving me more sass."

"Don't be such an ass, Shannon."

"Ah-ha! I'm right. Right?"

"Maybe."

"Yes," he shouted. "I knew it. It has us driving to the airport this very minute. The entire scenario down to us fighting over you reading the damn thing."

Dani rolled her eyes.

"Who cares? How many books have been written about couples driving to the airport?"

"Only one I can think of. That one you have in your hands. Right there. Read it."

"Shannon, don't we have more important things to deal with than some book and a coincidence?"

He relaxed into the seat putting both hands on the wheel. He was getting nowhere like this. It didn't make sense to keep badgering his wife, whom he had only just cheated on. It was time to change tactics. Shannon softened, letting his sadness show.

"When will you be coming home?"

Dani avoided his gaze. The green highway sign signaled the airport off ramp was coming up. She began to gather her bags.

"Terminal one. Drop me off. I'd prefer if you didn't wait with me."

He shook his head.

"Please, can't I make sure you get on the plane safely?"

"Not today, Shan."

Shannon nearly sideswiped a passing car as he changed lanes without looking.

"Watch the road!" Dani screamed.

The driver honked, and Shannon beat the old Ford's horn in reply.

"A week? Two weeks? What?"

"Shannon, you promised to get me there in one piece."

"We're fine. I could drive this route in my sleep... Are you planning to come home at all?"

"I need to figure out if what we have is a home. At this moment, I don't know."

Dani watched Shannon grind his jaws. She knew his anger was boiling just below the surface. The truck's rusty squeaks and the roar of the tires grew louder as the silence between them returned. Dani began to relax. Then, the truck swerved hard, sending Dani into the passenger side door!

Barely getting control of the truck, Shannon maneuvered towards the farthest right lane.

"What's wrong? Shannon?! Oh, my God."

Nearly out of breath, he gasped. "Did you see him?!"

"Who? What are you talking about?"

"Where did he go?!" Shannon looked frantically out the windows. Suddenly, the truck lurched forward as he stomped on the gas pedal. Dani was rocked back into the seat.

"I can't handle this! Get yourself together!"

"I need to show you."

"Show me what? All you need to do is get me to the goddamn

airport. That's it!"

Dani braced herself holding onto the door handle and dashboard, as the truck raced down the highway. From her window, the other cars on the highway seemed to stand still as they raced past.

Shannon held his head low studying the road and traffic in front of him.

"The guy in the car next to us. You didn't see him? You didn't notice?! He had no face. Do you hear me? He had no face!"

Dani looked at her husband. Her mouth fell open, and she shook her head.

"You've finally done it, Shannon. You've cracked. Are you doing this to make me miss my flight?"

He pulled his gaze from the highway ahead and caught her eyes.

His eyes burned.

"Dani, he didn't have a face. I swear it. I saw him last night at the gallery, and then in the Treasure Island parking lot. I thought it was some drunken hallucination, but I was wrong. He's following me."

"A man with no face? You couldn't see his face? It was burned? What are you saying? I don't understand."

"It was like one of my busts. Before I carve out the face. Just a... a... head."

"Jesus, Shannon, listen to yourself.'"

"Dani, I know what I saw!"

"Pull over," was all Dani could muster.

It was clear that he believed what he said, and that, in her mind, meant that he could be losing his. But hadn't she seen something similar? She let that thought evaporate into her panic.

"What? On the highway?"

"Do it! Pull over. Right now!" she screamed.

"If I don't catch him, you won't believe me!"

"I don't believe you, and I won't believe you. How can I? It's the most ridiculous thing I've heard you say since you told me you loved me. I can't figure you out, Shannon. Are you trying to kill me?"

His mouth moved, but before he said any more, he thought better of it. Shannon focused all his attention on driving. It took several minutes for him to navigate the truck over onto the shoulder.

They sat silently as eighteen wheelers and assorted cars whizzed past them. With each passing, the truck shook violently and rattled.

In the center of the bench seat between them, the paperback waited. As gusts of cold air blasted into the truck from the rushing traffic, its pages lifted ever so slightly.

Dani picked it up and flipped through the front pages looking for any signs of a title. The title page was gone, as it had been before, but one tiny sliver of the copyright page was still glued to the binding.

What was left read: © Paul Steale

She tapped the name into the note app on her smartphone.

Shannon opened the driver's side door and hopped out, slamming it shut with a loud clunk. Dani watched as the wind whipped around her husband, sending his hair flying every which way.

He moved in front of the truck away from the onrushing cars and up the side of the berm. It was brown with dying grass. Kicking the dirt, his head hung low. He was thinking. He sat on the ground and plucked a blade of Bermuda grass that was still somewhat green. He stuck it in his mouth and twirled it with his tongue.

Inside the truck, Dani kept checking the time on her phone fearing she had less than an hour to grab her boarding pass. She didn't know how to ask him to get up and get going. Too much had been said that made so little sense to her, and that had shut down their communication.

Much more, she was too scared to open the door and step out.

After five minutes that seemed like an hour, Shannon hopped up, spat the grass out and marched back to the truck.

Inside with a slam, his face grew flushed as the warm air inside the truck met his cold cheeks. He cranked the engine on.

As they pulled out onto the highway, he said, "I want you to believe me. I know what I saw."

Dani closed her eyes searching her thoughts. She had nothing to say, and anything she did say would come from the swirl of emotions in the pit of her stomach. Until she was well enough away from him, those things were best left unsaid.

"Talk to me, please."

But she kept quiet.

As he pulled off the highway at the airport exit, her hazel eyes opened and found him. It was a welcome surprise to him.

"Thank you for getting me here. I've got to rush. My flight's leaving soon. I'll be lucky to get my boarding pass."

Shannon pulled the truck curbside at her terminal as fast as he could. Jumping out, he untied then hefted Dani's bags out of the pickup bed.

"You want me to carry these for you?"

She pulled her backpack on.

"No."

"Let me sit with you while you wait. Please."

Dani turned away from him. She could not bear to see him and his sad eyes. Slipping her hand underneath his, she took the carry-on bag from his fingers.

"Go home, Shan. It'll be easier for both of us."

With that, she walked into the terminal, disappearing behind the sliding doors and leaving him standing.

Alone.

CHAPTER SEVENTEEN

He thought better of throwing the book across the cold loft. Had he done so, it would have disintegrated. In his mind's eye, he imagined the hundreds of brown and tattered pages floating down over the concrete floor like leaves from a wintering tree.

Instead, he dropped the paperback onto the end table near the sofa. Dani had forgotten it on the old truck's bench seat, her threat to take it with her unfulfilled.

Shannon scanned his empty home.

In the far corner of the loft, where he had kept Dani from putting up curtains, his unfinished canvasses mocked him. He walked to his set of stretchers. On his easel he found his box cutter. His bad "children" would be punished. He slid the knife out on the box cutter and slashed through each canvas, some nearly finished and imminently sellable.

He hated that he considered these his children. It burned that he had no real ones, nothing in the flesh, to commemorate his love for her.

His screams echoed off the concrete walls.

Shannon turned to the unfinished sculpture. The hottest hatred he saved for it.

Moving towards the stone, he removed his clothes. His bare feet pressed against the dust and shards from his work of the day before. Several slivers pinched his skin likely slicing through the soles of his feet, but he absorbed the pain.

If he had cleaned up like Dani had wanted, he would not be

bleeding. Then again, he never did what she wanted. He was paying for that now.

He wanted to pay.

He slid his safety goggles on.

With chisel and hammer in hand, Shannon's first strike was electricity shooting from his body. The blow was so hard that shards sprayed and bounced off the glass windows. The clank rang in his ears.

He beat at the rock again.

And again.

And again.

And again.

CHAPTER EIGHTEEN

Staring out window of the airliner, Dani tried forcing his face from her mind. When she told him to leave at the terminal, she knew it broke his heart. She saw it written on his face. Whether he could see through her, she didn't know, but with those her last words, she left Shannon very little opportunity to think otherwise. She had turned away, as fast as she could, and rushed inside the airport.

Never looking back.

But he had shattered her heart the night before.

How did I ever become so cruel? she asked herself.

Despite what he had done–repeatedly–she loved him still. It burned in her heart. After everything, sitting alone on her way to Florida in the jet, Dani desperately wanted to be back with him.

If he's started to see things... Faceless people... He needs me. What are you doing, Dani?

She felt tears gathering in the corners of her eyes.

Turning from the bright sunshine streaming through the window, the roar of the engines and the slicing of the jet's superstructure through the air became the focus of her senses. She allowed the sounds to fill her mind. They soothed her, and she closed her eyes.

"Excuse me, miss."

Startled, Dani opened her eyes. The youngest stewardess—the one who reminded Dani of her baby sister off at college across the continent—stood over her, the beverage cart behind her.

"I'm sorry to wake you. Thought you might like something to drink."

"Thanks... Uh... Yeah, I'll take a soda."

The stewardess snapped open an aluminum can and poured soda and ice into a cup.

Handing it to Dani, she said, "Sweetheart, if you need anything else. Let me know."

All Dani could do was smile, wanly.

She sipped her soda and leaned back into her seat. The cool liquid comforted her. Closing her eyes again, the words from that musty old book kept rolling back into her mind:

Her love for the man seemed boundless.

But her love for Shannon hadn't been. She left him completely alone when he proclaimed his need for her the most. She thought it absurd that he could believe that the old tome was telling the story of his life, his present. It couldn't even accurately reflect how she felt.

Her love... Her love... My love... I am a liar, she thought. *Not the book.*

I should have thrown the damn thing in the trash when I found it.

A book with no cover.

No name to claim it.

CHAPTER NINETEEN

With a TV dinner in hand hot from the microwave, Shannon walked across the open space of the loft. He scattered the largest pieces of stone out of his way with kicks, but it was still tough going on his bare feet. The stone he was sculpting was now whittled down by hundreds of pounds over the last several days—all of which, he thought with a hint of sarcasm, still waited to be swept off the cold concrete floor.

And he had no plans to do it any time soon.

A full beard covered his face. It was itchy and reminded him that there were other things that he had failed to take care of, as well.

Like sleep.

It had been days or rather, nights, since he had had any.

He dropped the dinner on the coffee table, and some of the turkey meat and gravy splashed onto the glass.

"Oh, fuck."

He picked the slices up. They burnt his fingers before he plopped them back into the black tray.

"Owww. Shit."

He sucked on the tips of his fingers.

I'm no good without her.

Grabbing the TV remote, Shannon clicked the flat-screen on. He hoped that whatever terrible crap that passed for daytime programming would distract him and stop his pining.

He scanned the channels. Finally, disgusted at the dearth of entertainment, he shut it off.

"Local news. Talk shows. Shopping shows. Movies I've seen thousands of times," he recited to no one. "How do they continue like this?"

Out of the corner of his eye, Shannon caught the yellow fringed stack of pages. They were under the lamp on the end table where he left it.

"Oh, no. You don't. I will not be reading you. You're lucky I don't throw you into the sink and light you on fire. Just shut up over there."

Instead, he picked up his phone, and ordered, "Call Dani."

The pleasant phone voice replied, "Calling Dani's cell."

Shannon closed his eyes and wished, *Please, baby, pick up. Talk to me. I miss you so much.*

He listened to the phone ring and ring and ring.

Finally, her voice mail message answered.

"Hi, it's Dani. Leave a message!"

Shannon hung up.

CHAPTER TWENTY

NYC was an unexpected detour. A detour from what–other than her normal life as of late–Dani did not know.

Carol Strause, her mother, decided they needed to spend several days shopping their cares away in the most expensive stores on the east coast. It helped that after her four divorces she was an alimony multimillionaire and could whisk away on a whim.

Dani left her mother on 47th Street between Fifth and Sixth Avenues, the famous Diamond District, looking at jewelry. They were to meet later for dinner at Delmonico's.

She had taken the subway across the water to Prospect Heights to find a book.

The book.

Dani would be satisfied to find any book with his name, Paul Steale, on it. The name from that ragged, old paperback.

Having searched Amazon and the Internet for him, Dani could find nothing but the easy writings of his publicity representatives. Wikipedia housed a quick paragraph or two about the elusive Mr. Steale, a many-time bestseller. It basically summed up his class schedule at City College of New York. Everything the man had written prior to his college tenure was out of print or halfway across the world and would take eons to have shipped to her—in this day and age where everything was available at your fingertips!

None of the man's books were e-books, yet. There were rumors, though, that he had been working on a much anticipated new novel.

At this point, she wanted to have anything he wrote in her hands if only to prove that he actually wrote a book. She had little hope to find the one that so prominently figured into her life and her husband's, however.

So, she had braved the underground towards the biggest bookstore she could find.

The store smelled like moldy towels. It was not quite pungent, but the stink did curl her nose. Other patrons, mostly greying, lonely-looking men in their 40s, shuffled amongst the 10 foot tall aisles. Inside the aisles, on loose tables, on any counter top, there were stacks and stacks of dingy, old books piled everywhere.

It took her a moment to figure out the layout. Placed at various heights throughout the store were placards marked "Ab, Ac, Ba" and such—alphabetized not by title or subject but by author last name.

Thank God for small miracles, she thought.

It meant that she only had to find the "St" section. The title of the book—which was a mystery to her—was something she need not know. She counted nine aisles in and found "Ss." A quick walk up and to the right, past several ogling middle-aged men, she found it. Dani pulled her finger across the book spines whispering the last names as she read them.

A smile formed across her lips. As she crossed to "Stanley," her phone rang and rang loudly. It was practically the only thing audible in the whole store and interrupted the abnormally quiet patrons.

Shaking her head, she fished the phone out of her purse. She had meant to silence it but forgot. It was Shannon calling.

Two more rings and a loud, "Shhh" from somewhere in the store forced her to answer instead of turning her phone off.

Holding the phone up to her ear, she said, "Shannon, I can't really talk right now."

"Come home, baby. Please." He sounded pathetic and small, and she knew that wasn't a magic trick of her cell phone.

"Really, Shan, I can't talk. I'm in a bookstore. People are staring. You know? Talk-free zone."

"Don't make me beg."

"You already are. Let me call you in a few minutes. I've almost found the book."

"What book?!" The little speaker nearly burst.

"Jesus. No screaming. You know. The book."

"I knew you believed me."

"Look, gotta go. I'll call. Bye."

She held the off button until the phone shut down.

"Sorry," she said to anyone who was listening.

Flashing a smile, she deflected the clerk who approached with a scold at the ready.

"It's off," she nodded with her apology.

The corpulent, middle-aged man in faded denim pants and a tweed jacket turned to return to his duties at the counter, and Dani realized she yet had a use for him. "Oh, sir. Sir? Since you're here, would you be so kind? I need to find an author."

The man cleared his throat. "Uh. Sure. Who you lookin' for?"

"Great. Thanks. His name's Paul Steale. I have this paperback that I just can't seem to find in good condition."

Squeezing past Dani, the clerk smoothed his wild hair down and straightened his glasses on his nose. She tried to avoid his breath which even in whiffs was strong with coffee and pipe tobacco.

"Right. Paul Steale. One of my favorites, actually. At least, his later work, when he was still good."

He pointed along the spines. Suddenly, Steale's name was everywhere accompanying titles like *Song Bird*, *Filthy Hands*, *Dark Ages*, *Second Story Guys*, *AKA*, *The Harbinger*, *Saugus*, *A Legacy*, *Love Child*. But nothing that struck her close to describing what she had read from the old, tattered novel.

He handed her one of the hardbound books. She flipped it over and got her first look at Steale. His portrait was taken atop one of the towers of the World Trade Center much before 9/11. Even in a turtleneck, the black man was handsome, and she imagined he would still be.

She frowned. "The problem is that I don't know the title of the book. Maybe I could tell you about it, and you could tell me which one it is."

"That could be a problem. I'm pretty current with him, but he did write some obscure stuff in his early years. Give it a shot."

"It's about an artist and his wife. A young couple. Does that ring any bells?"

The clerk cocked his head in disbelief.

"You sure it was Steale?"

"Pretty sure. The paperback was missing it's title page and table of contents, but I did manage to pull out the remnants of the copyright notice with his name."

"You have it with you?"

Dani shook her head.

"No, I lost it. I was right in the middle of it, and I really enjoyed it. I'd like to finish."

"C'mon back to the desk." He pushed past her again and waved her forward. "We need to check with someone who's an expert. A real Steale fan."

Climbing over piles of books on the stairs leading to the second, smaller floor, surprisingly Dani had trouble keeping up with the large man. She attributed it to him knowing his way around rather than his athletic ability.

Overlooking the aisles and aisles of books, the information desk was situated in the far corner of the floor. The man dialed an ancient rotary phone. He knocked off a stack of books from a chair and motioned to her. "Have a seat."

"Thanks, but that's not necessary."

"—It's such a mess—Oh, hold on—Hi, Tom, it's Ken. Down in fiction. I have a customer here looking for a Steale book, and I know you're an expert. Right?..." Ken turned to Dani and asked, "It was about an artist?"

"A troubled artist. He cheats on his wife... His beautiful wife," she smiled eagerly.

"Did you catch that? Yeah, an artist... That's what I was thinking. Sounds like Steale's early stuff. Out of print. Yeah. Before the bestsellers. Hey, I didn't say sellout I said bestseller." He chuckled. "Okay. But you can't remember the title? Right. Got it. Thanks." He hung up the phone with a frown. "Well..."

Dani's eagerness dampened. "You don't have it?"

"No. Probably not. Tom can't think of the title. He thinks he read it, but it was too many years ago to count. And if you know Tom that was a very long time ago. It's most likely out of print. I'm afraid, and it's rare enough that even we wouldn't have it." Blowing a raspberry, she sighed.

"There is hope. He said that you might find it at the public library. Main branch. They have everything."

"What time do they close?" she asked excited once more.

"Five or six. I think." He pulled back the sleeve of his jacket and checked his watch. "You could make it. If you caught the subway very soon."

Dani checked her cell time and dashed towards the stairs.

"Thanks so much for your help."

"My pleasure. We don't get many young people here anymore. Much less pretty ones. Hope you find it. But come back. We've got other good ones here!"

Shushes came from everywhere, and the man shrunk in his chair.

"Oops."

Dani poked her head back up above the second floor landing.

"Does he still live in the city?"

"Who? Steale?"

The clerk lightly banged his cherry wood pipe on the desk.

"Yeah."

"I believe so. Upper East Side. Rich. Rich. Rich. That's what just one bestseller will do for you."

"Thanks!"

She was gone.

CHAPTER
TWENTY ONE

Once Dani hung up on him, the pain and guilt from the previous week's parting rushed back to Shannon. He nearly threw his cell against one of the windows that created the panorama, but he thought better of destroying $500 worth of electronics.

The paperback wasn't so lucky.

It mocked him from its perch on the end table. How an inanimate object managed to mock him, he didn't know, but it did.

No sooner than he had gently set his phone down, the old book was flung across the room. It remained intact through its flight until it exploded against the concrete wall dividing the glass plates.

Pages rained everywhere.

Instantly regretting his throw, Shannon dropped to his hands and knees.

"Come here, little pages," he sniggered. "Come out. Come out. Wherever you are... Christ, Shannon, you're an idiot. Note to self: when you get the urge to throw shit, don't."

It took him about an hour, but he picked up every page and sorted them by their page numbers. It was easy work but tedious. When he found a clump of pages still stuck together, he felt like he'd won the lottery.

"By God, Dani does this to you. Are you going to let her continue to do this? Better question: Are you going to lose her?"

It was a question whose answer he did not know.

Staring at the stack of pages that was once a bound book, Shannon decided to read.

He may not know the answer, but he could find it.

The book knew.

CHAPTER
TWENTY TWO

A massive building, whose Roman columns buttressed its three arches, the Stephen A. Schwarzman branch of the New York Public Library abutted the copse of trees known as Bryant Park. Guarding the steps that led to its main doors were two stately, giant stone lions that Dani had seen in countless movies.

Instead of waiting one more stop, she had rushed off the subway at Grand Central Terminal and ran the rest of the way up 42nd Street. She hooked a harried left at Fifth Avenue. Fumbling with her phone and dodging pedestrians along the way, she wished she had gotten off as planned. Time, running too, was short.

At the library, tourists were loitering on the steps snapping photos. Dani snaked to and fro through the throng.

It was 20 till six. She did an instant calculation.

Twenty minutes which means 5 minutes to find the guy I need. Ten minutes to explain the situation and find the book. Shit. I need to apply for a library card. And they'll probably want to close the doors and kick everyone out five minutes before official closing time. Girl, you might not make it.

Her phone rang as she reached the glass entrance. It was her mother.

"Arghh." Dani stopped and caught her breath. "Yes, Mother."

"My dear, what time is it?" It wasn't hard to imagine

her mother's frown from the tone in her voice. "We have reservations."

"I'm at the library in mid-Manhattan. I have to get a book."

"I was just in mid-town! A book?! From a library?! Can't you just buy the stupid thing online? You know how much meals at this restaurant cost?"

Every minute she was not inside was a minute closer to her losing the book. Dani had to move and move fast.

"Mom, please. I will be there in less than an hour. This place closes very soon."

"Just get here. I suppose I can use this as an excuse to have as many cocktails as I want. Goodbye, dear."

Her mother hung up, and Dani rushed through the door. Immediately, the metal detectors went off, and the security guards waved her over.

"Geezus."

Dani handed over her bag to be X-ray scanned.

"Sorry, guys, I know it's late."

The head security guard, a middle-aged Asian man with greying temples, smiled.

"Hey, we love readers here. We have to be safe is all."

Moving through the metal detector again, Dani was clear, and the guard handed her bag back to her.

"Thanks. Uhhh, sir, where's the information desk?"

"It's all the way at the end of the room."

Dani raised her chin. It was the first time she looked past the entrance and into the enormous hall.

The walls were lined with shelves and shelves of books above which light from the fading day streamed in through giant, arched windows. The floor was populated with rows and rows of reading desks.

Dani was relieved when she saw there were still about a hundred of people reading at the desks which meant the librarians weren't terribly strict with time.

Quickly moving down the center aisle, Dani cut towards the wooden archway where the librarians waited to serve patrons.

The librarians' archway was fabulously decorated, located at the very end of the great room. The whole building was a marvel from the marble tiled floor to the ornate, wood-carved, frescoed ceiling and the beautiful chandeliers.

The young woman, though, had no time to appreciate her surroundings properly. In buildings like these, she could get used to reading more.

"Hi. I was hoping to find someone to help me," Dani breathlessly said to the seated librarian who seemed to be the least busy.

The woman, though, was not shy in hiding her annoyance at being interrupted.

"The computer search terminals are available right over there." Dani tried her best supplicating grin.

"I'm pretty sure this requires a real live person to help me."

"The computers work just fine, miss."

The woman gave a curt smile and turned her back on Dani.

This is New York City, Dani, she reminded herself.

"I'm sure they do. Anyway, miss, I need to ask about a book. And I can't simply look it up."

"This is a library. We have books."

Again, the woman, after adjusting her glasses, turned away from Dani.

"I know who the author is, and what the story is about. But that's about it. Do you or anyone here know anything about the author Paul Steale and his books?"

The librarian scoffed and turned up her nose.

"That washed-up hack?"

"I don't know enough about him to describe him that way." Dani was a bit taken aback.

"Obviously."

"Can you, please, point me to someone who can help?"

Finally, the woman relented, "Why, certainly. We even have librarians with poor taste among us."

The woman grabbed the phone and dialed two digits.

"Front desk, Jim. It's ten to closing. Do you have time to speak to someone about a Steale book... She doesn't know the title. Thus, she wishes to speak to an expert... Are you sure?"

She rolled her contempt-filled eyes with no effort to hide from Dani.

"I'll send her back. But I'm leaving at the usual time for your information. I will not wait for you or her."

The librarian slammed down the phone. She pointed towards the door in the carved facade. "Meet me over there."

Dani gathered up her bag and phone and moved as fast as she could to the door. She heard the deadbolt slide unlocked. The door cracked, and the librarian stuck her head out to make sure no one else was following.

"Okay. This is highly irregular. No patrons are allowed back here, but I'm past caring at this point in the evening. We close in eight minutes. He's all the way in the back through the shelves." Letting Dani through the door, the woman waved her off. "Hurry."

Dani was dazed. The main floor of the library was cavernous, but these rows of bookshelves occupied the same space that the reading desks did on the opposite side of the divide. There were hundreds of thousands of books in front of her.

Again from behind, Dani heard, "Hurry!"

Okay. Through the shelves.

Unsure, she pulled her bag close to her and moved through the nearest aisle. Despite the early evening sunlight still streaming through the giant windows, inside the aisles it was surprisingly dark. Dani nearly stumbled into a cart, overfilled with books waiting to be sorted. It was the first of several that she needed to navigate around until reaching the long table at the end of the room.

She wouldn't have known he was there if it hadn't been for his humming. The stacks of books on the table were nearly as tall as she was, and certainly taller than him.

As she crossed the table end and peeked behind the stacks, Dani waved with a weak smile at the bookish little black man who lovingly appraised the spine of a hardbound book. If a person could be the opposite of another, he was nearly the opposite of the clerk at the bookstore in every way.

"Hello, young lady," he said in a high and precise voice. He smiled invitingly. "I see you've caused quite a stir with Imelda up front. Don't you mind about her. Come. Sit."

He motioned at a chair beside him.

"Thanks so much for talking to me. It's really rather stupid, but it's one of those things that gnaws at you."

"Books have a magical way of doing that to people. So, what is it that you need?"

Dani took him up on the invitation and sat.

"Paul Steale. I have a ratty old paperback of his back in Chicago that I cannot for the life of me find its title. I'd love to get a better copy, and—"

"—Steale's been a personal favorite of mine since the '70s. We were classmates at Bronx Community College. It's incredible really. I've followed his career from the bongo drumming coffee houses of Alphabet City to the high-rises of Park Avenue. All the way up the New York Times' Bestseller List."

"That's funny, because I never heard of him until this paperback fell into my lap. It just looked so lonely on the ground. I felt sorry for it. I didn't have the heart to throw it into the trash. Strange. Don't you think?"

Dani was still at eye level with the man. She thought his eyes were kind and sincere.

"Oh, no. Not at all. A good book deserves a loving home. Like friends and family."

He gathered up one of her hands in his two very small ones.

"Some people see books as the only real family they have. By the way, my name's James Herald. What's yours?"

"Dani."

"Dani, such a pleasure. Now, tell me about this book."

Her cell interrupted. It was her turn to roll her eyes in exasperation. She dug the device out of her bag.

"I'm so sorry. I should have turned it off. It's probably my mother. We have a dinner date. But, it's a book about a sculptor

_—"

She was wrong. The screen was filled with Shannon's face. Herald's smile dissipated once he saw the face.

Maybe, he thinks he has a chance with me. Weird, Dani thought noting the man's reaction to seeing Shannon on her phone.

"Normally, we don't allow those things, but go ahead and answer it. We're pretty much closed. And nobody out there," he pointed towards the outer library, "can hear you in here."

"Thanks."

Dani stepped away from James who turned to tend to his books.

"Hello?" she said.

CHAPTER TWENTY THREE

L ounging on the sofa with the pieced together paperback laying across his chest, Shannon waved his phone in the air. Reception was tricky for some reason in the loft. He fished for the best position to hold the phone to find a good signal.

His bluetooth earpiece was in his ear, and its blue LED flashed intermittently.

"Hey, babe!" He was genuinely surprised that Dani had answered this time. "I thought I'd get your voicemail again. You don't know how happy I am to hear your real voice. I mean, your live voice."

"Shannon."

Uh-oh, he thought. There was a sternness in her voice that spoke volumes without having to actually say anything.

"Look, I'm busy right now. I told you that."

Shannon sat up barely catching the newly reconstituted book from falling onto the floor. Had it, it might've split into several hundred pieces once more.

"Of course, you did," he tried to sound conciliatory and reasonable. "I forgot. I'm sorry. Forget I called. Uh… Give me a ring later?"

"Oh, stop it, Shan. Please, I have to go."

"Okay. Call me, though. It's important."

"Stop the guilt trip. Bye."

She killed the connection.

"You want time. You got it," he said pulling the earpiece off and laying back down on the sofa. Shannon rifled through the loose pages until he found his place in the book.

"Yeah. Here it is. What does the book say for me to do? What does the book say? Wife won't talk on the phone. Yep."

What he hadn't had a chance to tell Dani was that he called her as a test. In the book, the wife refused to talk to the artist, and Dani had just proven that she would also not talk to him. His theory was falling into place.

Now, Shannon read to find out what came next.

> During the course of their marriage, it was the arguments that kept them engaged. This night. This last argument drove him further away. He left their lonely apartment and sought the company of women. Any would do. As long as they were beautiful.

This was a passage he was not eager to prove right, because it would prove her right. Shannon sat up and folded the book closed. He grabbed the duct tape that lay on the end table next to the sofa. He pulled a carefully measured strip off the roll and tore it with his teeth. He pressed it down the length of the paperback's spine. *Not a bad job. It should hold.*

He flipped it open, and the book fanned without a page falling loose.

The young artist thought about reading some more, but his eyes hurt.

Across the cold room, the unfinished sculpture sat, untouched. As tired as his eyes were, Shannon's arms and back ached from pounding against the stone the day before.

His mind started to race. Alternating emotions about Dani flashed on the edges of his mind. He remembered his and Billy's conversation—or rather—one-sided screaming fit. Billy had lost more orders for his work today.

"Word is spreading about how much of a cad you really are," Billy chided him on the phone that morning. "If it wasn't for my reputation and the fact that you do have an undeniable talent, you'd be done for."

"Don't give up on me. I'm learning my lessons. I can't lose my wife and my career. I can't. Stick with me, Bill. Stick with me. I'll make it up to everyone."

The call ended without a firm declaration of loyalty, but it wasn't a declaration of separation, either. It was a small victory for Shannon in a sea of recent defeats. He had promised himself long ago that he would never beg for anything in his life, but he begged Billy, and he was begging Dani.

"Fuck!"

He stood up and stretched. His joints popped putting an end to even the smallest thought of going back to work on the stone.

At the giant plate glass window, Shannon scanned the street below.

It was growing dark.

Very little traffic, car or otherwise, passed by. Further south, the Chicago skyline lit up the night.

He pulled himself away. If he stared much longer, he would be the proverbial moth drawn to the city's flame. There was always trouble to get into there.

Go take a sleeping pill. Get some sleep.

If he closed his eyes in sleep, he hoped the temptation would be silenced.

CHAPTER TWENTY FOUR

"**I**'m sorry. I shut it off, James. Otherwise, I'm afraid the next call will be my mom. She's waiting for me at Delmonico's."

Dani followed the little man up the aisle against the wall. The sun was down now, so the only light in the giant room came from the ornate hanging lights. They were beautiful but wholly inadequate. It was still very dark.

He must have owl eyes, she thought. Where she squinted in the darkness, he glided along the book spines effortlessly.

"I don't pass out demerits, so you won't be getting any. Librarians are not elementary school teachers. Thus we lack their punitive habits." He let out a small giggle before stopping abruptly.

Dani stumbled into his back.

"Oh, sorry… Again."

"Aha! We made it. Maybe you can recognize one of the paperbacks we have collected here."

He pulled out one at random. Studying it like it was worth its weight in gold, he opened it, and the old tome's spine cracked loudly.

The little librarian raised an eyebrow.

"These are old. Like me. But, the stories they tell, create worlds."

"You've read all of them?"

Dani scanned the section–nearly three rows on the shelve–all with books printed with the name Steale.

"To my knowledge, yes."

"Shit. Err... wow."

"...Let me think. A young artist? Sculptor mainly. Gosh. I can't recall." He faced Dani. "Why is this book so important again?"

Dani swallowed her initial answer and considered whether to tell him her real reason. If she did, he would likely throw her out thinking she was crazy, leaving her without any answers. A moment passed, and she decided. Her father always said that honesty was the best policy, even though it was something he never practiced—something her mother never let her forget.

"It's nonsense really," she said after the pause.

"Why spend so much valuable time on a goose chase?"

"You're going to think I'm an idiot or worse."

Smiling, the little librarian placed his hand over his heart.

"I promise. I won't."

"You wanted an answer." She smiled but her embarrassment was apparent. "My husband—the one who just called—we're separated—just a few days so far. I can't take his cheating anymore."

He nodded.

"Understandable."

"This time it was very public... I know he loves me. I know it. He's an artist. A sculptor, in fact. Like in the book I'm trying to find. To me, the book was just a book. But to him, it was a little like reading our lives in action. He saw that it was mirroring my life, his life. But I know it's only an illusion. Something he wants to believe. Anyway, he started reading it. Now, he swears by the damn book. Ridiculous. A book written 20, 30 years ago. About him?!"

"Your life sounds exciting. Like quite a good plot for a book. Errr... I mean, the plot for a good one. You understand."

She shook her head stopping the man from continuing his train of thought.

"Oh, it gets better! He's been seeing a faceless man running around. Following him."

"Perhaps, he needs to see—"

A door slammed somewhere in the vicinity of the entrance to that room. The sound echoed off the high ceilings making the room sound cavernous.

"Jim, dammit. We're leaving!"

The pleasant demeanor of the little librarian soured.

"That's fine! I'll lock up!"

"Against the rules, but I don't give a shit!"

The door slammed again.

"Oh. Bitch does not begin to describe that woman. I'm sorry. Go on." His smile returned. "You were saying, 'faceless man.' Does your husband need medication?"

"More than he needs the book. Finding the book's really to satisfy my curiosity."

The little man tapped his pursed lips with the tip of his finger. Dani could see something had jogged his memory.

"Faceless man..."

"Intellectually, I understand it's all nonsense. From the mind of a paranoid schizophrenic, my husband. Emotionally, I need to give it one last try. That's why I'm here."

Almost knocking Dani over, James rushed passed her to the section where she was standing.

"Here it is! I knew it. A few hundred pages: *The Faceless Men.* That's the title. His first book! Steale's that is. Almost always lost, because it was such a small printing as a hardback and only a test printing as a paperback. Very little noticed even by his most ardent fans."

He handed the dusty hardback book to Dani. She turned it over in her hands. It felt ancient, the fibers in the cloth on the cover separating after all these years. On the spine, a red stamp from the library service marked the book as "Rare." She opened it to the title page where Paul Steale's autograph was written over his printed name.

"Oh, dear."

James shook his head.

"What?"

"It can't be loaned out. You'll have to read it here."

"Great. Can I start?"

She thought of her mother sitting alone in Delmonico's, but this was her chance to sort her life out.

"Tomorrow. Security will kick us both out soon."

Dani was crushed. So close to answers and denied at the eleventh hour.

"I suppose I can wait until morning. Will you be here?"

"Yes. 10 a.m. Sharp."

"Ten, so will I."

James the librarian was unabashedly excited by the opportunity to see Dani again.

"Good. I look forward to it."

"Darn it. I left my purse on your desk."

"Follow me, young lady. Once it gets dark in here, it can be a trial to navigate."

He waved her on.

At his desk, she gathered up her purse dropping her cell into its maw.

"Well, thanks. You've been too kind. I will see you bright and early."

"You're welcome. Perhaps we can talk more after you finish the book, too. I'd love to hear your thoughts."

She smiled, waved and moved into the most lighted aisle.

"Good night."

" 'Night. Let Charlie know I'll be another 10 minutes, please. Tell him I'm hurrying. I hate to make them wait to lock up, and I refuse to be here alone for very long. Too creepy at night. Ghosts, you know?"

Dani moved along the aisle back towards the center offices and information desk. Halfway along, she fished her cell out and turned on the flashlight app. Without daylight and only every other fixture casting light, it had become very dark. She held the phone up. The dim light from its screen illuminated only a few feet into the cavernous interior. Her heart began to race as she shuffled slowly forward.

What's wrong with you, girl?

She was sure she was overreacting to the dark. As a child, Dani had been known to spend nights either sleeping with her parents or insisting that the lights were left on in her bedroom. To her adult mind, it wasn't that she had been afraid of the dark, but rather, she was afraid of being abandoned—something she could admit to herself.

She let a smile cross her face. It helped to calm her heart. Still she wanted out of the library, so she quickened her pace.

With the stained wood-paneling of the office in sight, Dani's uneasy feeling returned. Then, she heard it. She stopped and listened.

A scuffing across the stone tiles.

Oh, no you don't, she scolded herself.

"Hello?... James?"

Dani searched the darkness hoping to hear the librarian answer her back.

More scuffing.

Her heart pounded. The sounds were coming from the aisle opposite!

She bit her lip and slinked to the other side of her aisle. The light from her phone was dimming. Her battery was undoubtedly running low, but the LED light had never done anything similar.

Again, more cautiously, she whispered, "Hello?"

Something moved in the darkness! She reeled around and into James, nearly knocking him off his feet.

"Oh, dear!"

Dani held onto his arm.

"Sorry, James."

She began to laugh as her fear became shame.

"How many times do I have to apologize to you today?... I got turned around. I heard noises. My mind was playing tricks on me."

"Easily done. Especially in here at night. Now, you know what I mean about this place being creepy in the dark."

He took his arm in hers and guided her into the offices and then the main floor of the library.

"It's the books, you see. They come alive with all the souls they've touched over the years. Their bodies have passed, but their minds are still attached to this Earth and the things they loved in life, like these books. My grandmother told me that. She was a librarian, too. She felt that books became a tether for souls who have no one left to haunt."

"Are you sure there was no one else back there with you?"

"I don't believe so. I can never be 100 percent sure, but I am confident that we are alone. Save the ghosts of course."

He chuckled.

Dani looked back over her shoulder toward the offices. In the darkness, she saw a shadow move. The figure crossed under one of the dim hanging lights. It caught the light for the briefest moment.

It was a man with no face.

"Who?!" she blurted, stumbling back into the librarian. He caught her from falling.

James raised his eyebrows over the rims of glasses.

"I'm sorry. I didn't mean to bump into you. What did you see?"

"Huh?"

Dani turned from him to look again. The man, or whatever she had seen, was gone. *If he had ever been there, you silly little girl.*

She inhaled, "Nothing. An overactive case of the spooks is all. This place is really bad at night."

"What say you, we get out of here for the night?"

Nodding eagerly, they rushed towards the security desk at the building entrance and said their hurried goodnights to the guards who eagerly left.

James waved goodbye to Dani as he paused at the doors.

"I must lock the doors as the last librarian to leave. Have a good night, and I will see you in the morn."

" 'Night…" she said moving down the steps. "Nice to meet you!"

The overwhelming bustle of Manhattan was a welcome sound to Dani. It replaced the silent gaping maw of the ghostly library. The sun may have gone down, but the city was still alive and haunted with the living.

Her cell phone beeped in her purse. She found it. The battery was nearly dead, but it did manage to give her the time before it went dark. If she was lucky, she might still find her mother waiting at the restaurant. Dani raised her hand at a passing taxi. How the driver had noticed her, she didn't know. She ran for the yellow car as it pulled over.

"Miss! Miss! Dani!"

She stopped and turned. James was running after her.

"Yes, James?"

"Maybe we could share a cab? I live close to Delmonico's just north of it in Little Italy. Cut our expenses, and I won't have to ride the subway with the great unwashed illiterates."

Dani giggled. She could tell he was joking, but likely meant it. "Sure. Let's hit it."

They both hopped into the taxi.

Slamming his door shut, James poked his head through the plexiglas divider and instructed the driver, "Delmonico's and be quick about it, my friend. This young lady's late for a dinner date with her mother. And we should never be late for our mothers."

The hybrid—all the traditional yellow cab sedans had been replaced by hybrids—buzzed into motion as the driver, a young man from some country in Africa, put the pedal to the floor. Dani and James were rocked back into the seat. She motioned toward the seat belts.

"I suppose we should."

"Quite right," James said.

Once buckled in, the little librarian pulled his briefcase onto his lap and made a show of popping it open.

"Oh, dear. How did that get in there? It must've fallen in."

Dani wasn't paying any attention. Her attention was on the driver's reckless maneuvering.

Finally, James cleared his throat, and she looked.

"Oh, I—"

Steale's rare first book sat in his briefcase plain as day.

"—Bring it back to me tomorrow. It's a quick read. I hope that's not a commentary on your future given the current predicament your husband thinks you're in. Promise to meet me at the library at 10 sharp. Promise?"

"I really appreciate this."

She reached for it with some reluctance.

He nodded his approval, and she took it from his case.

Carefully, she put the old tome in her bag.

"I will see you tomorrow first thing. Promise."

"It's a deal. I do run the place, after all. I have one additional request."

"What's that?" she asked.

A myriad of terrible suppositions shot across her brain. She hoped her face hadn't betrayed her suspicion.

"We must have coffee tomorrow and discuss this book. I want to know what you think of it, but more importantly, what you think about your future once it becomes clear."

"Oh, yes, of course!"

"Great!" His face was flush. "I mean, I know you're married and having a rough go, but I'm confident my company will do you some good. I have literary insights, young lady."

She laughed.

"Do you know where he lives?"

"I assume you mean Steale?"

He raised an eyebrow over the rim of his glasses.

"Indeed I do. I pass by every time I do my run in Central Park."

"Any good coffee shops nearby his place?" Dani said.

"Why, yes. There are a few. It is Central Park."

"Here's my number."

Dani wrote down her cell number on a piece of scrap paper.

"Call or text me the location, and I will meet you there before you have to go to work. What do you think?"

"A morning adventure! I haven't had one of those in—oh...

forever!"

CHAPTER
TWENTY FIVE

"**D**aughter dear, are you dead-set on ruining my good time?" Carol Strauss said.

She rolled the ice cubes around in her nearly Scotch-less cocktail tumbler with her wild gesticulations. The woman was on her way to being completely sauced much to Dani's dismay.

"If the atmosphere and the waiters weren't so nice here—" the 63 year old woman—though with all her South Beach plastic surgery she looked more a mere 45—said. "I'd be positively pissed."

The older woman winked at a passing busboy.

"Mom, how many times do you want me to say it?"

Dani picked at her pasta.

"Oh, honey, we're done apologizing for tonight. I'm talking about tomorrow. I had our shopping day planned to the T. Now, well, it looks like I go solo. Unless I want to spend my morning inside some dreary library."

"It's quite beautiful, actually."

Carol waved her freshly empty tumbler at a passing waiter. He smiled and eagerly grabbed it for a refill. The cougar, and she was one, pulled her long, platinum blond hair away from her ample, and very apparent bosom.

"Mother, you're embarrassing me."

Leaning across the table and letting her breasts hang, Carol smirked at her daughter.

"You're lucky you have my genes. You'll be thanking me when you reach my age. Of course, I will be in heaven plucking my harp by then."

"The multiple marriages, I can do without."

"Those aren't inherited unless you're talking money."

The waiter returned with a fresh Scotch. "Ma'am, here you are. Scotch on the rocks."

Dani's mother furrowed her brows.

"Ma'am? I don't see any ma'ams around these parts. Do I look like a ma'am to you?"

She threw her head back, laughing in her best, throaty Bacall.

"You look like an actor. Have I seen you in any shows?"

The towheaded server flexed in his very tight uniform into which he stuffed himself. He flashed a toothy grin.

"I'm between shows right now. But auditions are picking up."

In a flash, Carol reached out and grabbed a handful of the young man's ass.

"A dancer. I could tell. Great body, I'm sure. If you goofy-foot the heterosexual way, give me a ring. My lovely daughter, here, is fucking up my plans for a great time in the mañana. Maybe there's an alternative that we can call plan B."

He took her card, studied it and then slid it into his front pants pocket, way, way down. It was impossible to miss his sizable bulge.

Dani shielded her eyes trying her best to both look inconspicuous and not look at all. She started eating if only to avoid the situation. The other well-to-do patrons, most of whom were blue-hairs, were beginning to pay attention to her mother's lioness' roar, however.

"If you don't mind, I better get back to my other tables. But I will be calling… Ms. Strauss."

With that, he was across the restaurant.

Like the proverbial cat who ate the canary, the older woman slipped back into her chair, smiling and satisfied.

"Okay, you have my permission to spend your day with that moldy old fish-wrap collection. I'll be spending it on some young, hung boy. Which, since you're planning on divorcing that no-good asshole, you should be doing."

"Mom, I never said anything about divorce."

"Ha! I can smell it. I've been down that road too many times not to know where a separation of this kind leads. Loosen up, Dani. Enjoy your life for once. Don't let a man tie you down. You're young and beautiful—thanks to me—I'll remind you yet again. You have time for many second chances. Let this one off the hook. Other than him being fantastically handsome, I have never liked him. Never approved."

Carol grabbed Dani's empty water glass and poured some of her Scotch into it.

"Here. Don't stick with that dry old Cabernet. This will get you where you want to go faster."

The younger woman pushed her half-eaten plate away. She put her nose to her water glass. The whiskey's aroma was pungent. It opened her sinuses with one sniff. She sipped.

"Don't you want to know, Mother?"

"Know what?"

"About my life. What I'm going through."

Strauss straightened her back. She sighed.

"In my experience, it hasn't ever mattered what the gory details are. My first husband decided to spend us into the ground, so I got out with enough money before he crashed and burned. The second, well, he was a typical rebound. I got bored, and he was too nice. His best friend, the third, was a mistake that earned my first millions, once I threatened to expose his kinky little habits to his family. That was the great lesson. Your father hit me. Once. That was enough. So, really, Dani, what is there to surprise me with?"

"I thought you could offer some advice. Some insight that might help me save my marriage."

"Why would I ever want to do that? Better question: why would you? Hmm... Of course, I can see that his star's on the rise, so sticking it through could earn you some very big bucks."

"Mom, I love him."

"Your first mistake."

"And he's going insane. I think it may be catching."

Dani reached down into her purse and felt inside for the book. It was still there.

Waiting for her.

CHAPTER
TWENTY SIX

With her mother planning to spend the day with the waiter from their dinner at Delmonico's, Dani was able to grab a cab and head towards James' favorite coffee shop untethered.

She spent most of the night and into the early morning reading the book James had lent her. It surprised her that the book was such breezy reading. Turning the last page at sun up, she was afforded a half-hour of much-needed shut eye.

When she arrived at the coffee shop, a line of people waited impatiently out the door. Dani's excitement fell into the pit of her stomach.

Oh, no. We're never going to be able to get a table in time.

She desperately wanted to discuss the book with the kind librarian. Hearing his take on her thoughts was invaluable to her.

Dani scanned the crowd hoping to see him. But he wasn't in line. She was about to give up until she caught James waving frantically from behind the shop window. He had secured a table inside and had coffee waiting for her.

Squealing with giddy happiness and waving back at him, the young woman drew covetous eyes from the miserably cold throng forced to wait outside.

It was as loud in the shop as it was on the street. Clerks

shouting at customers, and customers shouting back orders all above a constant din of acoustic, new age music. She pushed past the line at the main register, and the warm air and deep, rich roasted coffee smell wafted around her. It jolted her alive and swept away any remaining anxiety.

The little librarian stood up. His chair made a loud screeching scrape across the floor as she approached.

"I got here early. This place is so popular that I knew precaution was the watchword of the day," he said with a flourish.

James beckoned for Dani to sit in a chair he pulled out for her.

"Wow. You aren't kidding. This place is crazy busy."

She reached into her purse and pulled out the book. Handing it over to him, a rush of relief fell over her.

"Thanks again, James. Is there anything I can do? Buying coffee is the least—"

"—Why, no. And I already bought ours. My reward will be this discussion. I'm not sure you guessed, but I don't have much of a life beyond books. You've presented me with an opportunity to see that excitement exists beyond pages and now, those dreadful, tiny pixels."

Dani thought for a moment then rose.

"I'm starving, and our conversation will need some fuel. How 'bout some pastries? Please? My treat."

"Oh, yes, all right. Blueberry muffin, please," James said, smiling.

She skipped like a schoolgirl to the bakery counter. This line was much less of a problem than the one to get coffee, and she returned to the table with muffins and scones in the blink of an eye.

James checked his watch.

"I have an hour and a half before they'll be expecting me at work. So? My interest is piqued..."

Dani savored a piece of sweet lemon cake that dissolved in her mouth.

She swallowed, and then, she said slowly, "It was a good book. You were right. Took me only a few hours to get through.

Didn't sleep much... But I have a problem—"

"—Let me think," he paused cleaning his glasses with a handkerchief. "The female protagonist leaves her husband and searches for the author of a book that holds the keys to her husband's madness."

"Yes."

"Sound familiar?" he asked.

"You knew..."

Dani sat back in the stiff wooden chair. She sipped her coffee.

"I did. It rang a bell, but I didn't want to spoil the surprise for you. What do you think it means?"

"I don't really know. James, if you're asking me if I think this book is prophetic concerning my life, I have to say, no. And the damn thing is missing the last whatever number of pages! So, I still don't know how it ends!"

"What? I don't understand."

"Check for yourself. They're gone. Fell out. I guess."

James opened the book and checked the binding at the rear cover. A flap of glue, with grooves where the pages had set were the only evidence that any pages had been there at all. He stared at it for a long time. Finally, he put it down on the table.

"I did that." He pulled apart his muffin and slathered butter on one half. "Dani, I've known you for less than 24 hours, and I haven't read that book in 30 years, but you've made me remember a terrible episode. A mood so strong and foreign to me overcame me, once, because of this book. I had finished the damn thing. The ending filled me with such anger that I ripped the pages from the binding. I've never ever abused another book in my life. But this one sent me over."

"You did that? Why?"

"I'm trying to remember, but I can't recall exactly why. The anger is what I remember."

Washing the muffin down with a swig of coffee, he raised his eyebrows, surprised and delighted by another remembrance.

"I'm in the book! I'm in the book just like you are!"

"What?"

"Running the risk of sounding like the literature minor I was, let me say that I find his lack of character description a strength of Steale's writing—despite the endings. He invites more people to identify with his characters, because they are so vague. There is a librarian character in that book. I remember that much. Now, whether the characters are a perfect match for you and I and—"

"—Shannon," she finished for him.

"—that doesn't negate any similarities to us. You did see those similarities? Right?"

When she first set out to read the book, Dani thought she would be evaluating Shannon's madness. She considered the questions that swirled in her mind concerning the paperback ridiculous. *How can a book foretell our future? A faceless man is real? An author, old enough to be our father, knows the secrets of our lives and wrote them 25 years before we even met?* And on they went.

All of it, though, was not able to shake her first conclusion. She was sure that Shannon was purposely giving the book the power of prophecy, so he could get off the hook for being a despicable cheat. When James mentioned vagueness, that reinforced her thinking.

"I did see them, but coincidences happen," Dani said. "Right?"

"What about this one?"

James pressed his finger against the shop window between the letters that made up the signage.

"Do you see that building?"

Dani followed his finger which pointed to a high-rise on 5th Avenue.

"Yes," she said.

"That's his building."

"Whose?"

"Steale's. Exactly as it is in the book. I checked the address. It's the same. And our meeting in this coffee shop?"

The pages were still fresh in her mind, and the scene in the book was as it was happening now.

"But how?"

He pulled his finger from the window and wiped the smudge away with his napkin.

"I don't know. Maybe it's not to be questioned. Only fulfilled. Like I fulfilled both of my parts: pointing you in the right direction and destroying the last pages, so you could write your own ending. I hope that my shameful vandalism has given you and Shannon the chance to make your own future. One that Steale, himself, never dreamed."

"How am I supposed to believe any of this? Look, I don't even know if I believe in God. I'm completely groundless when it comes to things remotely supernatural."

"Shakespeare wrote, 'There are more things in Heaven and Earth…'"

"James, other people tell me ghost stories. I have none of my own."

"I don't have answers for those questions, either. My experience as a Catholic did not prepare me for prophecies other than those in the Good Book. I think, if you feel uncomfortable—and, let me be honest—I do, too—walk away and never think again of it."

She looked at Steale's building in the distance.

"Have you ever seen him on the street?"

"No. I haven't. Why?"

"I need to know how that book ended. I need to know what he meant our future to be."

James grabbed her hands.

"Dani, my gut says, leave it be. With those pages gone, I bet whatever you make of your future will be of your own writing. Don't lose that power."

She slowly pulled her hands from his grasp.

"Tell me more about Steale."

"He takes his dogs for walks in Central Park every day according to Page Six. You aren't planning something dangerous or… criminal? Are you?"

Dani smiled.

"No."

The little librarian, relieved, mimicked her.

"Good… He was divorced several years back, and only has his dogs. Very lonely. Like me."

CHAPTER TWENTY SEVEN

His mind went wild with speculation.

Did she meet some guy at the hotel bar? Was she ignoring his calls while in the arms of another man? Or, was she spooning with the bellhop who delivered her room-service breakfast?

Shannon punched his fist in the air as his call went to voicemail once again. It was the fifth time.

"God damn it, Dani! Answer your fucking phone!" His voice echoed off the concrete walls.

He howled in anger.

It was early, but the neighbors had all gone to work, so he was reasonably sure no one would be calling the cops.

He continued to howl in anger.

After several minutes, when his lack of air and lightheadedness was too much for him, he let his anger dissipate. Shannon dropped onto the sofa where his imprint, from the last several days of sleeping on it, accepted him eagerly.

"This is not fair!"

The irony of the situation was lost on him. Shannon was always able to compartmentalize his behavior and minimize it according to his needs. But even the hint of Dani being unfaithful was unforgivable to him.

Unforgivable, and still a complete figment of his imagination. He moved to the window, his favorite place in the loft since Dani left.

Left me. She left me. For ever and ever, he thought staring out at the city.

Having finished the paperback that morning, or as much of the book as he had in his possession, the book was no longer a diversion from his real life problems. At first, the missing last pages were a mere annoyance. He figured they must've made up the pages of the last chapter, but there was no way for Shannon to know. The book could be lacking whole chapters for all he knew.

He had flipped wildly through the book to make sure his repair job hadn't simply mis-ordered the pages. But when the pages weren't there, he flung it across the room, again. It drove him crazy not knowing what happened to the young couple. They were on their way with a new friend to meet with the book's author, and then it ended.

No more inky black letters on faded, tan pages for him.

In the dark of the morning, he had pulled the sofa apart. He had pulled the bed, which had not been touched since Dani had left, out. He looked in cupboards, closets and drawers.

The pages were lost to him, and he was lost to the book.

He wanted most of all to ask Dani about the ending.

Maybe she had the pages? Did she take them as a trick? Was it one more thing to make him yearn for her?

She took them. The bitch took the ending with her. To make me crazy.

His mind began the circle of illogic anew. He always blamed Dani. It was probable that she did not take the pages, but it was so much easier to think she did.

As he stared out at Lake Michigan, its slow waves calmed him. The water was unusually still.

On land, the traffic down the lakefront highway wormed towards downtown.

Shannon turned to his unfinished rock.

He had a choice. He could stay in and work away his anxiety by pounding on the stone, or he could run out there into the big city.

The decision was easy. He would pop into the shower then put on his best cologne.

Dani, baby, with or without you. With or without you.

CHAPTER TWENTY EIGHT

Central Park was overflowing with people even on a workday. Between the throngs of tourists and homeless squatters, she could not find a comfortable spot to sit, and her mother, Carol Strauss, was intent on making Dani's morning worse.

After James begged forgiveness for having to go earlier than expected to work at the library, Dani decided to trek into the park to scout out Steale's apartment building, herself. But her mother's tryst with last night's waiter ended both early and badly, and Carol demanded that she be able to join her daughter.

Dani had no intention of commiserating with her. Instead, she was determined to get, at least, a glimpse of the author, so if that meant enduring her mother's pouting and general bad behavior, she would.

Her mother would not deter her.

If she doesn't like it, well, she's in NYC with a plethora of things to do by herself.

As soon as her mother found her in the park, Shannon started calling. He called and called. And called. And called.

With Carol bitching and moaning, there was no way Dani would add his complaints to the mix. It would freak her out. So, Dani decided to power off her phone.

Truth was, she missed Shannon and would have loved to talk to him and tell him what she had found out. It pained her to ignore his calls. She wanted to tell him that she read as much of the paperback as possible. That it corroborated what he had been saying, but before speaking to Shannon, she needed to get away from her mother. More importantly, she needed to verify, from Steale himself, that his book was only a work of fiction and not some magic prophetic vision into the looking glass.

The coincidences were too many and spot on for her to ignore any more.

"Mother, maybe you can take an area up there, and I will scout over here."

She pointed north up Fifth Avenue.

Carol rolled her eyes.

"Why can't we go spend some money? Explain this goose chase for me again."

"It's not my fault you picked another waiter slash actor who just happened to be gay."

"Oh, not that again. Look, it would have worked out swimmingly if I hadn't asked for sex."

"Mother, please!"

"Don't play disgusted with me, missy. How do you think you happened? My wicked, wicked ways. That's how. I may be past planting season, but I'm still a woman with needs."

Dani pointed up the sidewalk and waved her mother onward.

"If you don't come back here in five minutes, I'll assume that you found a bench where we can watch that door!" She pointed again at Steale's building. "If I'm not here, you assume the same and come find me."

"Oh. Why must you make this so complicated?! Turn on your damn cell phone."

"No! I don't want to keep ignoring his calls."

"What do you think you're doing by shutting it off?!"

Carol, exasperated, turned and stomped up the sidewalk away from Dani.

She has a point, Dani thought.

She sighed and returned to her surveillance.

One thing that stuck in her mind, from her breakfast with the librarian, was that he could not remember how the book ended. It seemed too coincidental—in a string of coincidences—that the final pages of the library copy were missing. She wondered if Shannon's copy had its ending. As soon as she could, she would call Shannon and ask.

She had to.

CHAPTER
TWENTY NINE

Above the northern tip of Grant Park on Michigan Avenue was Shannon's favorite Chicago hotel. It also housed his favorite bar.

Dressed in his best Italian suit—the same suit he wore at his wedding—he pushed through the hotel's revolving door and into the lobby. He cut a swath through the crowd of conventioneers who clustered about tables picking up their name tags and lanyards for the day's activities.

They were doctors attending a plastic surgery conference. The giant printed sign saying, "Welcome, America's Best Plastic Surgeons" was a dead giveaway.

Shannon scanned the crowd. He was definitely the best dressed and the most handsome of the men—without being falsely modest. For every five men there was one woman, and one out of every three women was passably attractive.

Not the odds you would expect from people trying to sell body improvement, he thought. *But they also know the cost of looking beautiful.*

He moved to the opposite side of the lobby from the busy convention hall entrance.

The glass enclosure for the restaurant and bar always seemed a bit out of place in the turn of the 19th Century-era building. It was too modern for a building more than a hundred years old. It offended the artist in him, but his offense lasted up until they handed him his cocktail, which, in terms of alcohol content, was the healthiest in the city.

So, out-of-place glass facade or no, Shannon tolerated the setting.

At the host station just inside the glass doors, the very young and very pretty hostess greeted him with a smile.

"I'm afraid, Doctor, that we're not quite ready to seat for lunch," she said, clutching a plastic covered map of the restaurant tables.

She had been busy wiping off names of the servers from the night before.

"Not here for lunch... yet, and I'm no—" Shannon caught himself. "Doctor" fit him.

Let's see how much play I can get.

"Thanks, Miss. I need a drink before listening to more blah blah blah from my deadly dull colleagues."

He pointed over his shoulder.

"Well... The bartenders are serving. Have a seat at the bar over there. They'll be happy to help you."

"Music to my ears."

He trotted to the far side of the room where the bar stood against the glass wall. The waterfront shone through in vivid blues and tans, and reflections of the outside world twisted and turned in the liquor bottles that lined the glass shelves.

Shannon sat at the end of the bar. The three tall chairs to his right were empty, but the chairs in the middle of the bar were already occupied. Two men and a woman, professionally attired and wearing lanyards from the convention, happily imbibed Martinis. The woman, in her 30s, was pretty, with shoulder-length red hair that almost matched the bright red of her lips.

Shannon wondered how long it had taken her to find that particular shade.

He waved at the bartender who was chatting up the threesome. The man nodded, finished his pleasant chit-chat and glided towards Shannon, and as he did, Shannon noticed the interested, yet quick, glance from the lady doctor. The just-right tilt in her head allowed her to steal a glance at him without her companions noticing. He returned her smile before she looked away.

"What may I get you, sir?" the bartender, a hefty man lost somewhere in middle-age, asked.

Shannon noticed his name tag which read, **Lloyd**.

"How about the 'hair of the dog that bit me' ?"

Lloyd smiled broadly an indication of a practiced politeness.

"Ah. Yes, I've heard that line before. It never gets old."

"I bet you have. I couldn't resist. Uh... Let's go with a good old Kentucky Bourbon on the rocks." Shannon beat out a drum rimshot pattern on the bar. "You must be new, Lloyd. I've never seen you before."

The bartender, giving Shannon a ten count on the whiskey, nodded.

"Local doctor? Enjoying the convention? I work the day shift around here. You come here days?"

"I'm... Del Cummins."

Shannon held out his hand for a shake, and the bartender took it.

"Pleasure."

"No, I am a night customer mostly. That explains it."

He took the Old Fashioned glass off the bar where Lloyd slid it and sipped the cool caramel liquid. It burned his tongue, before it chased down his throat hotly.

It felt good and reminded him that he was alive.

"So, tell me, Lloyd, what's the story with my colleagues down there?"

This time, he drank the brown liquor until all that remained was ice.

Lloyd, as was likely a habit, folded his bar towel in fours and dropped it out of sight.

"Well, like you, they're here for the convention, and like you, they really aren't here for the convention."

The whiskey, having gone down smoothly, was taking effect. He caught his reflection in the onyx glass bar top. His eyelids were heavy and pulling midway over his eyes. He smiled, looking a bit like that cartoon cat.

A warm cloak had lowered over him.

"My friend, Lloyd, you pour one hell of a good glass."

Shannon pulled out his billfold from his jacket pocket. He slapped $40 onto the bar.

"Hit me again, and let's treat the trio down there with some of the goodness we know over here. How 'bout you, too? Try the hair, barkeep?"

Smiling, the bartender lined up three more glasses, but refreshed Shannon's tumbler first.

"No, sir. I'm on the wagon. A friend of Bill, as they say."

The artist's face curled with disappointment.

"Oh, no, Lloyd! They got you?"

"I'm afraid so... Err—would you like to present the drinks?"

"No, no, Lloyd. I'm happy to be a bystander."

"Right. I'll just take these down, then."

Lloyd put the glasses onto a silver tray and walked down the length of the bar.

"Good," Shannon said, watching.

Slouching over the bar, Shannon nursed his new glass. He straightened on his stool as Lloyd pointed down the bar at him. He felt his cheeks redden.

Am I really embarrassed? I didn't know I had it in me anymore.

Shannon cleared his throat and lifted his freshly emptied tumbler into the air returning their toast.

"Right with you, Mr. Cummins." Lloyd noticed and was customary in his response, but there was a twinge of annoyance in his voice.

As Lloyd made his way back down to Shannon, the redhead followed. Approaching Shannon, she held her whiskey glass in two hands and dipped her chin with a smile.

"Thanks for the drink..."

Shannon pulled himself out of the bottom of his empty glass.

"Simply proving the old truism that we midwesterners are a hospitable lot."

She held a hand out.

"Ellen Krueger, Seattle."

Shannon, after wiping his hands with a cocktail napkin, shook hers. He slyly inspected her lanyard. Indeed, she was who she said she was. But he was unable to remember the name he gave the bartender.

Finally, after fumbling through the lies in his mind while still holding her hand, he answered, "Del Cummins, Chicago."

"Very nice to meet you, Doctor. Rhinoplasty specialist, myself."

Once more, Shannon was caught flat-footed. He grabbed his refreshed drink off the bar. Sipping, he hoped she wouldn't remember that he hadn't provided her a reply.

Ellen motioned at the empty seat next to him.

"Mind if I join you?"

"What about those fellers, over there?"

"Those boys?" She looked over her shoulder and waved to them. They waved back—warily. "Those boys're my partners. Fred, my brother, and Stan, our cousin. We took over my father's practice a couple of years ago once I finished my residency. Carrying on the family business."

"A family of plastic surgeons? Aren't the odds pretty long on that."

She chuckled.

"I don't have any idea about the odds. I work with my hands."

"Are you sure dear old dad would approve of doing so much business in the bar?"

"Ha! Where do you think we got this habit from?"

Ellen hoisted herself up onto the tall chair. She straddled it as if she were riding a horse. Her skirt hiked up revealing more of her thighs.

Shannon's eyes wandered up the nicely firm and tanned skin of her long legs before locking with hers. In that instant, he knew she knew what she was doing.

"So what's your specialty?" she asked, sipping her whiskey.

Any pretense at coyness was dropped.

"Pounding… actually."

Ellen nearly choked. She looked at Shannon with an amused, questioning grimace.

He continued, "I'm not a doctor. Or, whatever that was just now passing through your mind."

She giggled.

"Double entendre? Or slip of the tongue?"

"Oh, no double meanings here," he said with a smile. "I'm an artist. My specialty is sculpture."

"Ahh. The pounding. Now I get it. Very clever."

"I've been known to be."

"Don't you think it's a little strange for an artist to be at a convention full of doctors?"

He caught her eyes again and held them with his.

"Not if you happen to need one."

CHAPTER THIRTY

Cops, New York City cops most of all, have a reputation of never liking back-talking broads, and, Dani's mother was the most back-talkingist broad anyone ever met.

"—Who the hell do you think you are?" Carol screamed at the mounted policeman.

The police horse whinnied and tried to back away from the crazed woman, but the officer pulled on the reins and kept the beast still. Dani's mother, on the other hand, teetered on her high heels waving her finger angrily.

"Ma'am," the cop's voice was salted with a thick Brooklynese accent. "Ma'am, please, calm yourself."

"If you ask me to calm down again, I will call my lawyer!"

Dani pulled on her mother's arm.

"Mom, stop it. You're going to get arrested."

"Arrested?! A woman exercising her rights?! They wouldn't dare."

Carol stomped back to the bench where she left her bags.

"Officer, I'm terribly sorry. My mother can be... How can I explain?"

Dani tried a smile.

"Look, you are both lucky I am a patient man. I won't cite your mom this time, but if I catch her littering again, I will arrest her."

"Yes, sir. Thank you, sir."

She watched the horse and rider trot off onto the pathway that led into the park.

Dani joined her mother on the crowded bench.

"I don't know why I love this city so much. With men like that here."

"Mom, you aren't supposed to throw your gum at oncoming traffic."

"I didn't try to hit that cab!"

"But you did, mom. And you upset a lot of people."

Carol sulked and rifled through her handbag. She pulled out a pack of cigarettes and lit up.

"Mom, you promised!" Dani whined.

Dragging on her cigarette, the older woman savored the smoke in her lungs.

Exhaling, "It calms my nerves. Not every day. Sometimes. What are we still doing here? It's past lunch. I'm famished, and I need a ladies room in the worst way."

"A few more minutes, Mom. I want to see if we can catch him."

"Who again?"

"An author. Paul Steale."

"Never heard of him. Therefore, a waste of my time."

"Ten more minutes. That's all. Can you do that for me?" Dani pleaded.

She hated sounding like that little girl she thought she had outgrown, but her mother's influence was like gravity.

"Fine. I'll have you know, young lady, that if I poop my pants, you will be doing my laundry." Carol took another drag.

Dani winced then giggled. Her mother choked out smoke and joined her.

"Oh, don't make me laugh too hard. I'm not wearing my diapers!"

Their laughter subsiding, Dani looked back across Fifth Avenue at the building James identified as Steale's. The sheer numbers of honking and jostling cars made the street look far wider than it was. She had to constantly bob up and down, to and fro to keep her gaze steady on the high rise's front door.

And then there he was.

"Ha!" Dani nearly fell off the bench. "Mom, that's him!"

"Who, dear?"

"The guy. You know, the writer!"

Across the street, Steale had emerged from the building trailed by two, sleek black dogs. He nodded to the doorman. He and the dogs headed towards the crosswalk which led to the park.

"C'mon, Mom. Get your bags."

She scooped up her canvas purse and several of Carol's loose shopping bags.

"Hell's bells, girl. Hold your horses."

The older woman wrenched herself off the bench and gathered up her things. Her daughter was already halfway toward the crosswalk.

Steale stepped onto the sidewalk which encircled the park. Dani, several feet away, stopped almost frozen and locked her eyes onto him. Though only moderately well-known as a celebrity, his reaction bespoke of a man clearly aware of the dangers of stalkers. He pulled the dogs behind him as he watched her suspiciously.

Oblivious, pedestrians streamed around them.

It took Carol, hobbling up to her daughter on her flimsy high-heels, to break the silence.

"Well, don't stand there! Introduce yourself, silly."

Dani snapped out of it.

"I'm sorry, Mr. Steale. My name's Dani McClarty... I'm a fan."

Steale relaxed and allowed the dogs to move to his sides.

"Miss, any request can be made with my agent, Sue Cornstein, at WMe East. Thanks for your cooperation," he said curtly.

He guided the dogs towards the park entrance.

"Oh, no, Mr. Steale," Dani chased after them, "I don't want an autograph. I want to talk to you about one of your books."

Steale abruptly turned catching Dani mid-step. She nearly stumbled.

"Do not make me call the police."

Dani flashed back to their very recent problems with officers of the law.

"There's no need—"

"—Then stop and let us go about our business!"

She stood still for a minute, and when Steale was satisfied that he had gotten through to her and started to move again, she called out, "It's about your book, *The Faceless Men*."

He stopped and kicked at the pavement. Dani noticed a tinge of something cross his face, but before she could recognize it, it was gone.

Finally, he said, "What about it?"

"I have so many questions. I don't know where to start... How... How does it end?"

Of all the questions that were swirling in her mind, that was the most important.

"I can't remember the last time anyone asked me about that book. I can barely remember it, myself. In many ways, I'm not proud of it. It was an attempt at horror. I think I failed."

"I don't think you did."

Carol, puffing on a cigarette, sidled up next to Dani.

"What the hell's going on?"

"I read it last night. I... I liked it. Except, I have no idea how it ends. And I'm kind of compelled to find out. It's more important than you can imagine."

CHAPTER
THIRTY ONE

By the time Ellen managed to pull Shannon into the conference hall, they were both stumbling drunk and were lucky that the lights were dimmed. A live procedure was being projected onto screens throughout the room. The participants were seated around tables already set up with plates, silverware and glasses for lunch.

Shannon tripped into a table, and nearly knocked a water glass over, but he still had faculty enough to catch it before it spilled onto an annoyed doctor.

Several times, they were shushed. Shannon shushed back making Ellen giggle. Finally, they found empty seats around a table in the rear.

As he sat, the image on the screen stunned him. It was human, but barely. Shannon knew it was a woman, because it was talking and its voice was undeniably feminine. His brain pieced together the situation. The skin on her face had been pulled away from the underlying muscle and bone and lay as a flap across her neck.

The image started Shannon's alcohol-filled stomach churning. "What the hell is that?" He leaned over to whisper—very loudly —to Ellen.

She giggled on cue.

"I don't quite know... Oh, this is a facial reconstruction. The surgeon had to lift the face off to repair—"

The patient's eyes darted about.

For Shannon, no aficionado of horror films, to watch the damp, bloody muscles relax then contract in speech, the eyes being led by their strap muscles, the tongue lick the teeth through the holes in the muscles was too much.

He fell off his chair and pulled his table's tablecloth, and the settings resting on top of it, onto the floor with him.

Ellen, no longer able to stifle her laughter, burst.

From the stage, the sounds of a rustling microphone and feedback shot through the air. Heads turned to the rear, and the presentation stopped—with the skinless skull staring, also looking for the source of the commotion, from the silver screen.

"Security," the voice called out on the microphone.

Shannon extracted himself out from under the tablecloth, broken plates and glasses. They tinkled and further shattered against each other as they fell from him onto the floor.

On his feet, Shannon stumbled in a daze. He felt a hand tug against his arm. Expecting abuse at any moment, he instinctively pulled away, but it was Ellen.

"Hurry! Let's get out of here," she said.

He let himself be dragged out the emergency exit of the banquet hall.

Instantly, they were in the access alley behind the old hotel. The bright daylight blinded them. It was an eternity before their eyes adjusted, but until that happened, it was Shannon's turn to pull Ellen towards the sounds of the street.

She tottered trying to stay up with him. The click of her high heels was loud against the asphalt.

At the street, he saw the streaks of passing cars and the bright yellow of a taxi. He wolf-whistled, and the cab pulled over up the street near the park—almost a quarter mile away.

"Ellen, we got a cab. Can you run?"

Behind them, the emergency doors slammed open. Shouts soon followed.

What was left of their buzz was wiped away by the rush of

adrenaline. The young woman pulled off her heels and ran behind him.

As they hopped into the cab and slammed the door behind them, Shannon prodded Ellen. "Where we going?"

She shrugged her shoulders.

"Drive!" Shannon ordered.

The cab rocketed forward. They turned and looked out the rear window to see the hotel security scrambling after them and then giving up when they were too far away.

"Oh, my God. How am I going to get back into the conference?" she asked before bursting out laughing once more.

Shannon looked at her wide smile. The allure of adventure was writ across her face.

"Not my problem," Shannon quipped. "If you just learned to control that laughter of yours…"

"What? It's my fault?"

"I'm not saying that, but when you're trying to be sneaky, it helps to be quiet."

"You should talk, mister." She drifted into his chest. "I haven't seen a drunk so clumsy since my father."

"You do have daddy issues. Aha!"

"I wouldn't start a psychoanalysis competition, Del. I've only just met you, but I can be pretty sharp."

"You only have to say it once. My God… That thing on the screen was really freaking me out. I've had some hallucinations before. Freaky shit. But none of it compares to that. Makes me really appreciate skin."

"Hallucinations?"

"Ah. Did I say the wrong thing?"

He noticed that he had aroused the cabbie's curiosity, too. The black man's eyes shifted from the street to his rear view, where he could see Shannon and Ellen in the backseat, and then back again.

"Don't worry about it… Okay… I don't know what they were. I mean, I know what they were, but I don't know medically. I haven't seen a shrink about them, but I have been overworked lately. I chalk it up to stress... Or they could really be real. They seemed pretty real at the time. Fuck. I don't know."

Ellen pushed herself up from his chest.

"You saw what? UFOs?"

Shannon chuckled.

"No. Nothing like that. No little green men."

"Sasquatch? The Loch Ness Monster?"

"I didn't know girls knew about Bigfoot. You're different."

"I have brothers. Remember?"

She lazily looked out at the Great Lake from the passenger window. Its water was choppy with a rising wind.

"Oh, yeah. Anyway, I saw a guy with no face. Not like the no face we saw back there. No face—like a smudge of skin where his mouth and eyes and nose should've been. He was chasing me, too. It's not as crazy as it sounds. It happened just like in this book I was reading—"

Twisting from the window, she looked at Shannon with raised eyebrows.

"—Now, that sounds crazy," he continued.

She shook her head, yes.

"While you still can, you might want to stop digging the hole deeper. Next you're going to tell me that you're married."

"I must admit..."

Her face drew taut in anticipation of a confession.

Shannon leaned lower to meet eyes to eyes, nose to nose.

"...I haven't had this much fun in a long, long time. Let's continue having fun."

CHAPTER THIRTY TWO

The pressure that she had been feeling was gone.

It surprised Dani that it only took Steale's promise to send her one of his remaining copies of *The Faceless Men* —signed to Shannon at her insistence—to allay her anxieties.

"Dani, dear?" Carol called from the bathroom of their hotel room. "Would you mind calling down to the concierge to see if he can recommend something within walking distance. I refuse room service. I don't care how tired you say you are."

The toilet flushed, heralding her mother's emergence from the commode. Dani rolled over on her bed smothering her face into a pillow. The day had exhausted her.

"You, young lady, are coming with me if I have to drag your ass out of this room."

"Mom! No! Let me sleep."

"I wasted my entire day waiting with you for some damn, has-been writer, author—not even a potential marriage prospect for me. No sane person would waste a night in the greatest city on Earth!"

"Can't you find some other unsuspecting waiter?"

Carol smacked Dani on the ass.

"How dare you speak to your mother like that? Now, get up. Take a shower, and pretty yourself up. Who knows? You may meet someone yourself."

"Arghhh."

She twisted prone and put her feet on the floor. She pushed off the bed and tramped to the bathroom.

"It better not still stink in here," Dani said.

"Oh, hush. I still have scar tissue in my nose from changing your diapers, missy."

Dani shut the door behind her, but made sure her mother could hear her.

"It was probably all that coke you snorted in your oh-so-long-ago youth, Mom."

"Fine. You're paying for your own booze tonight!" Carol spat.

"I don't drink, so I beat you again."

She could hear her mother harrumphing in the room proper.

Their conversation could sound vicious and nasty, but to them, it was shorthand for a relationship born out of the turmoil of her mother's numerous relationships. They could be venomous to each other one minute and then laugh about it the next. For the most part, it worked for them.

Shedding her clothes, Dani stepped into the shower. The lukewarm water fell from the head in spurts. It was maddening that in one of the most expensive hotels in Manhattan the water pressure was so poor.

Letting what hot water there was pour over her, she thought of getting back home to Shannon. Her heart ached for him.

The water came faster. It felt good and reminded her of his touch.

Closing her eyes, Dani thought about his arms, and the way they felt as they held her. She could smell Shannon's sweat. She could taste his lips and feel him push inside her.

Her hand moved between her legs. Her fingers were a poor substitute for him.

They would have to do.

CHAPTER THIRTY THREE

Carol laughed at the top of her lungs.

The constant shrill whine of the passing taxis could not diminish her joyous voice. The rich dinner with a never ending stream of wine—and then the pot she scored on the street—coursed through her veins and found release in her laughter.

As her daughter, Dani still had that nagging sense of embarrassment one could only experience with a less-than-appropriate parent, but the adult woman in her admired her mother's ebullience. It was something that she rarely—if ever—witnessed when she was a girl.

Carol had always been in a state of disarray or anger because of her suitors or husbands.

"Mother," Dani said, arm in arm and providing support for her teetering mother, "I feel like something sweet."

The older woman cackled and the force of which was so great that it almost sent them both tumbling into the street.

The pedestrians, in typical New Yorker fashion, walked around them as if they did not exist. The two women could have fallen over on the sidewalk, bashed their heads and been gushing blood, and Dani doubted that any of them would have stopped to help them up.

"You're right," Carol slurred her words. "Some ice cream would hit the spot. Then..." she paused for dramatic impact, "we hit the strip joint. They have the sexiest men I have ever seen. And they dance around in next to nothing! Sometimes, if you're lucky, nothing at all!"

"Do you always have sex on the brain, Mom?"

"Why should a woman not think about one of the best things in life?"

"I never thought of it that way."

"Sweetheart, it's not always a chore to be endured."

Carol leaned on Dani. They were stopped at the intersection while waiting for the walk signal.

"Whew. I need to catch my second wind. That Cabernet was worth it. See, Dani? Wine and women only get better with age."

As they began to cross, Dani felt uneasy. The haze from the wine evaporated. Her spine was alight with tingles. She knew they were being followed.

"Mom, let's skip the strip club. You're a little too tired." Dani barely hid the concern in her voice. "What do you say?"

"Are you kidding me? This's our last night in the City! No way. On we go."

Dani steadied her mother stepping up onto the sidewalk. She took the opportunity to glimpse over her shoulder. None of their fellow pedestrians stood out. She shrugged the feeling off.

Half a block ahead, the lights of Sweeney's House of Men flashed in neons of orange, green and blue. The sign's decoration featured an outline of a heavily muscled headless male torso topped with a bow tie.

Several gay men ahead of them, unable to control their excitement, skipped towards the box office window. Dani heard them giggle like schoolgirls—like she had only moments before—before the foreboding feeling.

She tried to relax.

"Let me tell you, Dani. The last time I was here, they had a young man from Europe with the bi—"

"—Mother, let them make me blush."

"You'll do much more than that unless those queens ahead of us use them all up!"

Carol leaned up against the outer counter of the box office. The young man behind the glass smiled at the women. With his greased back black hair, tuxedo and rouge, he reminded Dani of Liza Minelli strutting in male drag.

"Do you ladies want tickets to tonight's performance?" he said with a sweet lispy drawl.

He tilted his head in a move that could have been misconstrued as a condescending put-on, but Dani understood the performance.

"Yeah," she said. "What's the damage for two?"

Her mother straightened up from her slouch.

"Oh, no, you don't. Young man..." she paused getting a better look at him, "I'm buying those."

She pushed Dani away from the hole in the window. All Dani could do was roll her eyes. He smiled and winked back at her.

"Tonight's a two for one special. That's why you see all these queens crawling up out of their hidey-holes for the show. $30, please."

Dani cringed at the price, but Carol didn't even bat an eye as she snapped open her billfold and passed the money through the hole.

The tickets they received in exchange were large, pink plastic penises.

Carol, as she handed her daughter a ticket, let out a belly laugh crossed with a wolf-whistle. Dani had never heard such a sound, much less one so filled with lust.

Dani took her ticket with pinched fingers, like it was contaminated and dirty, and a raised eyebrow. The crude thing felt like a boarding pass she got for a flight. She did not want to think about whether it had ever been cleaned.

"Do you know what this means, Dani? My lucky daughter, you and I are going to see some grade A prime beef!"

Before Dani could share another look with the ticket boy, her mother had her by the arm and was dragging her through the lobby. Inside, the walls were draped with deep purple velvet. Red spotlights traced paths, on either sides of the lobby, to billowing curtains that gave a tantalizing peek inside the Sweeney House of Weeney Auditorium with each gust of wind from the air conditioning. Framed head shots of Sweeney's star performers were suspended from the ceiling. Most were between the ages of 18 and 24 in Dani's estimation, and all very attractive.

Old Blue Eyes purred about very good years in a pleasing pre-show auditory ambiance. Her mother danced to the crooner.

"Oooh, I can't wait," Carol said.

She still hadn't let go of Dani's arm, and she relentlessly pulled her towards the theater doors.

"Mom, take it easy. We're here. There's no rush."

"We have to get the best table! I want to ensure that we get up close and personal."

When they crossed the threshold, they were met by cocktail tables arrayed around a stage that jutted out into the middle of the room like the root of the letter T. A table sat empty at the very end of the platform, and Carol scampered towards it. She did not let up on her grasp of Dani's arm and pulled her daughter with her.

"It's like I called, and they saved my favorite table!" Carol was ecstatic. "Whoa!"

Unable to control her mad, drunk dash, Carol bounced off her favorite table. That, too, she found hilarious. She laughed as she sat.

"It's nothing another vodka tonic won't cure!"

Dani was more graceful taking her seat.

Almost magically, a young, shirtless waiter wearing a bow tie appeared with menus. He held out the menus, but Dani did not take hers, because she was stunned by his black curly locks and emerald green eyes.

"Ladies, thank you for joining us tonight. We have about six minutes before the show starts. I can take your order up until the curtain rise. Would you like to start with drinks?"

"Oh, young man, you are a handsome thing. Aren't you? My unattached daughter, Dani—do remember that name, my boy —and I will need vodka tonics, stat. That's a medical term. I know, but our particular need is medicinal in nature. We most likely will only be drinking unless we decide to have some dessert. Make it your mission to keep us wet, all night."

Carol handed the young man back the menus. She licked her lips for emphasis.

"Wet."

The waiter smiled and blushed, his face to his navel burning pink.

"Yes, ma'am."

"Ma'am? Do I look like a ma'am?"

"Mother!"

"No ma—I mean—miss."

Carol winked. "That's better. Now, hurry up before the meat is delivered!"

"You are insufferable," Dani said.

She shook her head. Her mother's boisterous debauchery never ceased to surprise her.

"Oh, you act like a cranky old biddy. Lighten up. These boys love the attention. Soon, their prime will pass them by, and they'll relive every naughty moment like it was the winning touchdown in their last high school game."

"If you say so."

The waiter returned to their table with a silver tray atop which he balanced their liquor.

"Your drinks, ladies. Did you give any more thought to dessert? The house specialty is a banana split. I can have those ready right away."

He placed Dani's tumbler onto the table with a dancer's grace, but Carol's glass, she plucked it from his hands.

"And why would we have that, *mon belle garcon?*"

"Because, they are big and sweet beyond compare. Like me." He laughed, winked and said, "Two splits coming right up."

CHAPTER THIRTY FOUR

Ellen's back arched in his embrace.

Shannon felt her hot skin burning against his.

There was no going back. With every kiss, every caress, she was giving herself to him, and he was taking her.

With Ellen's fingernails scratching his shoulders, her tongue probing his neck, her hard nipples pressed against his chest, he lost himself. Shannon's vow to Dani was as meaningless as words to feral dog.

Again.

God, himself, could threatened to strike him down for his adultery, and it would not matter to him. He would make love to this woman who was not his wife.

"Yes... Kiss me," she said breathlessly. "I want you inside me."

He kissed her then rolled off and reached for his wallet. It was sitting on the table next to the bed. He had a condom hidden in it.

Only a few months old, it should still work.

Ellen's hotel room was in the more trendy north waterfront with a giant panoramic view of the lake. He fumbled with the metallic packaging as waves churned outside. The whitecaps beat against a rock jetty. Despite the soundproof glass, Shannon could almost hear the howl of the wind off the water. "Damn, my fingers are too sweaty. They can't grip this foil."

She reached between his legs.

"You do have one appendage that works."

"Ha, yes!" he said, noticing how cold her hands were. "It's just fine, but as a doctor, I'm certain you'd appreciate the use of our little prophylactic friend here."

"Not so little, I'd say."

"That's the alcohol talking. Can you get this damn thing open?" Shannon handed the condom to her. She bit down on the wrapper and pulled it open with her teeth. The oily latex rolled out of the tear flopping onto the floor.

"Oops!"

"I hope the carpet's clean."

He snatched it up off the light green shag.

"You want me to roll it on?" Ellen asked.

She laid her head across his thigh.

"Sure."

With a deftness that should not have surprised Shannon knowing that she was a surgeon, she had him sheathed and ready to go in seconds.

"You've had practice."

"Not any more than any other modern woman."

She scooted back onto the bed, lying flat. Her naked body was an open invitation to him.

"For the record, I've never had an STD nor surgical fetal removal."

Shannon's erection was softening suddenly.

"The object is to help me maintain a hard on, or all this was wasted time."

"T-M-I, I get it. Let's both shut up, then."

She pulled him by the shoulder on top of her and pushed his head to her breasts.

"I don't feel much like talking either."

He kissed the space between her breasts. The musk of her skin was perfume to his nose, and his erection returned. She felt for him and guided him into her. Their mouths met intermingling the sweet taste of alcohol still on their tongues.

CHAPTER
THIRTY FIVE

At the rate she had been drinking, Dani was surprised it had taken her mother as long as it did before she was up on the stage with the boys.

Even more surprising was her own reaction. She whooped and hollered with the crowd when her mother was bent over with one nearly naked man at her rear and another holding her face in his crotch. Thankfully, both men were still wearing their thongs.

When the two young men finally lifted her from the stage and out of the spotlights, Carol was a sweating mess. Her once perfectly styled hair was now akimbo. Streaks of eyeliner trailed down her face. She reminded Dani of those awful oil paintings of sad clowns.

Plopping back down in her chair, Carol reached for her cocktail and downed it without pause. With a dopey drunkenness, she looked up at Dani.

"Aren't you going to eat your split?"

Carol's was already eaten, but Dani's remained intact, one oversized, peeled banana with a trail of whipped cream spurting out at one end and two scoops of ice cream at the other. The two mounds of ice cream were topped off with coconut shavings not so curiously dyed brown.

The waiter had delivered the desserts with the quip, "This's sure to split ya!"

"I think I've had too much to drink, Mother. Every time I look at it, my stomach feels queasy."

"It's the best dick I've had since I got to the city!"

Carol cackled and slammed a fist down onto the table rocking the silverware and glassware.

"I take it back. Those boys who had me up there—" she shook her head "—Lordy, they were yummy."

"Did you enjoy yourself?"

The older woman cocked her head as if she had just heard the strangest thing.

"Did you see me up there? Of course I did. You want one of them?"

"What?" It was Dani's turn to be confused.

"Stupid girl. We can rent any of these boys for the night."

"Mother! No. I do not want to buy a man."

Carol rummaged around in her purse shaking her head and tsk-ing.

"Oh, fuck, here we go again. 'Boo hoo. I'm married.'"

"Do we need to have this argument again, Mother?"

"Let yourself go. You just might like it."

"Adultery is not my idea of fun."

"Your marriage is a joke, daughter dear. You cannot commit adultery on an adulterer."

With a bent cigarette held between her index and middle finger, Carol pointed at Dani.

"Forget about that no-good rotten son of a bitch, and have a good time for once in your life!"

Dani grabbed for the cigarette, "You can't smoke in here!"

Carol was too fast. Already lighting up, Carol said, "Bullshit."

"This is New York City! You can't buy a large soda! They're going to throw us out of here."

"So what? I've had my fun."

"Do you always have to be so pig-headed?"

Spying the pointing waiters, Dani grabbed the cigarette out of her mother's mouth and drowned it in a water glass. The other patrons were too enthralled by the latest act to be bothered. Though a few were waving smoke away from their faces.

Carol snickered, "How did my daughter become such an old maid?"

"Mom, please. I'm too drunk to get thrown out right now. Behave."

Reaching across the table, Carol slid Dani's banana split towards her side of the table. She plucked the banana up and began sucking on it—garishly performing faux fellatio.

Dani shook her head and then turned her attention back to the stage. Another woman had taken her mother's place and was being accosted on the stage by a giant, muscle bound man who, Dani was sure, was barely legal.

"Are you quite through molesting that poor fruit?"

Carol bit the banana nearly in half. With her mouth full, she spat, "Nasty little girl. I want to pull your hair." Pieces of banana flew across the table erupting from her mother's mouth.

"Like you did when I was a little girl? That's it." Dani rose from the table. "I'm going back to the hotel!"

"Go right ahead. I'm staying and enjoying myself!"

Dani grabbed her purse from the back of her chair and bolted towards the exit. She was guided by the violet curtains billowing outwards from the lighted lobby.

As she stomped her way out of the lobby and onto the street, Dani could not understand why she became so suddenly and violently angry with her mother. The whole episode was fantastic.

The cold night air bit into her. The residual warmth from the theater dissipated. It brought her thoughts back to the moment. She was grateful for having worn a jacket which she cinched tightly around herself. Dani was prepared for Manhattan's autumn weather which was just cold enough to make her breath visible.

She scanned up and down the avenue for a taxi. Traffic was uncharacteristically quiet. Dani decided to move down the avenue to the intersection. The street seemed to be a little bit busier, and she assessed her chances of hailing a cab as better there.

At the corner, the neon sign at the all-hours pizza joint flashed "Open," and the blue-white fluorescents burst through the clear glass walls so brightly that they made Dani squint. Despite it being such a beacon in the night the benches inside were empty.

The smell of baking pizza enticed her, and even though Dani had had no appetite for banana splits, a slice of pepperoni pizza made her mouth water.

Pushing open the door, she was startled by how loud its electronic alarm chimed. Dani let go of the door, and it slammed shut with a metallic crack. She grimaced hoping nothing had broken, and no one of account had noticed.

The night had put her on edge.

"Hello?" she called out timidly.

The warmth from the ovens inside was a stark, but welcome, contrast to the biting cold outside. She loosened her jacket.

Dani waited for a moment then called out again, louder. "Hello? Anyone here?"

She studied the pizzas inside the glass counter. They looked to be hours old, but still hot under the heat lamps. Orange grease from the cheese was pooling atop some of them. It didn't matter. She would have eaten any, if handed one.

From the kitchen, a large, middle-aged man ambled behind the counter. He had salt and pepper hair, but a black as night mustache sat on his lip that Dani could not help but raise an eyebrow at.

"May I help you?" the man asked with an accent straight out of Central Casting.

Dani would have bet a $1000 that he was New York Italian, born and bred, and if she was going to have pizza, who better to get it from?

"Yes, please. I'd like a slice of pepperoni," she said cheerily, bending over the counter and pointing at a slice.

He smiled, but shook his head.

"You don't want one from the case. Listen, I got a fresh pie in the oven. It'll be done in a couple of minutes. Can you wait?"

Dani smiled.

"Of course. Wow. Thanks. Uhhh, can I buy a soda now, though?"

"No problem. Diet or regular?"

"Any diet without caffeine? How about a medium, too?" she asked.

"I can meet you in the middle. Just diet."

Shrugging her shoulders, she nodded.

"That'll work."

She paid for her drink and the slice then sat at one of the empty tables. The man disappeared back into the kitchen to tend to his baking.

Sipping her soda through a straw, Dani looked out at the cold street corner beyond the glass. It still confounded her that there was so little activity in the most heavily walked city in the world.

Maybe it's too late, but the thought was plain silly for Manhattan.

"Okay, here we go," the man said, carrying a piping hot pizza on a pan. In his other hand was a stand which he placed in front of Dani.

"I hope you don't mind if I join you. This was going to be my dinner."

Surprised, Dani happily agreed.

"Please."

He placed the pizza down on the stand, pulled off his latex gloves and extended a hand.

"You'll never guess, but yes, my name's Sal. Just like on the sign."

She shook his hand and returned his smile.

"Dani, pleased to meet you, Sal. So, this is your place?"

"Well, it's my mom's, but she doesn't get up here much. She's finally retired at 90."

"90? Wow. That's one tough lady."

Dani bit into a steaming hot slice. It was so hot that it almost burned her, but the wonderful tomato sauce and melted cheese tasted so fresh and vibrant.

"Oh, wow, this's so good."

Sal had folded his own slice down the middle and took a bite so big that nearly half of it was gone.

"Been making pizzas since I was outta diapers. It better be good."

"It is," Dani said.

"What's a nice young lady like you doing out by herself so late?"

Dani rolled her eyes.

"Errrm…"

"The strip joint!" He smiled widely. "I knew it."

She laughed while her cheeks grew red.

"I took my mother. Or, more to the truth, she took me."

"Your mother?!"

"I'm not that old!"

"I didn't mean anything like that. I mean, she's probably one tough lady, too."

"Yeah, she probably should not have enjoyed herself as much as she did—a woman her age."

Dani stifled her laughter with another bite, but her eyes did the laughing for her.

Sal chuckled.

"That's okay. I'm a believer in never getting old. Sounds like I'd really like your mother."

"I love her for sure. But she still has a knack for embarrassing me."

Finished with her first slice, Dani looked at the rest of the pie longingly.

Sal noticed.

"Go ahead. I can't eat the whole thing. My doctor won't let me."

"Here, I'll—"

She reached for her purse.

"—No. It's on the house."

"Are you sure?"

Sal nodded nibbling on his slice.

"Thank you so much, Sal. It's such a nice thing to do."

"On a night like this, good company is payment enough."

He looked out the windows of the store at the very quiet street. "It's too weird. The last time I saw these two streets so... so dead was 9/11. Things've been very weird lately. Something's in the air."

"It's late. Maybe people decided to stay home," Dani offered.

"On a Friday night? If you say so."

He chuckled easily as he started on his third and last piece. "It ain't so bad, though. I work pretty damn hard on busy nights. Could use the money, but, hey, could use the relaxation, too."

"Do you work nights by yourself?"

"Yeah," Sal said.

He swallowed and abruptly looked away. He cleared his throat. "Yeah. Since my wife passed. My kids used to help, but I got one boy in the Marines and another in college in Washington State."

"Oh, I'm sorry. About your wife."

"Ahh, I'm thankful she was mine for the time we had. She was a wonderful woman, and she gave me two great boys... Are you married?"

Dani popped a piece of crust into her mouth and chewed. She thought about her answer. Finally, she said, "Yes, but, we're having problems."

"That's a shame. I don't mean to give anybody any advice, but life's too short. If you love each other, work it out."

Dani broke his eye contact. It was her turn to look away out at the street. Truth was, Sam's wisdom felt intrusive. She was tired of the unasked-for advice.

"Eh, don't mind me. I only know from my life. You got a different story to tell."

"I... Well," she stopped mid thought. There was nothing for her to say.

Sam focused on eating the remaining pizza.

Several moments passed as Dani watched the empty streets, until it occurred to her that her being at a pizza shop was not in Steale's book, nor her and her mother's adventure in the strip club. A giant smile of revelation grew on her face and a giggle turned into a laugh.

Sam, puzzled, watched her with a raised eyebrow, chuckling himself—her laughter was contagious.

"Something I said?"

She raised a hand to her mouth and struggled to say, "No, it's..."

"I'm all ears," he said, still smiling.

"Sal, you ever been caught up in somebody else's crazy ideas? Stuff you started believing even though you knew it was all bullshit?"

"That's a dangerous question, Dani. I mean, we believe in lots of things we got no real evidence for. I suppose, but I never believed enough that it stopped me from doing what I thought was right or doing what I wanted."

Movement down the street caught her eyes. A tallish woman was walking sandwiched between two men in suits. They were walking on the opposite side of the street and just now moving parallel to the pizza shop. The woman stumbled, laughing, and the light caught her face. It was Carol. The men caught her from falling and hoisted her up.

The men were bald and had no faces.

Dani backed away from the glass wall, her chair scraping against the floor with a metallic, stuttering whine. She could not, however, take her eyes from the people as they cut around the corner, moving away and getting smaller and smaller. Her face grew pale and all expression left.

Sam noticed.

"You okay there, Dani?"

When her mother and her faceless companions had become shadows, she pulled her eyes from the window but did not speak.

"The pizza's still nice and hot. I'll leave those last two for you."
Sal patted his sizable belly. "I have to watch my weight... get bigger!"

He tested a laugh. Dani wasn't biting.

"You need me to call a cab for you? You feeling okay? I hope it ain't the pizza."

"No, Sal."

Dani bolted up.

"Wait a second. Don't—let me get you that cab!"

Before he could stop her, she was up and out of the pizza shop after her mother, leaving Sal to watch as she ran up the street and into the darkness.

CHAPTER THIRTY SIX

Shannon laid wide awake. He tried to sleep, but once the alcohol began to fade, he was left avoiding the wet spots in Ellen's hotel bed.

The clock on the table next to the bed—which must've been 20 years old—read, in big red, digital letters, 3:13. The little 'am' in the upper right corner blinked with each passing second. He could hear the whole device hum over the slow, deep rhythm of Ellen's breathing.

It wasn't the first time he had ever contemplated escaping the post-sex bed of some pretty young woman who had lost her luster in his eyes.

Gently, Shannon threw off the sheet and slid himself into a sitting position at the edge of the bed. He looked over his shoulder to be sure Ellen was still asleep. Her small back was exposed as the bed sheet crumpled about her waist. Her ribs expanded and shrunk with every breath. She was undisturbed by his movements.

Carefully, very carefully, Shannon stood, then gathered his clothes. He put them on as silently as he could.

With the curtains open, the lake at night stared back at him. Its whitecaps churned luminescent. The full moon hung low in the pitch black sky and drew a long reflection across the water. Ellen stirred.

Sprawling across the empty bed, her legs wiped across the sheets pulling them from her chest. Her breasts slowly rose and fell.

She was porcelain in the moonlight.

He decided to leave before she did wake, and before his nagging regret finally killed what was left of his buzz. He pointed himself toward the door.

An urge rushed over him like the flush of a fever. He looked down at the woman.

He desperately wanted to kill her.

It was red hot all over him.

She was the reason he had failed Dani, the reason he had broken his vows.

Shannon stood over her. She filled him with a rage that pounded against his chest.

Ellen drew her hand up to her mouth and flicked absently. A little moan escaped from her parted lips.

He scanned the bedside table to his right. The lamp was a fixture bolted into the wood. There was a hotel pad, with her scribbles on it, and a pen.

Shannon had nothing to kill her with.

Nothing but his hands.

His heart jumped into his throat. *What the fuck is wrong with you?* he thought.

He bolted for the door. He could not get out of the room and away from Ellen fast enough.

In the hallway, he pulled the door shut but held it until it slowly and quietly clicked closed. Once he heard it fasten, a weight fell from him, and he let out a sigh of relief, slumping against the wall and hanging his head.

Shannon caught his reflection in the polished, black floor tiles. It struck him. He could make out his clothes up to his neck, but his face was blank. He stared hard, but he could find no eyes.

He was faceless.

Shannon shook his head hard trying to erase the image from his mind. He looked again, and there he was looking haggard.

Pulling himself up from his slump, he moved towards the elevators. His heels were clicking against the tiles and were louder than he wanted. Shannon slowed his pace and began to walk on the balls of his feet. The last thing he wanted to do was wake up the entire floor.

It was an odd thought. He wanted to get out of there, away from her, without being witnessed. *Why?*

His heart began racing again.

She was breathing when he left her. He distinctly remembered unconsciously counting the number of breaths she took as he stood and watched. That memory calmed him, but he pressed the elevator down button impatiently. It clicked and clicked and clicked, but it didn't hasten the ascent of the elevator.

He glanced over his shoulder. The stairwell was behind him. Shannon wanted so much to be gone that 15 floors of stairs was a price he would gladly pay. The truth was that he was afraid of being overcome again. He could easily bust down the door to her room and finish what he had longed to start.

Shannon just couldn't do it with waking the entire floor.

He looked up at the elevator indicator lights, and the elevator was stuck between the first few floors. That was it. He threw himself into the stairwell.

Instead of the stylish mauve, mint and black of the hallway, the stairwell was a tannish yellow-lit brightly with orange halogens. Shannon's artistic sensibilities were instantly offended. He looked below towards the endless circle of steps. The bottom floor rushed up at him, and he pulled his head back away from the railing. Tasting the remnants of the evening in the back of his throat, he shook off the alcohol-fueled vertigo and began his descent with a sigh.

By the time he reached the last set of stairs, his thighs were aching. Shannon had had more than his daily share of hip-centric exercise. No longer able to lift his legs properly, Shannon tottered down the final steps.

He wished he had waited for the elevator. His body was one big cramp. His head pounded with an oncoming hangover.

Shannon stopped at the exit door that led to the lobby. He held his forearm against the wall. Lowering his head against it, he allowed his eyes to close while he tried to find a second wind.

He hesitated before entering the lobby and watched for a few minutes at the cracked exit door. It looked empty from this vantage. But he wanted to make sure he didn't have to explain himself to any prying front desk clerk or security guard. It was bad enough that he was and had been on security cam this whole time. It was a wonder that he wasn't being interrogated at that very moment.

Finally satisfied that the time was right, Shannon walked briskly through the open lobby toward the glass front, past the empty, black leather chairs and sofas and past the water fountain made of a single glass sheet. Pushing through the main door, he glanced over his shoulder and stopped.

At first, he thought it was the distortion of the room through the glass fountain. Water trickling down the smooth, transparent surface scattered the light from the room behind it, but when he realized that he was actually looking at a man standing at the side of the fountain, his heart dropped into the pit of his stomach.

The man, dressed in a black, Italian cut suit and tie nearly identical to his own, coolly approaching him had no face.

Shannon was frozen. His mind could not process what he was seeing so clearly. When he previously witnessed a faceless man it was from a distance. This time, there he was, bold under the bright lights of the hotel, only a few feet away. His body filled with adrenaline, and Shannon scrambled out of the lobby and into the parking round.

He slid across the cobblestone driveway but managed to maintain his balance. He looked over his shoulder. The faceless man stepped from behind the glass door.

Though he had no mouth, Shannon heard his voice.

"We need to speak with you."

Suddenly, there was movement all around him. His eyes darted over his right shoulder, over his left. Spinning on his heels, there was another and another and another. From the shadows, everywhere he looked, there emerged more faceless men.

"No. This is not happening."

Shannon clutched his eyes hoping that this was all some sort of alcohol-fueled delusion. *What are they called? Delirium tremens?*

Then, he screamed, "You aren't real!"

He pulled his hands from his eyes expecting to see them gone, but they remained and inched ever closer to him.

"What do you want from me?"

"We don't want anything from you, Shannon," the one who exited the hotel said—though how Shannon knew it was him, he did not know. "It's what you want from us."

"What? What are you talking about?"

He spun looking for an escape, but there was none.

He could not even count how many faceless men there were. They were infinite.

They closed in on him, a mass of flesh dressed in black suits.

CHAPTER THIRTY
SEVEN

The clicking of her own heels was, oddly enough, the only thing that Dani could hear. In New York City, no matter what time, her ears should have been inundated with honking horns, rushing traffic and people: people talking, people whistling, people being people.

But there were no other sounds.

The street was deserted.

Carol Strauss, on the arms of faceless men—yes, she acknowledged what she had seen—cut across the street far ahead of her and then disappeared. Dani assumed that they had moved up the nearby avenue, because they were nowhere to be seen, now.

Dani fidgeted inside her purse. She pulled out her phone and dialed her mother. Listening to her phone ring, she looked up and down the street before crossing it herself. She wasn't in any danger as the nearest headlights were miles away.

The building on this side of the street was under construction, and the sidewalk was covered by a safety tunnel of scaffolding and wood. Dani ducked under the tunnel's railing in order to step onto the sidewalk.

With her heels clicking on the sidewalk once more, she concentrated on the path she supposed her mother had trod. The construction tunnel ended at the next intersection where she hoped to turn and catch a glimpse of Carol stumbling in the distance on the arms of two men whose facelessness did not bother her.

A laugh.

A very light giggle.

Dani stopped and listened.

She must've imagined it.

There was no time to waste, and she started to move once more.

But there it was again followed by hushed whispers.

She looked for any source in the windows and nearby alleyways, but there was not a soul in sight who could have made those noises.

This time, the laugh was loud and long enough that Dani could trace where it was coming from, and it was coming from the construction site behind the wooden tunnel she was in. Scrambling along the wooden planks, she looked for a gap or an open knot-hole, a crack, anything that would give her a peek inside.

Dani found a place at the end of the street. There was a gap wide enough for just one of her eyes to see through.

She found her mother. Carol Strauss—her drunken, beloved mother—sat atop a pile of steel I-beams being fondled by the two faceless men. Deeply kissing one of the men, Carol's lips touched skin that bulged outward toward hers, most unnaturally.

Dani pulled her head back. It made her sick to her stomach and frightened for her mother.

These things weren't human. They were terrible facsimiles. Unformed imitations, like the clay figures a child might sculpt if they forgot or didn't know how to complete a face.

She bolted around to the end of the street. The wood paneling gave way to chain link fencing, but the area where her mother was being fondled was invisible to her, now, behind the temporary building that housed the construction manager and architects per the sign hanging off its side. A little further down the fencing, an entrance was set into the mesh, but it was locked with a chain.

Dani studied the height of the fence. If she dropped her heels over first, she'd be able to climb up and over herself. That it had been years since she had climbed anything gave her a short pause.

Flipping off her heels, she slung her bag's strap over her neck instead of just her shoulder.

Up and over, Dani was surprised at how easy it was, but it would not be so for her mother. She let thoughts of how she might escape with Carol slip from her mind. *One thing at a time.*

As she dropped to the ground, she heard her mother's muted voice speaking. Carol still sounded as if she was having the time of her life.

Crouching low, Dani pressed herself against the outer wall of the temporary office and surveyed the site. Behind her was the fence. Ahead of her, climbing up to the sky well over the roof of the office, was the unfinished skeleton of a high rise. Every other incomplete floor glowed dim and brown by a safety light somewhere in its interior. In the darkness of the night, it looked less like something being built and more like something dangerous and hungry.

Sharp-edged gravel bit into her bare feet, and she suppressed several "ouches" as she moved, in a crouch, around the outside of the office. Dani wasn't sure that there was anyone in the office, but if there was a security guard, she intended to avoid him. Though, with all the noise her mother made, anyone guarding the site would have already descended upon her mother and her faceless lovers. That there hadn't been any interruption pointed to no actual security of any kind on premises.

Coming up to a window for the trailer, Dani decided to peek inside. Slowly, slowly, she popped her head up over the lower sill. Inside the office, the blue and white light of the security cameras flashed in the darkness, but the guard seat sat empty.

She slowly turned the doorknob to the guard shack. It was unlocked.

Slipping inside, Dani closed the door carefully, hoping it wouldn't make too much of a racket. Her attention turned to the security monitor. The flatscreen displayed multiple camera views, each labeled accordingly. She sat in the chair and placed a hand on the mouse connected to the console. Starting in the upper left corner, Dani clicked on the camera feed.

The whole of the flatscreen filled with the footage from the first camera. It was of the front gate. Mostly dark with some light streaking through the links in the gate, it provided Dani nothing. She clicked on the image and the panoply of feeds returned.

Dani methodically searched every camera, but there were nothing but shadows and indistinct shapes. There was no sign of her mother.

She was going to have to hope that Carol continued to be noisy. With still no sign of a guard, Dani moved out of the office trailer without fear.

The night was catching up with her. She yawned, and could not think of anything more inviting than a warm bed—even a hotel bed.

But, her return to normalcy was broken when Dani heard her mother shriek.

She looked up at the construction site searching for any signs of movement or origin point.

Another shriek!

Dani sprinted as fast as she could—still without shoes and feeling every sharp pebble—toward the first floor of the building.

"I'm coming, Mom!"

Entering through the gaping hole in a brick wall, Dani bolted into the hollowed-out room, but her purse strap caught on a stray piece of rebar sending its contents everywhere. She landed on a knee.

"Ow!" she snapped. "Shit."

Slowly, she got to her feet and listened.

There was nothing. Her mother had stopped making noises. Carol should have been more than aware of her presence at this point.

With a slight step, Dani tested her knee. She winced. She could walk, but there'd be no more running tonight.

Her billfold was the first thing she found. It took her several minutes to gather up her purse and its cargo—at least that which she could find.

She left her expensive heels on the floor, though. They were too tight, and she needed all the speed she could muster. They'd only serve to slow her down with a bum knee. The concrete floor, while cold to her stockinged feet, were for the most part clean of painful rocks and debris.

Dani ascended the stairs to the landing listening every step of the way.

Her mother's silence frightened her. Images of Carol laying crumpled in a heap on the concrete floor with blood pooling around her flooded her mind.

"Mother?" she half-heartedly called out.

There was no answer, but a shuffling and a clang of some falling metal led her past the empty second floor and up to the third. At that landing, Dani poked her head up over the guardrail. Unlike the two floors below, this floor had no central floodlight. This floor was dark. Only the light from below cast any shadows. Everything else was lit by moonlight or the streetlamps barely below.

Dani stepped into the shadows of this level.

Some boxes were stacked six feet high near the stairwell. Dani crouched behind them, listening.

There was movement coming from the other side of the floor. It sounded like dragging.

Dani glimpsed around the edge of a box. She searched for the source of the noise, but it was gone.

She stepped, in a crouch, around the stack. Dani moved briskly to another stack of boxes. Once there, she listened once more.

After several moments, Dani heard soft sobs. Her fear cautioned her.

"Mom?" she called out in a whisper.

More sobs.

Dani could run or face whatever was on the other side of the boxes. But her rising fear was powerful.

She knew she had to act, though.

Dani bolted around the boxes.

This time it wasn't her eyes that needed to adjust to her surroundings. It was her mind.

The thing on the ground was cloth, flesh and hair. A cold, wet hand brushed hers. It was trying to grab Dani to pull her into an embrace. She recoiled, but the hand clung to her. When it turned to look at her, it's eyes—her mother's eyes—saw her and recognized her before dissolving into the gelled mass.

"Da-n-i—h-eee-l—ppppp," it whined with her mother's voice.

The shape became a shadow, then a vapor, then nothing leaving only a horrible, wet moan that floated in the air around Dani.

Holding her hand into the light, she watched as the remnants of the thing that was her mother evaporated.

It took seconds before the panic caught up with her brain. Her legs had decided long before that she was not staying. Dani flew down the stairs, despite her knee, and then across the construction site in her bare feet. Finding the section of the fence that she had climbed earlier, Dani heaved herself up and over.

On the sidewalk, she caught her breath.

There was still no one around.

She could call the police, but what would she tell them? That she was trespassing in a construction zone following her mother with two faceless men only to see her mother dissolve into some Hollywood special effect?

In the distance, Dani saw the yellow of a cab. She waved for it and wolf-whistled, and it made its lazy way to her.

Dani sprinted towards the cab.

"Wvere too?" the cabby said in the English he barely understood.

"Drive!"

CHAPTER THIRTY EIGHT

S tars in the night sky twinkled above him, and the city lights twinkled below him.

Shannon was thousands of feet above the city on the roof of Ellen's hotel. The cold wind off the lake whipped around his body. It was chilling to the bone, but kept Shannon from falling asleep.

He had no idea how he got to be where he was: on top of a skyscraper.

Shaking off the fog that had collected in his mind, Shannon could not yet remember.

Moving up close to the barrier wall that bordered the roof, he leaned over the edge and looked down. The lights of the roundabout glowed brightly, and the face of the hotel was dotted with lights from occupied rooms.

At the end of the avenue running along the waterfront, red and blue lights of police cars flashed without sirens.

He felt a vibration in his pants pocket. Shannon didn't realize that he still had his phone. Without looking, he held it to his ear.

"Hello?"

"Shannon, where are you?"

It was Dani. She sounded upset.

"I'm... Well, I'm... It'll sound crazy if I tell you—"

"—I've seen terrible things, Shannon."

"Honey, what's wrong?"

He gathered up his loose clothes laying on the roof.

A sign reading **EXIT** signaled access to the roof exit. Shannon headed for it.

"Listen, to me. I saw my mother melt away."

Shannon stopped in his tracks. He remembered. He remembered the faceless men attacking him. He remembered their fists, their hands tearing at him.

"Shannon, are you there?" Dani's words were frantic.

"Yeah, yeah, I'm here. Babe, come home. There's something happening to me. To you. To us."

"I'm headed to my hotel room. I want to call the police, but I don't think they'll believe me. Am I going crazy?"

"Dani, if you are, then so am I."

As he turned to take the roof exit, the door burst open. Uniformed police officers flowed through the opening, guns drawn and shouting.

"Get on the ground!"

"Show us your hands!"

"Drop it!"

Shannon dropped the phone. With 9mm pistols in his face, he had no other choice but to do as they commanded.

Laying on the gravel covered roof, Shannon could still hear Dani screaming through his phone which laid nearby.

"Shannon? Shannon? What's happening?!"

"Hands behind your back!"

Once his hands were cuffed, the officers lifted him to his feet.

"My phone! I need my phone!"

Shannon could no longer hear Dani, but he knew she was still screaming for him.

CHAPTER THIRTY NINE

Dani bolted from the taxi as soon as she paid the driver. The graveyard desk clerk, alarmed by Dani running through the lobby, attempted to stop her, but passing her key over the elevator security scanner, she quickly boarded the elevator to her floor.

From memory, she had four hours to get to La Guardia for the first short flight to Chicago. Shannon was in trouble, and he needed her.

As soon as the elevator doors slid open, she ran to her room, slid the hotel key into its slot and banged into the room.

"Holy Hell!"

Carol shot up from her bed. She was outfitted in her night creams and curls. Only lit by the light from the hallway through the open door, she was hideous and not unlike the fleshy mess Dani had just witnessed.

Dani stopped in her tracks and nearly bowled over. She let the door shut behind her.

She'd taken it as fact that her mother had evaporated into nothingness. Had it been a hallucination?

The answer was obvious and staring out at her from behind her garish mask.

Now, seeing Carol Strauss alive and in the flesh, even at her worst, Dani was shocked and relieved and shocked some more.

Motionless, Dani's eyes were as wide as saucers.

"Girl! Where're your manners?" Carol snapped on her night light. "Didn't I learn you how to step lightly after 2 a.m. ?"

"Mom?" Dani said. The word caught in her throat.

The older woman moved by her stupefied daughter on her way to the loo.

"Mom? Yes, Mom. Spit it out, girl. You can't go out a-whoring without telling me the details."

The toilet seat creaked, and Dani could hear her mother relieve herself of the previous night's alcohol.

"You left me at the club, and I made the most of it. Let me tell you. I know most of those boys're queer, but that doesn't bother me one little bit."

The toilet flushed, and her mother moved to the sink to wash her hands.

"What use does an old woman like me have for chicken aside from heavy petting anyway?" Carol emerged from the bathroom with a laugh.

"I've had my fill of men in my life. Sometimes, a taste is just enough. What dragged you out of there? Or who?"

"I—uhh—I—I walked for a while. Had some pizza, and then took a cab back here," Dani said.

Carol jumped back into her bed.

"That was some long walk."

Dani moved to her bed and set her suitcase atop it. She reached inside and grabbed her fresh night clothes.

"I'm getting a flight out in a few hours."

"Oh, here we go," Carol said.

Instead of fighting, the older woman rolled over and pulled a pillow over her head.

"Don't wake me when you leave, either."

In the bathroom, Dani stripped off her dress. Feeling the water until it was a comfortable temperature, she entered the shower.

"I refuse to let you go back to that man!' Carol practically screamed.

"I'll call you when I land."

She shut the shower door. It was enough of a barrier that Dani would not have to hear any more bitching. But Carol was not done. She burst into the bathroom.

"Mother!"

There was a banging on the wall!

"Oh, shut up!" Carol yelled. "I practically own this hotel! Complain all you want."

"Go back to bed, please."

Carol slammed the lid down and sat on the toilet.

"Why are you leaving and going back to Shannon now? More sweet talk? Good Lord, it always worked on me. It's no wonder it works on you, the fruit of my loins."

"No, Mom. He's in trouble."

"So, what? Are you supposed to drop everything and rescue him? After the way he treated you? He's a grown man, and you aren't his mother," Carol said. "Didn't my life teach you any lessons? You just want to repeat all my mistakes?"

Dani finished her quick shower and popped open the shower door. She pointed at the towels.

"Pass me one, Mom?"

"All bullshit aside, Dani. I want you to settle down with a nice man and raise a family. I know I've said it a million times— enough so that you don't even hear it when I say it anymore— this man is not the one. He's wasting your time."

Dropping the newly dampened towel on the floor, Dani slipped on her night clothes.

"I love him, Mom. This life, it's enough for me. Let's get some sleep. I know I'm going to have a busy day today."

Dani left Carol sitting on the toilet, perplexed.

"How exactly does your busy-ness figure for me?"

From the outside room, Dani said, "You're coming with whether you like it or not."

"What? I thought you were leaving. Do I get a say in this?"

Carol moved back into the outer room. She jumped back under her covers.

"When did I get drafted?"

"I decided now, Mom. Just be my mother. Support me for once."
Fluffing up her pillow, Carol looked across the gap between beds at her daughter. In the darkness, she could see that Dani had already closed her eyes.

"I am your mother. I always will be."

Dani answered her with a light snore.

CHAPTER FORTY

Shannon would've welcomed even the roughest of street-hardened toughs into his cell. He'd been alone in the cold, small grey room for more than a day, maybe more than two days. The concrete walls surrounding him made it difficult to perceive time.

He craved human contact if only to remind him that he was not the only man alive.

Only occasionally had a guard checked up on him in all those hours. And during that time, In every shadow, he saw movement. He had fleeting glimpses of eyes peering at him from the dark corners of his cell.

Blinking in and out of existence.

Over and over, he replayed the events of the last several nights. It mostly seemed a blur, enough so that he really had no clear idea what had happened.

Did he drink too much? Did someone slip something into his drinks? Was it all his paranoid imagination?

Shannon heard the metal clanking of a prison door sliding open and the tapping of hard-soled shoes on the solid, concrete floor.

He righted himself. His eyes darted around the cell. There was nothing inside with him that he could use to protect himself.

"Shannon McClarty, back away from the bars. Do not move to the bars. Keep your hands in view. Any deviation, and I will tase you," the guard, with a name tag reading Velasquez, said.

He cast a giant shadow into the cell.

Purposefully stepping around the shadow, Shannon held his arms out as the bars slid open. Almost immediately, he was in cuffs threaded through the loops of his jumpsuit, so his hands were held fast to his waist.

"What's going on? Where are you taking me?" Shannon asked stifling his fear.

"You got visitors."

Velazquez held him by the shoulder as he guided him out of the cell into the hallway.

"Prisoner McClarty secure and coming through."

"My lawyer?"

"Not your lawyer." Velazquez snickered. "You probably won't see them until they show up to agree to cop your plea to avoid the death penalty."

"I didn't do it," Shannon said. "I swear."

"I'm sure. You're in a jail with a bunch of folks who didn't do it, either."

Pushed through the last set of sliding bars, Shannon was led into a holding room and forced to sit with a group of inmates also waiting to be admitted into the visiting room. Five guards communicated with more guards through a sliding slat cut into the metal door.

Two inmates were being ushered through to the holding room from the visiting room by two guards, their visiting privileges having expired.

Velazquez tapped Shannon on the shoulder and motioned for him to stand.

"You're up, prisoner McClarty. Let's go."

The guard guided him through the door and into the prisoner side of the visitors' room. Separated by a thick plexiglass wall, the room was further partitioned off by large metal dividers into a bank of eight desks completed on both sides of the glass. The guard snapped open Shannon's handcuffs.

At the last desk, Velazquez pressed Shannon into the seat. Opposite him sat Dani, a phone receiver pressed to her ear, with her mother behind her.

"Pick up the phone to talk," Velazquez instructed. "You have 15 minutes. Get to talking."

Quickly, Shannon grabbed his telephone.

"Dani, oh my God. Dani!"

"Shhh, shhh, shhh. Listen to me. We don't have time for anything other than forming a plan. Understand?" she said.

Her all-business demeanor shocked him.

"I got it," he said, still confused.

"I read the police report. Everything. Be honest with me, Shannon. Did you kill that woman?"

He felt his face contort into anger.

"No!"

Her gaze burned into him. She, of all people, would know when to believe him and when not.

After an interminable silence, finally, Dani said, "All right. We'll get the details of what happened later. But I need you to allow me to take control of your legal counsel. The guards will pass you a form to sign. It's to affirm my right as your spouse to make decisions on your behalf. Mom has made some calls. We're getting the best attorney in Chicago to review your case. Hopefully, he'll take you on. Then, we fight. We fight all of this."

Shannon smiled at her. No words he could say would convey to her exactly how much he appreciated his wife. He needed her.

Yet, he had to ask, "Have you seen them?"

Dani paused, "What?"

"Have you seen the faceless men?"

Dani looked around the room nervously then leaned into the plexiglass that separated them.

"Do not say another word about them... "

Velazquez abruptly returned.

"Time's up, McClarty. Let's go."

"My time can't be up so soon!" Shannon said, dropping the phone from his ear. "You think this's 15 minutes?"

Dani rose from her chair, and Shannon could see her yelling after her guard minders on the other side of the glass.

"No arguing, McClarty. You're the prisoner."

Velazquez put a powerful hand on Shannon's shoulder with enough strength to compel him to rise.

Shannon could feel the anger welling up inside him. He was going to strike the guard, but Dani fell against the divider and locked eyes with him. He felt a calmness overcome him. She was crying. Crying for him, but that made it all right.

"Fine! Fine. I'm coming," he said, but he mouthed the words: I love you to Dani before he was dragged away.

"C'mon, man. I'm going," Shannon protested.

But Velazquez ignored him. His hand still gripped his shoulder like a vise.

"Shut your mouth, *puto*."

The guard pushed him through the prisoner holding room and then through to the main hallway.

"Prisoner McClarty!" Velazquez announced.

Another guard, a female, opened one of the office doors in the holding area. She held a pen and a clipboard.

"Secure him, Velazquez."

"Yes, ma'am."

She approached Shannon and held out the clipboard.

"Sign this. It's from your wife."

Shannon looked at the paper held on the clipboard. It read in bold letters at the top: Power of Attorney Application.

"Sign the bottom, so we can move on, McClarty," the woman said.

He took the pen and scribbled, as best he could, his signature on the clipboard held by the guard. She quickly took the pen from his hands. Velazquez put the handcuffs back on him.

The female guard ordered, "Get him out of here."

Velazquez nodded then locked a huge hand on Shannon's shoulder once more.

The cellblock bars slid open, and they were practically running back to his cell. His cuffed hands made it difficult, and he nearly tripped over the track for the last sliding door.

"I thought I had 15 minutes. What happened to that?"

Velazquez thrust Shannon through the open door to his cell.
"Hold your hands steady."

Breathing heavily, Shannon did his best to catch his breath.
He turned around and held out his cuffed hands from their
restraint at his waist.

The guard slipped off the cuffs and quickly exited with a slam
of the cell door.

"Aren't you gonna answer me?!" Shannon yelled after him.
"Why didn't you give me my 15 minutes?!"

He kicked at the metal door sending shooting pain through his
foot. He fell onto his meager bunk. Instead of shoes, prisoners
were issued flip flops, and they provided no protection against
a reckless prisoner jamming his toes against a metal door.

Shannon pulled his foot up towards his head. Luckily, no toes
were bleeding. They were just smashed and slightly swollen.

"Damn it," Shannon said to himself.

He released his foot and stretched out across his bed. Counting
backwards, he estimated that his next meal was hours away
yet. Considered a high-risk inmate—having been accused of
homicide—Shannon was not allowed to eat in the commissary
with other prisoners, so his needs were provided by a direct
delivery to his cell.

He imagined that shower time—which was long overdue as
his last shower had been never—would not be far behind his
dinner.

His cell stunk, and he was certain he was the cause.

There was one saving grace to his dingy prison: it was next to
the yard. Despite the thick glass that served as his one, tiny
window, he could faintly hear the outside and see shadows of
the real world. Birds, cars, people noise. He concentrated on
those sounds.

It was hard for him to imagine what would become of himself
were he to stay in such a place for a long period of time. If his
situation were hopeless and he was sentenced to life in prison
—for crimes he did not commit, he reminded himself—could
he survive? Would he go mad? *What would I do without her?*

He needed her. She was his rock, his anchor. It calmed him to know that she was out in the world fighting for him.

Fatigue fell over him as his adrenaline rush was expended, Even his throbbing foot couldn't keep him from becoming drowsy.

When his eyes closed, though, the nightmares came. They started with him lifting his hands from her throat, and then he would catch Ellen's glassy, dead eyes staring back up at him.

He couldn't bear it: dream or reality.

With each fresh nightmare, his belief in his own innocence was faded.

But he did fall asleep, and in this sleep, like the others, his hands gripped tightly around Ellen's neck.

And he squeezed.

And squeezed.

So hard until he heard the bones in her neck snap.

Ellen's dead eyes pierced to his very soul.

CHAPTER FORTY ONE

"**D**amn it, Mother," Dani said. "Let's not complicate this. I don't want to lawyer shop. Pick the best one, so we can have this public defender dismissed."

Dani looked down at Shannon's signature on the power of attorney form.

"You said he was the best of the best."

"Look, darling daughter, I don't have much experience with criminal defense lawyers. My expertise is limited to divorce attorneys."

Carol led Dani through the throngs of civilians awaiting their turn, rather raucously, to have their visitations.

Outside the prison in the parking lot, Carol tossed Dani the rental car keys.

"You drive. My vision's shot at sundown. I'll make a call to Richard. He'll shoot me straight. I don't want to get any old ambulance-chasing, TV lawyer. If you love him, then I want the best shot at saving him. Don't be impatient."

They settled into the rental car, and Dani headed them off towards downtown Chicago and her loft.

"Oh, for heaven's sake, where's my cell?"

Carol fished through her enormous designer bag.

"I've got enough makeup in here for a parade of drag queens—oh—here it is."

She activated the phone and spoke into it, "Call Richard Nance."

"Calling Richard Nance," the phone replied.

"I'll put it on speakerphone, daughter dear, so you can hear, but don't just chime in unless you've got something smart to say."

The phone rang and rang until, "Nance & Hill, attorneys at law. How may I direct your call?"

"Jenny, this is Carol Strauss. Be a good girl and patch me into nasty Nance's office, please."

The receptionist giggled, and the line began to ring again. There was no negotiating a hold or a call back. Strauss was his best, most lucrative client, and surely made it known that any calls from her were to be piped through immediately.

Dani could hear the cigar smoke wafting in the air when Richard Nance answered.

"Carol, what can I do for you? You haven't gotten married again and need a quickie divorce? Do you?"

He laughed, and Carol laughed, but Dani wasn't amused. She didn't like her mother's foibles called out on the table so brazenly—especially from someone who had profited so greatly from them.

Carol immediately recognized her daughter's disdain, and cut off any frivolity.

"Listen, Nancy my love, I need some very good advice."

"Shoot," he said. "Am I on speakerphone?"

"Yes, you are."

"Any reason for that? I don't really like to give advice if I don't know exactly who's hearing it."

Carol laughed.

"Of course, of course. It's my daughter, Dani. We're on our way to her house at the moment. From jail."

"Jail?" Nance asked.

"Long story short: we need the best criminal defense lawyer in Chicago," Carol said.

"For who? For you?"

"No," Dani spoke up. "For my husband. He's accused of murder. But he's innocent."

"Always are," Nance said. "Presumption of innocence. Look, let me make a few calls. I have some friends in the Windy City. I'll get you the best, Carol. Nice to talk to you finally, Dani."

"Yes," she said. "Thanks for your help."

"Thanks, Dick!" Carol said.

"Expect my call," he said, and the line went dead.

They were doing good time on the expressway. The high-rises of Chicago grew ever taller with each passing mile.

"Do you really think he's innocent, Dani?" Carol asked. Suspicion dripped off her tongue.

"Isn't that an odd question to ask, now? After you've gone through all this?"

"I'm trying to be supportive! But you never know. Do you? Look at Ted Bundy. Nobody thought anything was wrong with that man. He wasn't just a pretty face, either. Charisma. Everyone bought into it. Let's just make sure that we aren't," Carol said.

Dani wanted to lash out reflexively, but she didn't. Her mother did have a point.

"I hear you, Mom. But Shannon's ability to charm me has faded over the years. I can tell when he's not lying, because he's lied to me so many times. He's pretty much taught me all his tells."

She pulled the car off the expressway and maneuvered onto the small side street where she lived. Lined with cars, there was no space anywhere to park the rental car.

"Crap," Dani said under her breath. "I forgot how bad it can get."

"What's wrong?" Carol asked.

"We'll never find a parking space. I should've known."

"Forget it. Let's go downtown and get a hotel room. Five star, all the way for this queen and her princess."

Dani thought about it. A hotel sounded nice, and she didn't feel like putting her loft back together after the police had torn it apart for their recent murder investigation.

"Wait a second!" Dani said as if she'd just won the lottery.

She slowed the car and immediately turned on her turn signal.

"We lucked out, mom."

Carol rolled her eyes.

"Did we really?"

Instead of double parking, a delivery driver had pulled into a space and parked. He was just now coming from a nearby building to return to his vehicle. Pleasantly, the man smiled and waved at the women.

"Is this the poor man who's going to be delivering our take-out later? Where oh where will he park? Our food will get cold. Even the Wyndham would be better."

With almost certainly no good food left in the loft, Dani knew that her mother made a good point.

"Should we go and get food, Mom? Is that what you're hinting at?"

Carol blew a raspberry.

"And miss getting this primo parking spot in your little patch of heaven?"

The delivery car pulled out of the space, and the driver waved a hand out of the window.

"Should I get out and guide you into the spot? I don't have my orange flashlights, but maybe my scarves will do?"

Dani started to parallel park. She glanced back up at the departing delivery car. The driver watched her without eyes, without a face.

She slammed on the brakes. The car lurched jostling the women.

"For Christ's sake, Dani!"

"Mom, did you see it?"

"What?"

"Did you see it?"

"What, girl?"

"The driver had no face."

Carol peered out the windshield at the retreating car.

"I can't see anything. Is that confirmation?"

"You don't believe me?" Dani said.

"I didn't say that," the older woman held up her hands. "It's too damn far for these old peepers to see. That's all I mean."

"Well, it was there. Driving away and looking at me in the rearview."

Carol straightened in the seat.

"What do you want me to do about it? If you're so damn concerned about it, let's chase the damn thing down!"

"Should we?"

Carol shrugged her shoulders.

"It'd be more trouble. Could be dangerous."

Honk!

"What?" the women said in unison.

His patience exhausted, the driver in the car behind them honked again.

"Okay!" Dani said leaning out the window. "I'm trying to park!"

"Do me a favor," Carol said. "I want to see this faceless sumbitch."

The rental car rocketed forward as Dani pressed on the gas. Behind them, the honking driver was left in a cloud of burned rubber.

Dani looked hard up the street for signs of the delivery car.

"Good Lord, girl! I think my panties are still back there in the road!"

Carol scrambled for and finally held onto any available handle.

"You said you wanted to find it!"

She slowed the car as they approached the coming intersection. It was a four-way stop governed by a sign not a light. In the neighborhood, it was notorious for accidents, and Dani was not going to have an accident this day.

The more she thought about it, the more excited she got about intercepting a faceless man. She and Carol were formidable. *Could we actually interrogate it?*

Once she cleared the intersection—making sure that the delivery car had not turned—Dani floored it. They sped towards the industrial section of town. Brownstones made way for warehouses and cinder block buildings.

After five in the afternoon, the area was thin on traffic. Workers were already headed for home.

"Do you see him anywhere?" Carol asked.

Dani sighed. "I think we lost him."

"So much the better. I didn't bring my brass knuckles. I tell you what, missy, an Old Fashioned would hit the spot."

The younger woman turned the car around. She was disappointed her quarry had escaped.

"You won't be getting one at my place. I run a dry home."

Carol scoffed. "Then, stop at the first bar we see! I will not be subjected to your prohibition torture, my dear."

"This is Chicago."

"Not Chicago of the Twenties!"

At the upcoming intersection, with darkened warehouses at each corner, their corner just so happened to have a dive bar set into one of the old buildings. They hadn't noticed it from the opposite side of the street, because it's sign was not yet lit. Now, with the sun completely down and the night sky darkening quickly, the words "BeeBee's Bar and Grill" glowed brightly. A few motorcycles were parked up next to the wall on the sidewalk. Another stand up sign out front said, "Happy Hour! Parking in rear."

"Aha!" Carol said. "I win again. Pull over. Let's get a drink and call our little pursuit over."

Dani wanted to volley some smart retort to her mother, but she bit her lip. Turned out, a drink sounded very good to her, too.

She turned at the corner and followed the arrows to the rear parking lot where there were quite a few cars already parked.

Before Dani could shut the engine off after parking the car, Carol was out of the car and pulling the backdoor to the bar open.

"Get your ass in gear, girl," she said waving for her daughter to join her.

"Yes, Mother."

Dani hopped out of the rental. She made it a point to press the lock button on the key fob before following inside.

The bar was exactly what she expected. Dark, lit by neon alcohol signs, booths on the left, filled with men, and a few women, who had just finished a day's work, and the bar on the right where the bikers roosted together sitting on stools. In the center were a few tables sparsely populated with sad singles. Her mother, drinks already bought, waited for her at one.

A jukebox blasted a late '80s heavy metal ballad that no one seemed to be paying any attention.

Dani recognized it only because it was played incessantly on all of the FM oldies stations that Shannon loved to play so much when he was sculpting.

"I haven't been in one of these places, since I was a hippy dippy in college," Carol said as Dani sat. "I love it. The booze's the same here as it is downtown. Cheaper and without all the pretense. This promises to be a very good night."

Pushing her drink away, Dani said, "We still have to clean up the loft and finalize Shannon's counsel."

"It'll wait. Hell, if it could wait for a mad dash after some faceless creep, it can wait for a few good Old Fashioneds. Can't we hire some people to come in to clean anyway?"

Carol pushed Dani's cocktail back towards her.

"Some of the men in here are quite hunky. Don't you think? Bet they could really push a mop or a broom. Broom broom!"

Dani scanned the room. Most of the men were rough in some way.

"Hunky? Mom, aren't they a little out of your normal target demo?"

Carol laughed.

"You mean: aren't they a little poor? I don't need any more money, honey. I need a good time. Haven't you seen my metamorphosis?"

The cocktail did not burn her throat as she anticipated. Instead, the bourbon was sweet with a hint of cherry and orange only interrupted by a tang of bitters. It was good. Dani did not expect to like it. She expected the drink to be as rough as the clientele.

"See?" Carol said.

She had noticed Dani's reaction to her drink.

"Old Fashioneds are so good. The right amount of everything."

The smile on her face, Dani knew, meant her mother was

already up to no good. She noticed that most of the men in the bar were glancing over at their table. That was why Carol's mood had brightened. Men's attention always seemed to have that effect on her mother.

Two rather big and rough construction workers sidled up to their table.

The bolder of the two said, "Mind if we sit?"

Carol looked up in faux surprise. She batted her eyes.

"Why of course, gentlemen."

Here we go, Dani thought.

Instead of putting a quick end to her mother's frivolity, she decided to let it unfold. Besides, her mother usually did what she wanted, regardless.

The men pulled out chairs and sat opposite each other at the table.

"I'm Vince, and this is Bobby."

Carol extended a hand to Vince.

"So very nice to meet you kind men. My friend, Cecilia, and I—my name's Felicia—dropped in to have a cocktail or two. We've had a very, very busy day."

"I bet," the less bold construction worker, Bobby, said. "We been off work an hour—"

Vince broke in undoubtedly sensing a flameout. "Who cares about work? We ain't here for that. We'll be back at it in 10 hours. Let's relax and unwind. Right, girls?"

Carol said, "Absolutely."

She kicked her daughter under the table when Dani did more than remain silent and actually snorted into her cocktail.

"Right, Sissy?" She turned to Bobby. "I call her Sissy. My little nickname for Cecilia. You like it?"

Bobby, confused by the subject, said, "Uhhh—sure."

"You girls work down here?" Vince said. "You look like clerical types. No offense. Some of the best-looking women in the world can type 80 words a minute."

Dani dropped her empty, save for ice, cocktail glass on the table.

"I am not a clerk."

Bobby chimed in, "He didn't mean nothing."

"Yeah, I only meant—"

Carol kicked her daughter's leg yet again and gave her a look that said, "What are you doing?"

"I don't care what you meant. It's what you said."

"What's wrong with being a clerk, Sissy?" Carol said with a troubled smile.

"Nothing's wrong with it, but I object to being objectified as such! I am not just some pretty set of fingers with the ability to press buttons."

Bobby began to rise, "I don't think—"

"Sit down, Bobby. We're just having a little conversation. Nothing too serious?"

Vince smiled. It was, for Dani's taste, laid on a little too thick.

"Rhoda! We need more drinks here for these ladies!"

The big man waved at the bartender to round up a new batch of drinks.

Dani looked at her mother and motioned for them to go. Carol, ever so subtly, shook her head. It was clear to Dani that she was having fun and expected more excitement to come.

"These Old Fashioneds here are spectacular. I can't believe Sissy and I have never stopped in here before."

Carol chugged what remained of her drink. She mimicked Dani and set her glass down on the table with a thud.

Rhoda, the bartender, arrived at the table with a fresh round of beers and cocktails. "Who's tab?"

"Put it on me and Bobby's," Vince said.

"You mean, mine," Bobby said under his breath.

"You got it," Rhonda said, putting each drink down on the table and removing the empty cocktails. "Tip, too?"

Vince waved her off.

"Yeah, yeah. Tip, too!"

"A tip? Please, for slinging my drink across the rooms," Bobby muttered. It was an apparent source of contention.

"Thanks so much, barkeep," Carol said, already sipping her new drink.

"Enjoy your night," Rhoda said with a hint of sarcasm.

Dani looked down at her full cocktail. She was feeling light-headed from the first drink. She dreaded drinking this one—which she knew her mother would insist on, but then, who would drive them back to her loft? *Could they hail a car around here?* It was all part of her mother's impish plan. She should have kept on driving, searching for the faceless man.

"Ca—Felicia—I don't think I can drink this if we want to be driving ourselves home," Dani said.

"Nonsense," Carol said once again being the worst role-model a daughter could ever have.

"We can give you girls a lift," Bobby said.

"That's right," Vince added but with more menace than his wingman implied.

Dani straightened. A surge of warning shot up her spine. She recognized Vince for what he was. She smiled and made a motion with her hands to grab her cocktail, but intentionally knocked it from the table.

"Oh, crap. How clumsy of me!"

Dani grabbed the cocktail glass rolling on the ground. She rose and moved to the bar where she put it down with a clink.

Bar patrons noticed. Some laughed. Others sat unimpressed.

"Sissy, what have you done?" Carol said angrily.

Dani rolled her eyes at Rhoda.

"Can I borrow a bar towel? I dumped my drink."

Rhoda threw her a couple of long ago white towels.

"Clever girl. Wipe it up, and get your mother—at least she could be—out of here. The boys in here aren't to be screwed with. Get my drift?"

Dani shook her head.

"Gotcha, sister."

She dropped the towels on the ground to sop up her spilled drink, but left the rags for Rhoda to collect.

Returning to the table, she found her mother still trying to engage the two men.

"And what do you do, Bobby? You run a—oh, how do you pronounce it—"

"—backhoe excavator—" Vince interjected.

Carol giggled, "Right, backhoe. You run one of those, too?"

"Nah, I'm a cement truck driver. You know the truck with the big rotating drum on the back?"

"Of course, I've seen those things. So big and powerful looking."

"Time to go, Felicia," Dani said with a measure of sternness that took the two men aback.

"I'm not ready to go, yet. My drink's still full," Carol protested.

"Sit down there, Sissy. Let's enjoy each other's company for a little while longer," Vince said.

But Dani remained standing.

"Nope. Time to go. We have work to do tonight to get ourselves prepared for the morning."

"Now, hang on a minute," Carol said. "All of that can wait."

The young woman pointed to the back door from whence they entered.

"I'm walking out of that door and getting into the car. You have one minute. I'll wait that long, then, Felicia dear, you're on your own."

Dani turned around and walked toward the back door.

Outside, the cool, night air brushed her face and replaced the stale air—scented with faint reminiscences of cigarettes smoked long ago and worse—filling her lungs. Rising anger killed the slight buzz from her cocktail. She planned on being as good as her word, but Dani knew better. If her mother didn't follow, she would not leave her.

It crossed her mind, however, that this scenario was becoming a pattern that she might not want to repeat.

Pressing the key fob, the rental car lit up and squeaked to guide her to it. As she approached the car, a familiar one caught her eye. In the furthest corner of the parking lot, that to her recollection had previously been empty, the food delivery car she and her mother were previously hunting sat parked. The plastic placard sporting the logo of the delivery company was neatly stuck on the rear window.

Because it sat directly below a lamp, the windows appeared entirely black, and she couldn't see if the car was currently occupied.

A slight tremor in the pit of her stomach returned, but Dani still walked past her own rental and toward the delivery car.

Standing next to it, Dani looked inside it. It was empty of a driver but had all manner of detritus strewn within. Whoever owned it spent a considerable amount of time in the thing.

Delicately, lest the car had an active alarm, she touched the hood. It was still hot—which in her mind meant that the driver was likely still in the bar. But she hadn't noticed anyone enter the bar, since she and Carol had arrived, and she had the seat facing the front door that led to the street and sidewalk. Her back had been pointed at the rear, so it was possible that the driver could've entered and not be seen by her, but it wasn't like she had been completely absorbed by her mother's spectacle and her two playthings to notice who was in the bar at the beginning and the end.

A faceless man she would have seen.

She popped out her phone and took a photo of the car's license. What she would do with that information was unclear to Dani. But it was better to have than not have—especially if the driver was a faceless man—proof that such things existed and were not a figment of her and Shannon's imaginations.

The rear door of the bar opened allowing a momentary blast of hard rock to drown out the sounds of the night. When the door slammed shut, quiet returned except for the intrusion of her mother's laughter.

Dani turned and moved back to her rental. She watched as her mother, followed by Vince and Bobby, made her way to their car. Carol, still in full performance, carried on flirting with the men.

"See, boys?" she said. "Told you that Sissy wouldn't dare leave me. It was very nice of you to escort me outside. I didn't know this was such a dodgy neighborhood at night."

"Ladies need to be very careful at all times. Everywhere. That's for sure," Vince added.

Dani's original assessment of the men was improving with their show of chivalry.

"Mo—Felicia, did you see the driver of that car enter the bar?" Dani pointed at the delivery car.

Instantly, Carol's frivolity faded. "Well, I'll be."

Bobby looked at the beat up delivery car.

"What's so special about that jalopy?"

"Oh, that's one of those Internet delivery guys," Vince said.

"It just so happens that, when we were on our way over here, the driver of that vehicle—who is not a handsome man like you boys—practically drove us off the road. Completely reckless. It really upset my nerves—enough so that I needed a cocktail to calm them down."

Vince puffed up.

"Let's find the sonuvabitch. If he's in that bar, we'll give him a good talking-to. Maybe more if he lips off."

"Oh, he won't be lipping off to anyone." Carol winked at Dani. "You coming back in?"

Dani took a heavy breath and shook her head, yes.

"Wouldn't miss this for the world."

The boys were already marching back to the bar. Carol and Dani sprinted to catch up.

"Glad we have some muscle to back us up," Dani said to her mother under her breath.

"I've seen muscle in my life, and these boys have it. A little too much padding, but I've got no doubt they can crack heads when they want," Carol returned the whisper.

Again, they were blasted by electric guitar virtuosity when Vince pulled the door open.

"C'mon girls. Pick the bastard out!" he shouted.

Picking out a faceless man would be easy, but Dani wondered what exactly they would do if they found the man.

The crowd in the bar all seemed to turn in unison as they

reentered. But their interest faded nearly as fast as they looked.
"Maybe we should be stealthy about this, " Dani said at the top of her lungs, but her mother and the boys must not have heard her.

Bobby marched towards the jukebox, pulled it out from the wall and yanked the cord from the socket. The music died instantly.

"What the fu—"

The bar was filled with expletive-laden protests.

Her mother, the master showman, however, assumed control.

"All right everyone, I apologize for the momentary loss of those fabulous tunes, but they will resume shortly."

Rhoda moved out from behind the bar. "You'd better plug that back in, Bobby. Or, I'll have you banned from the bar. Again."

"You ain't bannin' nobody," Vince said. "This little lady here has a problem with some delivery driver in this bar. It's the car in the far corner of the parking lot. I suggest, for the good of your enjoyment, you all let us know who owns that car."

From the corner, "Who gives a flying fuck who owns that friggin' car?"

Vince made a move towards the man.

"You shut your trap, or I'll knock the crap out of you. Next person who talks better say something useful."

"Hang on, everybody. Let's not let this get out of hand," Dani said. "We just need to know who owns that car in the corner. Then, we can be on our way."

One burly man rolled off his barstool and approached Bobby menacingly.

"Plug that back in, and you people shut the hell up."

"Or what?" Bobby countered.

"Or, I'll break your fuckin' face."

Bobby smiled.

"I was hopin' you'd say that!"

In a blur, he rocked the man onto his heels with a solid uppercut.

Dani rolled her eyes. This was exactly what she feared would happen.

"No, no, no, no, no!"

She spun on her heels, but not before seeing Carol hop onto a barstool to watch the unfolding chaos.

"Mom, let's go!"

"Mom?!" Vince said.

Out of the blue, he was pummeled by a wooden chair.

Dani considered running back and grabbing her mother, but she noticed the delivery driver slinking his way out of the bar.

"Got you," she said under her breath.

She exited directly after him. The chaos of the bar fight left behind, Dani waited until the man reached the middle of the parking lot.

"Hey!" she called after him.

He stopped and turned around.

"I got no beef with you."

"What's your name?" Dani said.

She approached him with every caution, but hoped to put him at ease.

"I'm Dani."

His brow furrowed. Her tone confused him.

She could tell.

"I'm Reg."

"How long've you been delivering?"

"I—uhh—gotta run. Have a nice night, lady."

"Wait. What's the hurry? You still on shift?"

He turned to move towards the car, but Dani put a hand on his shoulder.

"Look, I just want to ask you a couple of questions. All that in there, it was bluster, and mostly a bad idea from my overzealous mother."

"What questions? Why?" He was less than angry but more than annoyed. "I don't know you. I've never seen you before in my life."

"I saw you delivering in front of my building a couple of hours ago today. You waved at me when I wanted your parking space."

"Do you realize how crazy that sounds? I wave to a million people every day. I couldn't pick out one face in a lineup if my life depended on it!"

Dani backed off.

"You're right. I'm sorry for bugging you."

"Thanks," he said.

Briskly, he moved to his car.

"One more thing," Dani said before he pulled open his car door. She heard his exasperated sigh from across the parking lot. "I'm a big fan of Columbo."

"Columbo? What?"

Dani figured, as a millenial, the man had no idea about the old TV show. The only reason she knew anything about it was her mother's late-night TV habits.

"Lady, you make no sense at all."

Trying to disarm him, she smiled.

"Probably not, but indulge me."

"I'm tired. I gotta get home."

Dani blurted out, "Who are the faceless men?"

"What?"

He stopped and slowly turned to face her.

"You don't have to lie about it."

He pulled open his door.

"You really are crazy. I was totally right. Faceless men? The fuck is that?"

"But I saw you. When your mask—that face you're wearing—fell off."

Without saying another word, the man folded himself into the car. He shook his head and laughed.

Dani thought about running over and opening the door and then dragging him out. She probably lacked the strength, and in the time it took her to muse about it, he had pulled the car out of the parking space and was maneuvering it toward the parking lot exit. He stopped next to her and rolled down the window.

With a smile on his face, he reached up and tugged at his face. He winked. Then, he folded up a flap of skin. He pulled it across his face, and it folded into his remaining scalp. His features disappeared leaving a completely smooth surface. No eyes. No nose. No lips. No hair, No ears. Just brown, smooth skin. He had taken off the mask. And as Dani predicted, underneath, there was nothing but flesh.

Time stopped between breaths for Dani. She wanted to congratulate herself and scream out, "I knew it!" But being confronted by something that filled her with such fear, her jaw went slack, and her feet were filled with lead. Her heart raced in her chest.

He sped away as Carol called for Dani at the bar's back door.

"Dani! What in heaven's name are you doing out there alone!"

The car sped out of the parking lot in a cloud of black, rubber smoke. The acridity of which finally shook Dani awake from the stony fear that held her still.

CHAPTER FORTY
TWO

Shannon awoke with the third blow. The first two, he definitely felt, but they were lost in the waves of sleep and melded into his dream—which consisted of him feeling the contours of a nude model he was sculpting.

His advances were being thwarted by the model. Playful slaps, timed perfectly to the actual physical blows, batted him away.

After the third blow sent waves of pain throughout his body, he awoke into a scrambling mass of arms swinging at him.

Now no longer muted by his sleep, every blow sent shooting pain across his body.

He raised his arms up and pulled his legs towards his torso trying to reach a protective fetal position. It did little to deflect against the hits, and even less to stop the pursuant pain.

"Stop!" he yelled, but they did not.

He ran over the scenario in his mind: if he did nothing, he would be pummeled to death. But what else could he do?

A shaft of sunlight pierced the cell from the small window above his bed. It struck into the inky black bodies that had been beating him. Where the light hit them, their bodies faded. They moved into the shadows.

If this was his initiation into prison life, he was going to do the initiating. It was his turn to fight!

Shannon rolled himself violently off the bed. He sent himself into the legs of his assailants. Some of the attackers fell around him.

Uncurling his body, Shannon reached out for the nearest person. He felt the man's legs and yanked himself up on top of the man. Without opening his eyes, he unleashed a flurry of fists at him.

He swept his legs out and knocked another of the men to the floor. Immediately, he set upon him. The other man tried to stand, but Shannon sent him flying with a roundhouse kick.

The third man, however, beat on the metal door of the cell, desperate to get out.

Standing now with the two men writhing at his feet, Shannon ran at the banging man. He sent the man's head into the metal door.

"No one's getting out of here. Who the fuck are you?" Shannon screamed.

He repeatedly kicked all the men rolling on the ground.

"You think you can come in here and fuck with me?"

Another kick, and Shannon felt a rib give.

His fists flew. His legs kicked. His teeth bit.

These men were no match for his fury. They screamed to be let out, but their screams went unheeded.

Shannon laughed at their weakness. He laughed at the top of his lungs.

The lights in the cell blasted on.

"What the hell's going on in there? Step away from the door, prisoner!" the night guard boomed.

The guard beat his baton against the metal door.

Searching the small room—sweeping his eyes back and forth in a terrible confusion, Shannon saw no signs of the men he was fighting. They had vanished under the green-tinged fluorescent light.

He looked down at his foot, the one he had been kicking with, and it was swollen and bleeding.

The door slammed open, and he fell onto his cot.

The guard took one look at the blood splattered everywhere

and pooling on the floor underneath Shannon's foot, and muttered, "Oh, fuck."

He reached for his radio holstered on his shoulder.

"I need a medic team on the cell block for prisoner McClarty. Stat. Lots of blood."

"Where are they?" Shannon asked the guard.

"Who?" the guard replied and withdrew latex gloves from his pocket. "You're the only sad sack piece of shit I see in here."

"They were here. In here with me. I swear," Shannon said.

The guard reached for his radio again.

"I'm also gonna need a psych down here for immediate eval."

The guard walked over the pool of blood on the floor. Twice as big as Shannon, he loomed over the cot.

"Now, I'm going to administer some first aid. If you make any sudden moves, I'm going take this baton and knock you senseless. Do you understand?"

He waited for Shannon to answer.

But all Shannon could do was mutter, "They were here. They were here."

The guard pushed him prone onto the cot with the baton. He grabbed the small sheet off the cot and wrapped Shannon's foot tightly.

The outer bar doors opened and closed down the hall. Sounds of boots pounding against the concrete floor echoed off the walls.

All Shannon could say was, "They were here. They were..."

CHAPTER FORTY THREE

James Herald stepped off the moving walkway near the arrivals section of the Chicago O'Hare Airport. He felt a long way away from his beloved Manhattan and the library he had known for 30 years and from where he had never once taken a vacation.

Strolling towards the baggage carousel, he stretched his neck, side to side. The flight was short, but the airplane was flown at full capacity, and he was forced to sit between two larger human beings. It made him sit up straight and stiff for the nearly three hours they were up in the air.

It felt good to be moving, though, in the brisk Chicago air— which was chillier than his beloved Manhattan surprisingly.

Things were going his way. As he approached the chrome carousel, his single suitcase slid down the ramp right in front of him. James waited a few seconds, and he scooped up his bag with barely any effort.

He and it rolled out of the arrivals area and followed the directions to the El with ease.

The journey from the airport to downtown Chicago was uneventful though it was the evening hours when people were packed into the train going home.

The city, much like Manhattan, was turning red and brown as all green drained from the foliage that existed between brick, concrete and asphalt.

When he first caught sight of the lake, he was taken aback. It was so large that it looked no different than the Atlantic on the east side of the island.

His mind drifted to the future. James liked this city. It was a place where he could find himself retiring. It was large, but not as large as New York City. It was always busy, but not nearly as crushingly busy as his town. It was pretty, both man-made and otherwise, and as pretty as the place of his birth.

Once the El entered the tall towers, the city closed itself around him, and it did indeed remind him more and more of home with the skyscrapers blotting out the blue of the sky.

At the stop for his hotel, James deftly stepped around the homeless sitting on the steps leading to street level. He did manage to "accidentally" hit a few with his bag as he descended.

Inside, he giggled about it. Outwardly, he feigned a surprised apology each time.

James wasn't trying to be cruel, but these people were just plain rude to block the way.

His hotel was less than a block from the stop. In the time James had extended the collapsible handle of his rolling luggage, he had arrived at the revolving door of the hotel lobby.

Inside, the briskness of the evening was replaced by a pleasant warmth and delicious smells from the attached restaurant and bar.

"Good evening, sir," the bellhop nodded at James.

"A good evening to you, sir," James said, sailing towards the front desk which was a long glass desk fronted by black marble.

"James Herald," he said, settling against the glass. "I have a reservation."

The beautiful young woman attending him smiled and said, "Mr. Herald, may I see an official ID, please?"

"Will a New York driver's license do? I don't drive. I don't even own a car, but I figured if I was going to have official identification, why not go all the way?"

He smiled effusively fishing out his license from his overstuffed wallet. Credit cards, business cards, old scraps of paper fell out.

"Oh, dear, I'm such a klutz. Look at me."

He handed over his driver's license to the still-smiling attendant though she was slightly unnerved at the small man's clumsiness.

"Thank you, Mr. Herald."

She studied his ID for a moment then started typing on her terminal.

"Here it is. Oh!"

"Something amiss, miss?" Herald giggled ever so slightly.

"No," she said, "Nothing's wrong at all. I see you're a rewards member, and you're booked into our presidential suite."

He handed over his Amex Black card.

"Only the finest for me. You see, I've spent most of my life on an island, and when I do travel for business, I expect my accommodations to be of the finest the host city has to offer."

"Well, this suite has the most incredible view of this city and the lake available. Also, it seems that all of your meals have been comped. Very nice."

"Fantastic. I'll have to thank your manager. Oh, and do you also have an El pass waiting for me, too?"

The attendant opened up a drawer on the back desk and retrieved a manilla folder with his name on it.

"I assume that everything you've requested is in here."

She handed it over to him.

"Great."

She returned to her terminal. A keycard machine spat out a hotel key.

"If you lose the key, just return to us, and we'll provide another."

The attendant handed over both his Amex and the key.

"Thank you for choosing us to stay with us while you're in Chicago. We appreciate it. And my name's Charlotte should you need anything further."

"Why thank you so much, Charlotte. Is your concierge service —"

"If you move past the elevators, you'll see our dedicated concierge desk. It's just before you enter the restaurant."

Smiling broadly, he pulled his bag in the direction she indicated.

"You've been so helpful. Thanks, Charlotte!"

Marching past the elevators and before he turned left to enter the restaurant, James stopped at the glass door of the concierge office. He poked his head inside.

"Anyone available?" he chimed.

From the corner of the office, a tall, Hispanic man sauntered up to the door. A smile graced his face.

"Come in, sir. How may I help you?"

"I was wondering if you have any idea where I might see the art of Shannon McClarty. I hear he's a very popular local artist."

The concierge grew excited.

"Oh, yes, he's local. Popular isn't quite the word. Maybe infamous."

"Do tell," Herald implored.

"He's a very good artist. To be sure. But he's recently been arrested."

"Arrested?!"

James let his surprise drip from his mouth. He couldn't help a wide smile from creeping across his lips.

"What on earth could the man have done to be arrested? A renowned artist like himself. Well, they are known to be somewhat loose cannons. Ear chopping and such."

"He murdered a woman."

"Oh my, oh my. Murder?" James said. His affectation was magnified. "What could that do to his resale value?"

The concierge chuckled, "Would anyone have bought a Van Gogh if he hadn't committed suicide?"

"Well, murder certainly trumps suicide. He was murdered. Not a murderer. So this adds a wrinkle. Anyhow, where can I find his work?"

The concierge moved to his laptop and clicked a few words out. He stared at the screen, and then began writing down an address.

He handed it to James.

"This's the only gallery in the city, and it looks like anywhere, that still shows his work. There's going to be a blacklist for sure."

James looked down at the address.

"This near here?"

"Yes, it's best to take a car rather than the El, though. I can arrange one for you?"

James smiled.

"I need to eat and make myself at home—" James finally noticed the man's placard. "—Julio. I'll be in touch this evening. I assume you'll be on shift?"

"Yes, sir," Julio said.

Nodding, James pulled his luggage out of the concierge office and made his way to the restaurant. He was growing very hungry, and he would need a full stomach this evening after all.

Before entering the restaurant, he hailed a bellhop. He handed the teenager a $5 bill.

"Son, here's my room number. Be a dear and take this up. I appreciate it."

"Of course, mister," the bellhop said and then was gone, the only trace of him the fading sound of James' rolling luggage.

Pushing open the glass doors to the restaurant, James was met by stronger smells of fresh cooking. Steak. Chicken. Potatoes. Grilled garlic vegetables. His mouth watered.

The hostess, another prime example of Chicago's crop of pretty, fresh faced ladies, handed him a menu.

"We aren't particularly busy right now, sir, so you have the choice of any open seating. How about this booth?"

She guided him to a booth against the wall-sized window facing the street. Rush hour traffic sped by on the street.

Pedestrians in their overcoats sprinted to meet the next El. The lights of the high rises started lighting up for the night.

"Lovely. I'll take it. And I'll have a regular iced tea and a Sea Breeze, please."

He scooted himself into the booth.

"Absolutely. Coming right up."

The hostess marched off with her orders.

James laid out the menu before him and started to peruse it, but his eyes and mind were drawn outside. He watched people weave down the sidewalk on the way to whatever their lives were. It wasn't until the hostess returned with his drinks and introduced his waiter that he thought again about food even though his hunger was biting.

"Oh, yes," he said sipping his drink. "I'm in the mood for a New York steak. Rare. Can you make those here?" He chuckled, the joke probably lost on the waiter. "With a baked potato. Let's start the whole thing off with a Caesar salad. What do you think?"

He waited while the man transcribed his meal. Finally, the waiter lifted his eyes from his pad.

"I think that sounds like quite a meal, and something our chef will appreciate making. He's from Brooklyn, so he understands a fellow New Yorker."

"Is it that obvious?" Herald asked.

The waiter just smiled, took his menu, turned and walked to the waiter's station.

Herald pulled out his cell phone. He forgot to turn the thing on after landing. It wasn't as if he was expecting to find important emails or voicemails waiting for him. But turning it on made him feel that much more connected.

Sifting through the latest headlines, he searched for news on Shannon McClarty. His incarceration was outside the city, but within taxi distance. He would have no trouble getting to a meeting, but how would he procure the meeting without Dani's permission—much less the authorities' permission.

Dani might allow him to speak with Shannon alone, but he

didn't think that was likely. She was as much involved in this story as he was, but her path did not yet converge with Shannon's. How could he make her understand? Or, could he somehow skirt her knowing at all?

The cycle was repeating.

Again.

CHAPTER FORTY
FOUR

"**B**illy, I don't care what you think right now. A contract's a contract, and if you don't abide by it, I will sue you out of existence. You got it?" Dani said into the cell phone while mopping up the forensic dust from their hardwood floor.

Carol sat at the corner of the kitchen island sipping her coffee and listening intermittently.

"All it takes is one phone call," she lilted.

"Why in the world would you want to unload anything Shannon's done? The notoriety alone will drive up his prices. Isn't that the way these things go? Besides, he stood by you when bigger galleries wanted him. He didn't cut and run. Have some balls, Billy."

Yawning, Carol pointed at the digital clock displayed on the microwave.

"We have a conference call in two."

Dani shook her head in acknowledgment.

"Okay. Yes. Look, Billy, Shannon's innocent anyway. Once he gets out, he won't forget his friends."

She hung up the phone.

"And?" Carol asked.

"He's keeping them on display. He'll pump up the price."

"That's quite the turnaround. Here I thought you were just

scolding the poor man, and you were instead beating him into submission. Show's you how much I know. You want to have this conference on the laptop or phone?"

Leaning the mop up against the refrigerator, she wiped her hands on her shirt.

"I wish you hadn't scheduled it for now. I needed some time to clean myself up."

"Wasn't my decision, daughter dear. When powerful lawyers clear time for you, you take it."

Right on cue, the laptop began chiming.

"Oh, shit," Dani said.

Carol calmly pulled the computer over to her and pressed a few keys to answer the incoming call.

"Well, hello, there!" she said.

Dani did her best to wipe off her face before joining her mother at the laptop.

On screen, two rectangles were occupied: one with Nance and the other with a lovely black woman not quite middle-aged and still graced with youthful beauty.

Nance spoke up, "Carol Strauss and Dani McClarty, this is Celene Felis, Esquire. You probably recognize her, but in case you don't, let me say she's the Windy City's best defense attorney specializing in police misconduct. One of the very best in the country no less. I had a long conversation about Shannon with her this morning, and she's agreed to speak with you about the case. Celene, please."

"Thank you, Counselor. I appreciate the referral. And let me say, ladies, you've caught me at an opportune time. My last case has just been adjudicated, and I'm looking for another at the moment."

Carol interrupted, "Oh, my goodness. You could not be a more welcome sight to us, Ms. Felis. I am a fan since that case of the actress killer—"

"Ah, Ms. Strauss, she was and is innocent. And therein lies my fascination with Shannon's case. You, Dani, swear he's innocent. Do you not?"

Shannon took a deep breath and said, clear-eyed, "I believe my husband. I believe what he tells me."

Carol and Dani watched the screen as Celene stared out at them. It was clear she was assessing Dani's truthfulness.

Done with her assessment, she said, "I believe you. Mr. Nance, thanks for introducing us."

Nance smiled and nodded. "Very good then. Do you mind if I sign off of this call? My work here is done."

Carol waved at the screen.

"I'll call you later about that little lawsuit we're currently working on. Toodaloo!"

Celene's face grew as the other box disappeared. She dominated the screen.

"Now, let's get any unpleasantness concerning your husband out of the way. I want to know everything. All the bad times. If he ever hit you. Did he steal money from his grandmother? I need to know him. Warts and all"

The words caught in Dani's throat. *Would this woman still help if she knew exactly what Shannon's done in his life? How badly he treated me? Should I lie?*

Carol broke the uncomfortable silence.

"Listen, Celene, Shannon's a shit. There's no other way to put it."

Celene's face hardened.

"Explain. Spare no details."

The two women waited for Dani to speak. The young woman gathered her thoughts and began with a sigh.

"He has been cruel, but he's an artist, and he's frustrated often with his work. It has nothing to do with me really... We have been in one physical fight. We've had terrible arguments. Mostly about money."

"But Shannon definitely raised his fists at you? That is public information?" Celene asked.

Dani shook her head, yes.

"I filed a police report, and almost requested a restraining order, but we worked through it."

"Was he under a court order of any kind? Anger management or the like?"

Dani nodded, yes, yet again.

"Completed an anger management course and 40 hours of community service cleaning a battered women's shelter. Of course, he was not allowed any contact with the women and children. He said it made him feel like a pariah."

"As well it should have. I assume you refused to press charges and were a character witness for his defense?"

"I was," Dani said.

"Carol, am I dealing with battered woman's syndrome here?"

Carol stuttered, "I'm not sure I'm the best to make that diagnosis. Look, I've been around the block and dealt with my share of men, good and bad, and maybe I didn't raise my daughter to be as worldly as I had to be. But she is smarter than I am, and I don't think she'd fall into that kind of trap."

"So, it's safe to say that you love your husband and would stand by him even though he hasn't comported himself with the best behavior. Be that as it may, Shannon McClarty, warts and all, is no killer. This isn't the best situation for me to defend, but we play the hand we're dealt. Be at my office in an hour, ladies."

The call ended without nary a " 'Bye."

Carol slurped her coffee.

"That girl's a ball-buster. I like her."

"She seems to enjoy putting me on the hotseat," Dani said.

She grabbed the mop and began scrubbing the floor once again.

"I guess I should've expected that. I've covered for Shannon too much. Maybe?"

Shrugging her shoulders, Carol harrumphed. "Like mother, like daughter. I've been known to suffer too much for the men I think I love."

"Mother, I do love him."

"I didn't mean you didn't. I was talking about me. I blame myself, really. I'm not much of a mother. And never been one."

Dani dropped the broom and rushed to Carol. She held her mother in a tight hug.

"Mom, I could not do any of this without you. That's how good a mother you are."

The older woman fell limp against her daughter's embrace. Her sobs started off slowly and muffled.

"Shhh. Shhh," Dani whispered. "I love you, and I don't want you to think that way about yourself. You did what you could. We all did. That's all. Okay?"

Carol sniffed. "I know. But…"

"No, buts."

"How can I ever make it up to you?"

Dani smiled, "Silly, old girl, what do you think you're doing right now?"

Carol lifted her head, sniffed and wiped her tears.

"Love you, Dani."

"I know. Well, we better get ready to go meet her. It won't do to be late."

The women took turns using the shower, and all in record time for each. They were on their way to the law offices in less than 45 minutes.

They were ushered into the glass-walled conference room in the center of the offices.

"I feel like a damn fish in a bowl," Carol said.

Dani, too, could feel all eyes of the office peering at them. Judging them. Judging her.

The few gazes she could see, she stared back at them until they turned away.

"I want a Coke. You want a Coke?" Carol asked. She moved to the glass door and opened it.

"Miss? Miss? Yes, you. We'd like several Coca-Colas for refreshment and a crudite plate. Thank you."

Carol let the door shut as she took her seat at the conference table.

"It's important to establish a pecking order when dealing with a bunch of hens, sweetheart."

"And here I thought we had to play Queensbury Rules."

At the end of the hallway separating the conference room

and the outer offices, both women's eyes were attracted to the bright flash of light as the door to the largest office on the floor opened. Silhouetted against the sunlight, they could see a woman wearing a suit-skirt walking towards them.

When their eyes adjusted, they knew it was Celine. She was smaller than her presence on the computer conference call suggested. But the confidence she demonstrated with each step in her high-heels augmented her much beyond her short stature.

She pulled open the conference room door with a smile.

"Carol, Dani, it's a pleasure."

Dani grabbed her hand.

"I wish it were under better circumstances."

The lawyer laughed and sat down next to Carol.

"I always wish it were under better circumstances. But, I make my money this way."

Celine waved in her receptionist who was pushing a cart stacked with exactly what Carol ordered for them.

"Well, I'll be," Carol said flummoxed as the receptionist laid out the crudite and drinks on the table.

As an added bonus, the woman put out a plate of, what smelled like, fresh baked chocolate chip cookies.

Carol grabbed one.

"I thought I was the one pulling a power play."

Celine smiled. "We do our best to make sure our clients are comfortable during hard times."

"We didn't mean to give your people a hard time," Dani said.

She shot her mother a scolding glance.

With her face stuffed with cookie, Carol managed, "Yes, we did."

The receptionist winked at Carol as she pulled the cart out of the conference room.

"If I wasn't such a cantankerous old broad, I'd think your front desk woman there was hitting on me."

"She was," the lawyer said, not missing a beat. "I've already informed the court that I'm assuming Shannon's case. That will be made official once the clerks return from lunch. I'll be visiting Shannon this afternoon."

Dani grabbed a Coke, filled two glasses with ice and poured.

"Would you like one?" she asked Celine.

Smirking, she replied, "I never touch the stuff without whiskey."

Carol's eyes went wide.

"Oh, my dear, we are going to get along famously. Too bad you're criminal defense, otherwise Nance would be out of a job."

"I have my area of expertise as he does, but mine is so much more fun."

Celine caught herself, "I don't mean to give you the impression that I don't take my responsibilities seriously."

Carol met her daughter's eyes.

"Not at all. Women in jeopardy need to stick together," Carol said.

"Speaking of jeopardy... The judge we think being assigned to the case, Rick Takio, is a former colleague. We go way back, and that's not good news."

Dani nearly choked on her drink.

"Why?"

"Early in our careers, we interned for the same law firm. He would not stop harassing me—asking for dates—so I reported him. Got him dismissed from the firm. It did not help his career, and he's kept a grudge all this time. Good news is that if he does get assigned and things do not go our way, we can use that as a foundation for grounds for retrial or dismissal."

Dani sighed. It was a little too much for her to hear. Carol on the other hand seemed delighted.

"Palace intrigue is always so fascinating. I love the way you think."

"If we're already talking about retrial, where does that leave us with Shannon's defense?"

Celine reached over and grabbed a soda and popped the can open.

"I'm not ceding anything, Dani. On the contrary, I think we have a great case. Just from the preliminary reports. I skimmed the camera footage, and where it places Shannon during that poor woman's murder. I can see holes in the prosecution, and they are the size of mountains."

Sitting back into her chair, Celine surveyed the women. Her smile was wide, and it appeared to Dani that she was waiting for them to praise her for her genius.

Dani leaned forward toward her, her posture inflated and challenging.

"Why did you really take this case?"

Celine's body language immediately countered.

"I'm a lawyer. It's what I do."

"Bullshit. What's your gain in doing this?"

"Dani, you stop right there. I taught you never to look a gift horse in the mouth!" Carol nearly spit up her soda.

"I'm not saying that this is a bad thing, Celine. I just want to know your angle. I seriously doubt that you're doing this as a testament to your dedication to justice."

Celine smiled again.

"I like it, Dani. You're a tough cookie in your own right. Yes, I believe in justice. It doesn't come cheap, and your mother has agreed to a very hefty retainer. But more than that—in all honesty—I get to fight on television. My own career depends on that face time. I like the sound of 'Madame Mayor.' "

"Good. I understand."

Dani considered and leaned back into her chair.

"You demand honesty from us. I demand it from you. We'll be stronger that way."

"That's a deal. We've got a few hours before I head to the jail. Let's make it useful."

Celine pulled the laptop on the conference table to her.

"Okay, I'm going to start asking questions, and my investigators will be vetting every answer. Speaking of honesty. Ready?"

"Do I need to be involved?" Carol asked. "I feel the need to visit a nice little spa I know. A facial, a massage, maybe a little trim here and there."

"Ms. Strauss, you can go, but first, I'll be needing some answers from you, too."

Carol rolled her eyes.

"Fine."

"Mom, don't you want to get your money's worth?"

"I suppose. But if I'm put in a situation where I have to marry another 90-year-old billionaire, I'll never forgive you, Dani dear."

CHAPTER FORTY FIVE

Herald waited in the rather colorless jail administrative offices. The paint on the walls was some very strange muted shade of green. The tile on the floor was checkerboard. The walls were occasionally decorated by the photos of current state, county and city elected officials.

He tapped his leather shoes absently on the floor as he watched uniformed officials move in and out. They seemed to be performing some duties, but the librarian had no idea what those could be.

James checked his watch.

34 minutes. His wait time was 34 minutes wasted.

This was exactly the kind of torture he and his fellows at the library regularly inflicted on their patrons. There, on the other side of the partition, he didn't mind the wait. On this side, it got under his skin.

What was it they said, he thought, *Karma is a bitch?*

"Excuse me," James called out to a passing officer. "Would you —"

But the man ignored him and let the administrative office door shut, cutting off Herald in mid-sentence.

The worst of his coworkers at the library never, on their most horrible days, ignored a customer so blatantly, at least, not without cause. When he returned to the library, he had half a mind to call for classes on customer relations—though it was anathema for his fellow librarians to see loanees as customers. They generally felt that the books in their care were the real objects of their concern, not the people who read them.

Finally, the nice woman who had first acknowledged him exited from the largest office.

"Captain Sidley will see you now, Mr. Herald."

James jumped to his feet and gathered his briefcase, instantly relieved.

"Fantastic. Thank you so very much for your help."

The secretary smiled with an air of skepticism. "Not sure I was too much help, but you're welcome."

She guided him into the outer office where her desk was, then opened Sidley's door. The seal of the city with his nameplate hung on the door prominently.

They take themselves seriously in these parts, James thought.

Sidley rose from his desk with his hand outstretched to greet James.

"Bob Sidley, Mr. Herald."

James took his hand and shook it warmly. He smiled from ear to ear.

"Thank you so much, Captain Sidley, for seeing me. You are doing the New York Public Library system a very generous and important favor."

Motioning to the seats facing his desk, Sidley sat in his own. Herald followed choosing the chair that, at first glance, provided the firmest cushions. He didn't want to sink into it to the point of disappearing.

"It's not every day that I get a request like this."

Herald raised his hands in an exaggerated gesture emphasizing the enormity of his request.

"We do indeed know what we are asking. And given the circumstances, we are equally surprised that you generously offered to help us."

"I've always been one to help other people," Sidley said, his obsequiousness on display. "But I'm not quite sure what it is you are asking us to do."

James moved to the edge of his chair shortening the distance between them. He pulled up his briefcase onto the edge of the desk and popped it open at an angle.

He pulled out two 8x10s of a sculpture.

"This… This is the sculpture in our possession. We don't know if it is a McClarty, and we need to verify it's provenance. I have been sent to ask him what he knows of this piece. If it is a McClarty, our library system would need to divest of it immediately. Politics and politicians don't like to court unnecessary controversy."

"I see. Why exactly?" Sidley leaned back and his chair reclined

"It is difficult for a public entity like the New York City Library system to own controversial—read, works created by murderers—artwork. There was a nasty public outcry over a purchase in the '80s of a John Wayne Gacy clown portrait. One of our councilmen caused quite a spectacle. Since then, we are very cognizant of similar situations."

"A McClarty piece would fetch a good price right about now. Don't you think?"

"Oh, yes. It will fetch a pretty penny. Private collectors love to speculate on nefarious people's artwork," James said.

Herald's eagerness excited Sidley, and James knew it.

"I want it."

James was mock taken aback. "I'm sorry?"

"I want to buy it." Sidley smiled.

A small chuckle built in James' throat, but he quickly muffled it.

"Usually, we sell these problematic items to select customers. Very high—"

"Let me explain it to you. You get your interview. I get the piece if it's a McClarty. And for a very good price. Understand?"

Herald fumbled his briefcase and dropped it onto the floor spilling its contents. He scrambled to gather his papers back up and stuff them back inside.

Sidley laughed.

"This is what we call the Chicago way, Mr. Herald."

"Well, I—"

"Well, I nothing. You know what I want. You agree to provide it now, and you get what you need."

James clammed up and considered. The photos he showed Sidley were of a sculpture found in the only gallery still showing McClarty pieces. Herald had taken and printed them that very day. His library did not own the piece of art. He was amused that the ruse was working, but there were risks.

"Now, you might be thinking, how can an officer of the law such as me request something that might be less than ethical? Easy. I did. You might also be wondering, how can you promise me what I'm asking now and then not follow through. You won't. You agree to it now. You will follow through. If you don't, well, let's say that there is such a thing as the long arm of the law. *Capisce?*"

James nodded. "I understand. We will need to forego the semi-public notification of sale. It will just have to disappear from our inventory. The Teamsters run our heavy deliveries. I'm sure a delivery to you can be arranged."

"That's the kind of talk I like to hear. You're a can-do man, Mr. Herald."

Sidley held out his hand across the table. James took it and shook. The librarian smiled. Their size difference would have been imposing to anyone else, but Herald had his own reasons to be confident this man, despite his implied threats, would not be able to do anything to harm him, regardless of the final outcome.

The jailer rose from his chair.

"Let's go see what our favorite sculptor is up to."

With Sidley guiding him through the various barred gates, it took them very little time to move from the offices to the jail proper.

At each gate opening, the guards would announce their arrival with, "Warden coming through."

Followed by, "Warden entering. Guest entering."

When they reached the prisoner interview and holding area, two large guards marched them to the last holding room. At the door, Sidley stopped Herald.

"Do not hand the prisoner anything. If you need to show him something, hold it up. If I see you handing him anything, I will terminate the interview, and then strip-search you both. Understand?"

James nodded. "Of course."

Sidley opened the door and made a move to enter.

"Captain Sidley, sir?"

"Yes?"

He stopped and looked down at James disdainfully.

"I thought it was possible to speak to Mr. McClarty alone. Per *our discussion*?" James said

Sidley, nonplussed, nodded and allowed James to enter.

The captain puffed his chest and bellowed, "We will be watching you both on closed circuit. No funny stuff."

Inside, James found Shannon, chained in place, sitting at a large metal table bolted to the floor. Across from him, a metal chair, also bolted down, waited for him.

"Mr. McClarty, it is a pleasure to meet you," James said taking his seat. "Thank you for agreeing to see me."

Shannon snickered.

"In case you haven't noticed, I'm not really in any position to turn down any meeting."

"At any rate, Mr. McClarty, I appreciate your time."

"What is it you need…"

"Oh, right. I am James Herald from the New York Metropolitan Library System."

The artist slumped in his chair wearing a confused frown.

"I thought I turned that book in. I'm afraid I don't have any money on me for the fine at the moment."

James let out a high-squeak of a laugh.

"Very funny, Mr. McClarty!"

"Call me Shannon. I'm in chains. Chains make me a prisoner. A 'mister' is a free man."

"That's quite poetic. Are you also a wordsmith?"

Shannon shook his head, no, and half-smiled.

"Flattery will get you nowhere with a man who has nothing."

"Oh, but on the contrary, Shannon, you have much more than you know."

Now, Shannon outright chuckled.

"Fine, I'm game. As long as you keep me out of my cell, I can't complain."

James flipped open his briefcase and retrieved the series of photographs.

The speakers in the room squawked, and Sidley echoed throughout the room. "Show him. But he does not touch."

Shannon and James looked over their heads searching for the source of the voice.

"Yes, sir," James said meekly.

"I'm watching," he said again.

"I hear you," Shannon blurted out. "We aren't plotting anything."

"There's no need to get angry, Mr. McClarty. I'm sure this is all very normal," Herald said, amused.

Shannon sunk into his seat and whispered, but loud enough for James to hear, "Nothing's normal in this prison."

James held up the photo.

He let Shannon raise his eyes to meet it before saying, "Does this look familiar, Mr. Shannon?"

The man in the chains stared at the photograph in Herald's hands. It was black and white. So strong was the contrast that the image was hard for Shannon to discern. He leaned forward, eyes squinting.

"What is it?" Shannon asked. "I've already had the shrinks in this place testing me. Rorschach test?"

James shook his head, incredulously, and turned the photo so he could see. The image was as he expected: a simple picture of a marble stonework. It was only a naked woman holding a flower near her heart between bare breasts. It was beautiful, a work that would have made Michelangelo proud.

"Is this one of your pieces, Shannon?"

Shannon looked again. He studied the photo. His eyes would not focus and instead a changing swirl of black and white filled what should have been the photographic image.

"There's something wrong with that picture, Mr. Herald," he said.

"What do you mean? It looks like a perfectly fine carved statue. Marble. Delicate detail of a beautiful young woman. The flower petals seem to blow about with her very breath."

"Is that what you see?" Shannon stared at the photo then at James.

"Yes, I see the statue. It's yours? Isn't it? Such extraordinary work."

A smile pulled across James face from ear to ear.

His voice grew deeper. "Admit it. It's yours."

The inky blackness that had been swirling in the photo now flowed from it and out across the steel table.

Shannon, panicked, pulled at his shackles.

"Guards! Guards!"

The smile that peeled across James' face pulled impossibly behind his head.

"Help!" Shannon screamed.

The blackness spilling from the photo was now inches from him.

"They can't help you, Shannon, even if they knew what you do now."

The rictus encircled Herald's head, and then, with the sound of skin tearing and wet body parts sloshing, the smile flipped, and James was no more.

Sitting across from Shannon was a faceless man. Shannon pulled against his shackles, but he was constrained securely in place.

"Stay away from me!" he screamed.

The Herald faceless man held up a hand. It undulated and bubbled until the skin broke and a black tendril flowed out from the torn flesh.

"Listen to me, Shannon McClarty. You have a choice to make. You can break the cycle or complete the cycle. There are those who want you to break the cycle. I want the cycle broken, and this world saved. To do that you must let go of everything. Everything."

CHAPTER FORTY SIX

Halfway through Dani's cross-examination, Celine's secretary rushed into the conference room, clearly distressed.

She leaned over and whispered into the counselor's ear. When the lawyer's eyebrows raised over the rims of her reading glasses, Dani knew it was not good news.

Celine whispered a few words back to her assistant, and the woman rushed from the room.

Dani waited patiently for an explanation, but the suspense was too much for her mother.

"Okay, what's so damn important?" Carol said.

Celine composed her thoughts.

"It's not good news. Not for our case, and perhaps not for your safety. Your husband," she looked into Dani's eyes, "just escaped."

Dani was taken aback.

"How? We were just there. That place is a fortress. We saw more guards than inmates for God's sake."

"I don't have the details for how he escaped. I just have word that he has escaped. My secretary has called the police department. I've asked them for a protection detail to cover you."

"Do you think he's coming after us?" Carol asked.

"I've never met the man, but let's err on the side of caution, ladies," Celine said.

Dani stood up.

"The police aren't going to protect us. They're going to use us as bait."

Celine raised her eyebrows again.

"That is a side benefit for them, yes," the lawyer said.

"Why do you think I would let them do that?"

Celine leaned forward.

"If we're talking about aiding and abetting a fugitive, you can count me out."

"My daughter doesn't know what she's saying, Celine. She's a troubled woman who just learned that her possibly murdering husband is on the loose."

"Mother!"

"What I'm trying to say is that she is not in a right state of mind to suggest anything. We will, of course, cooperate with the authorities."

Dani moved to the conference room door. Carol rose, as well, but Dani waved for her to sit. "Mother, you take the protection. I don't need it. Don't try following me."

She let the door close behind her. Backing away from the conference room and down the reception area to the outer doors, Dani watched the lawyer and her mother sit and stare, dumbfounded.

It was clear they had no idea what she was doing, but neither did she.

It felt right.

In the elevator, Dani paced back and forth. Her mind was scrambled. She was scared that Shannon escaped and what that meant, but she desperately wanted to see him.

Exiting the elevator, Dani scanned the parking garage. She didn't think that Chicago's police force could respond quickly enough to start trailing her now, but it didn't hurt to be careful. The last thing she wanted to do was to lead them to Shannon. That was where she was going.

Then again, Dani had no idea how to find him anyway. He would have to find her.

She ran to her rental car and popped it open.

Her mother could afford a taxi, and she had keys to the loft if she decided to return.

Would Shannon actually head back to the loft? Isn't that too obvious? The police were surely staking it out, or would be. Or, maybe they, too, would think it was obvious and not watch it.

Stop thinking and just go, Dani thought.

With a shriek of burning rubber, she pulled out of the parking spot and sped out of the parking garage.

On the street, Dani heard the faint sounds of sirens in the distance. She was sure they were headed toward her.

A 50-50 gamble laid out before her: turn right or turn left. Either way or both might lead her straight into the police and away from Shannon.

Her heart raced. She could not choose.

Sighing, Dani looked across the traffic to the opposing sidewalk. Directly in front of her, a suited man stood still amongst the pedestrian traffic. He lifted his right arm and pointed. He pointed her east.

A calmness and confidence fell over her. She knew which way to go.

The man nodded, and that was when she realized that he had no face, but she made the turn anyway when traffic allowed.

Maybe she was afraid of the faceless men, but she feared for her husband more. If they offered her hope for a reunion, she would take it.

In her rearview mirror, Dani watched as the faceless man disappeared into the crowd of normal people. Cop cars, with their lights flashing and sirens blaring, pulled into the parking garage she had left moments before.

At every intersection she passed, a faceless man showed her the way.

It did cross her mind that they might be leading her to danger, but with Shannon now a fugitive, it was a risk worth taking.

Before long, Dani was speeding out of the city heading northwest to the farmlands and the small towns. The highway quickly became a two lane road. Plowed and rowed fields lined either side of it.

There were no more faceless men, but Dani kept driving onward.

When the sun touched the horizon, doubt overcame her. She didn't know what to expect. The nagging feeling that she had overshot wherever it was that she was supposed to be crept into her mind.

The lights of the last small town she was driving through were switching on when she pulled onto the main street. Businesses that were only open during the day were dark with their blinds drawn, and businesses, like the market and restaurant and bar, were busy with people—mostly older.

Dani parked in an open spot in front of the restaurant.

She switched the car off and grabbed her fob. Something to eat sounded good and would probably help to clear her head.

Having not eaten for hours—and then only snacking on the food offered by the law office—her energy was waning. Suddenly, with the smell of hamburgers in the air, Dani needed to eat. A greasy plate of chili cheese fries, country style, promised to fill her belly and bring clarity to her confused thoughts.

Climbing out of the car, she popped the fob and locked the car with a press of a button.

If the smell of home cooking was strong outside, it was overpowering inside the restaurant. The sounds of silverware clanking against stoneware were a welcome cacophony to ears that had only heard silence and a mind that had only listened to its own terrible imaginings for the last several hours.

"Care for a table or a booth?" the friendly teenage host asked.

Dani shook out of her hungry daze.

"Whatever will get me food faster?"

The girl laughed and led her to the counter strung around the open kitchen as was the style of Midwestern diners.

"You can order from Helga. She works the counter. She may not seem fast, but your food will be ready in no time."

"Thanks." Dani managed a weak, hungry smile.

An ancient woman, dressed in a classic waitress outfit, lingered near the order wheel studying several of the hanging orders through her bifocals.

Dani cleared her throat to get the old woman's attention.

Her ears were in better shape than her eyes, because she turned in Dani's direction immediately. She looked at Dani, coolly, then returned to her green slips.

Shaking her head, Dani flipped through the menu thinking that the elderly waitress looked and acted like a familiar sitcom character. It was a waste of time, however. She knew what she wanted already and slid the menu on the counter away from her.

"Miss? Miss?" Dani called out for the waitress. "I'm ready to order."

Again, the old waitress looked at her dismissively.

The hostess passed by with another customer, and Dani stopped the girl, on her return to her station, with an "mhmm."

"Is this what you call customer service around here? She barely even looks at me."

The young woman asked, "Who?"

"Her!" Dani pointed at the old waitress.

"Helga's still on the floor. Over there," the hostess pointed away from the counter.

Dani turned back to the old waitress, and in her place, was a faceless man.

Whispering, Dani said, "What about back there?"

The hostess followed Dani's gaze.

"That's our kitchen."

It was clear that the hostess did not see the faceless man that Dani saw. The girl looked right through it.

Dani fought the urge to get up and run. While seeing it up close was disturbing at the least, she remembered that she had already decided that these faceless men must be neutral and of no threat to her.

She closed her eyes then opened them. What she had been looking at was the stainless steel backing of the kitchen hood. The polish on it was so reflective that it was nearly as good as a mirror.

Dani was looking at herself.

Helga, the real Helga—young, pretty and with a complete face, approached Dani at the very noticeable behest of the hostess. Dani pulled herself away from staring at her own reflection.

"Hi, I'm Helga. What can I get you to drink?"

"You and my mother would get along famously," Dani said.

The inside joke was clearly lost on the young waitress. Her only reply was to crinkle her forehead ever so slightly.

"I'll take an iced tea," Dani dead-panned.

Helga nodded and began to move off, but Dani stopped her.

"I'll take your biscuits and gravy plate. I don't need any more time."

"Great! I'll be back with your drink."

Helga took Dani's menu off the table with a smile. Dani returned it reflexively.

A classic '50s rock and roll song played on the jukebox. It was one of her mother's favorites, and she was surprised at how much she liked it, as well.

She missed Carol.

Absently, Dani drummed the song's beat on the counter top thinking that her mother would love the adventure of her current predicament. She turned herself on her swivel seat closing her eyes and dancing like a little kid. When she stopped spinning and opened her eyes, the old woman she had seen reflected in the stainless steel sat next to her, staring at her.

"Ha, you don't scare me anymore," Dani said to her. "None of you faceless things do."

The old woman looked at her unmoved.

"He's here. We brought him here, too."

"Who?" Dani asked.

The old woman, in an overt display of emotion, rolled her eyes. "Who do you think?"

Dani swiveled in the chair again toward the greater restaurant, her eyes darting around the room, but she could not find Shannon.

"You must promise us."

Dani turned back to the woman.

"Promise you what?"

"You must promise to help us."

"I'm on the run from the cops. What can I possibly do to help anyone?"

The old woman grabbed Dani's hand. It was cold and damp like a slab of meat cooled in a refrigerator. Dani swallowed a gasp at its touch, but grew strangely calm in its embrace.

"Our mutual friend will tell you what to do. You and Shannon."

"I want to see him. I want to see him. I can't promise anything until I do."

The old woman nodded then evaporated into the air like steam off a cup of coffee.

In her mind, Dani heard the woman's voice, "Go. He is in the last booth in the far corner."

Immediately, Dani rocketed out of her seat.

She marched to the far end of the restaurant through the constantly moving wait staff. The seated hungry eaters took no notice of her.

Her eyes were fixed on the corner of the room until they fell on two men, one hunkered over wearing the sweatshirt of the local university and the other wearing a tweed jacket.

She recognized both.

Dani slid into the booth next to Shannon who was wearing the sweatshirt. She studied him for several minutes before moving closer. He, likewise, studied her.

Opposite them, James Herald ate his Cobb salad unsurprised by her arrival.

Shannon, now ignoring his hamburger, stared at Dani as if she was an apparition.

"Is this one of your tricks?" he asked Herald directly.

Herald giggled.

"No."

"Wait… What? You're having hallucinations, too?" Dani said.

Her husband pointed over at James.

"I've seen this guy do some pretty crazy shit. Broke me out of jail and got me here. He's some kind of faceless thing, but I don't hold it against him."

"Him? James Herald? He's a librarian."

James looked up from his salad.

"I've got no face except the one I choose to wear. I like books. What's the surprise about, Dani?"

"Am I being acknowledged as real?"

"Of course—"

James was interrupted by the waitress Helga, "There you are! I knew I'd find you. Here's your plate of biscuits and gravy and one iced tea."

"Thank you."

Dani accepted her plate with a smile.

Helga added, "Not a bother. I'll make sure to keep my eye out on this table, too. Flag me down if you need me. Toodle-oo."

"You better eat up. We don't have long before we get on the road," Herald said.

"Are you talking to me?" Dani asked.

"Of course," Herald pointed at Shannon's plate, "he's almost done."

"It was good, too. After that crap they tried to feed me in jail."

"And where exactly are *we* going?" she said.

"New York City, my girl."

Dani dropped biscuit bits from her mouth.

"New York City?"

"Shhh. Don't say that too loud. You never know who might be listening," Shannon said.

"How can I talk too loud if I'm not really here?" she asked.

Shannon pushed his finished plate away and situated himself into the crook of the booth. He looked her up and down.

"If you are one of James' parlor tricks, you're pretty darn good. But there are a couple of flaws if you ask me."

Dani bit. "I'm asking."

"For one, Dani would never eat biscuits and gravy. She worries too much about her figure, and that is nothing but fat on a plate."

She looked down at her half-eaten plate. He was right. Dani felt like trashing the rest of the food, but she was incredibly hungry and the biscuits tasted too good to waste.

"Maybe," she said swallowing more than her pride.

"You look like hell. No offense meant, but my wife never wore her hair in a bun. Christ, you expect me to believe my woman's aged ten years?"

"Ten years?!"

Shannon turned to Herald, confused.

"Don't look at me," James said. "She's not one of mine."

Shaking her head, Dani picked up a biscuit off her plate and threw it at Shannon. It slopped onto his chest.

He looked down at it, picked it off his sweater and popped it into his mouth. Through a mouthful of biscuit, "Good gravy, that is my wife."

A lightness filled her heart. His innate good-hearted manner never failed to sway the young woman. Dani wasn't quite ready to reveal it, though. Seeing Shannon. Being with him. Knowing he wasn't in danger. It was a shock.

"I can't believe you said that. If I didn't have several other more important things to be very upset about with you, I'd be furious about that right about now."

Herald laughed.

"You don't act like you're sitting and eating with a man on the run," Dani said to the librarian.

Herald simply shrugged.

Finished eating the biscuit, Shannon reached over to Dani, but she scooted to the edge of the booth—away from him.

"That's not fair," he said.

"I don't care what's fair."

"Don't act like that, babe."

Herald cleared his throat.

"Now, listen up, you two. The last thing we need is to draw any unwanted attention. I can only do so much. Understand?"

"Naw," Shannon said sarcastically. "What are you afraid of? The podunk cops in this penny-ante town?"

James returned to the last remaining lettuce leaves of his Cobb salad.

"Like I said, I've seen what he can do, and I don't think James Herald, here, is afraid of any damn thing."

"Finish eating, lovebirds. We have to make the City by morning. Non-stop driving, and I can't drive. So, it's up to you two."

Shannon harrumphed. "What? You can't drive? But you sure can hotwire a car."

"There are benefits to being surrounded most of your life by books."

"I don't get it, James," Dani said. "You're a faceless, hot-wiring magician and sometime librarian?"

James pushed his empty plate towards the end of the table.

"I am a full time librarian. Magician, no. As one of my kind, I have different abilities. Or as Shannon has found out on his adventures with an unlucky young woman or with certain inmates, or as you, Dani, did minutes ago, we can take on identities that are not our own."

"What?" Shannon said. His realization was apparent on his face. "You mean, I didn't kill anyone?"

"That is correct," James said. "You, Shannon McClarty, never killed any person—of your kind or mine. It was an illusion, so that we could have your minds opened to the extent where you would be pliant enough to help us do what is necessary."

Pushing himself back into the booth with his jaw clenched, Shannon stopped himself from screaming at James. His face contorted by a confluence of emotions settled into tears of happiness.

Dani wanted desperately to comfort him, but didn't. She sensed this was a revelation for him to process alone. It was, however, a relief for her, too.

"Do you understand what hell I went through? Thinking that these hands could do terrible things to another person?"

"Yes," the librarian said while wiping his glasses clean with a handkerchief.

"What in God's name made you do this to me? To her?"

Herald straightened himself and placed his glasses onto his face with the fastidiousness of a man who spent his time pondering the Dewey Decimal System.

"We knew exactly what it would take for you to see us for anything beyond monsters who live in the shadows under your bed. It took showing you that the monsters you see in your head are really the stories your tell yourself. Now, that I've taken that away from you, you can see all of us for who we truly are."

Shannon wiped his face clean of tears. He hung his head until Dani found the strength to interrupt the silence between them.

"Does your magic include spells for hiding from the cops?"

Dani indicated with her head, as subtly as possible, toward the front entrance of the diner.

"How do you think you got here?" James said.

Shannon craned his neck to look above the crowd, and James slowly turned, but to Dani, their curious, purposeful looking was very obvious.

"I didn't mean for you to both look now!" Dani hissed.

On their dinner break, the two police officers smiled and chatted up the diner staff before taking seats at the counter where Dani had been sitting.

"They'll see us and recognize us if you two don't learn to be more discreet."

Her husband sat back down in the booth. He chuckled.

"What's so funny?"

Shannon grabbed another biscuit from her plate.

"They won't see us."

"That's right," James said.

"Invisibility cloak, Professor Dumbledore?" Dani continued

sarcastically.

"Something like it," the librarian answered undeterred by the woman's attitude. "Very nice reference. My people are born in the shadows, and we've learned to use the shadows to suit our needs."

Herald pointed at the television hanging in the corner of the diner. On it, Dani and Shannon's pictures were displayed with the chyron: **Fugitives from Chicago Jail on the loose.**

Dani sunk pressing down into the booth's cushion.

"Don't bother. They don't see you for who you are, Dani. Neither of you. Nor I, for that matter. We are familiar in that we have human faces but not recognizable faces to those who see us."

"I'm supposed to believe that?" she asked.

"Surely, you aren't going to start questioning me after all you've seen and all you've been through? You may think that these people see you as a beautiful young woman, but they don't. You are, to them, an old, grey-haired lady. I think you've seen her before. No?"

James met her gaze and did not flinch from it.

"If you were stupid enough to walk out of the diner leaving my protection, you would be recognized, and I do not know what would happen to you."

Dani took a deep drink of her iced tea and swallowed it slowly.

"I suppose I have a little too much of my mother's contrariness in me. I apologize."

Dani thought about the old woman who had been her reflection. *Was that a glimpse of my future?*

Shannon rubbed her back.

"Don't be that hard on yourself."

Dani shot him daggers.

"What?! Carol's my mother-in-law! I'm not allowed to like her," Shannon said.

James put an end to their cozy repartee, "I suggest we finish our meals. Time is of the essence."

Relenting, Shannon smiled, and they caught each other in the nonverbal apology habit that had formed from their courtship and marriage. He wrapped his arms around Dani, and this time, she did not resist him. His arms were familiar, and being embraced by them, felt right.

Shannon pulled Dani into him and finished the kiss she had started at their meeting moments before.

She was home.

With him.

CHAPTER FORTY SEVEN

Carol Strauss exited the car share in front of Dani's loft. The cops had cased the place and found no sign of either Dani or Shannon. They gave her the green light to return to grab her things.

She had her own set of keys, so that would not be a problem. Her flight back to Miami left in a little over three hours, and after promising to remain in contact with the Chicago PD, they agreed to let her fly home.

It did, also, take a good bit of cajoling from Celene.

Carol couldn't wait to see the bill for that—now that she was footing the legal bill for a fugitive from justice and an aider and abettor of said fugitive.

The loft was exactly as she and Dani had left it. The various cleaning tools and supplies were exactly where they were left earlier that day.

"What a shame," she muttered to herself.

The previous night, Dani slept on her old bed, and Carol had taken the sofa—across the loft. Her suitcase, still open, lay on the floor besides the nest she made of the cushions.

Checking her watch, she reckoned she still had time to make the airport and the flight with a stop off for a cocktail in the airport bar. Carol slumped onto the sofa. She really wanted to curl up and sleep—as was her natural tendency when confronted by depressing circumstances.

Did she think that her daughter was in danger from her husband? *No. Not really.*

Did she fear for her daughter's freedom now that she was being accused of a felony? *Yes.*

Any high-priced lawyer would simply be a plea-bargainer facing off with an antagonistic press and the cut-and-dried nature of an accused murderer and fugitives from justice. All Strauss' money would amount to how many fewer years in prison Dani, alone, would be facing. For Shannon, it would be a question of the death penalty or life in prison.

There was a bottle of Macallan's in the kitchen. It called to her, but Carol knew that if one drop touched her lips in that loft, many drops would touch them, and she would not be flying to Miami that evening. She would only allow herself a drink at the airport.

"Ahhh—shit," Carol said to the empty room. Her words echoed off its hard surfaces.

The place was the definition of lonely.

She sat up, righted herself and checked her luggage. It was ready except for her toiletry bag.

Time to go, she thought.

Carol moved to the bathroom. She snapped up her toothbrush, slathered on a helping of toothpaste and brushed.

On top of the toilet, a heap of pages caught her eye. It was a book—torn apart page by page—into a mess.

She decided to take it with her. It might be a chore to put it back together, but she had plenty of time once she was in the air, and once together, she could read it as a diversion.

It would keep her mind off her daughter's troubles on the flight back to her beach home.

Carol placed the pages inside a plastic bag. A few pages crumpled, but the book had seen better days, anyway, and a few more dog ears could not be helped. She put it back on top of the toilet.

After a thorough brushing, she pulled her toiletry bag together and headed back to her suitcase.

It was time to go.

She threw everything together, slammed the case shut and had to sit on it to lock it closed.

Carol set the case upright onto its wheels. She didn't feel like doing any more freshening up. She simply wanted to get the hell out of Dodge. Her daughter was a grown woman who had made her own decisions. Dani might have to live with her decisions, but Carol sure as hell would escape as much of it as she could.

At the door, she turned and surveyed the apartment—half in a state of clean-up.

Carol couldn't help it.

She was sad.

Closing the door behind her and ready to lock it with her key, Carol remembered the book. "Damn it."

She rushed back into the bathroom and grabbed up the mess of pages in the bag. Stuffing it into her purse, Carol dashed out of the loft.

The deadbolt snapped into position.

She looked at the big, black metal door. Sighing, she pulled her luggage down the cold, concrete hallway.

Carol hoped to return one day with her daughter.

CHAPTER FORTY EIGHT

Paul Steale smiled at Bob, the doorman he had known for nearly 30 years while living in his high-rise apartment building. He never knew much about the man —not even his last name—just that he was a pleasant sort who he was happy to give a Christmas card with several $100 bills inside every year.

The black, polished limousine waited for him adjacent to the front entrance.

"Mr. Steale," Bob said and nodded in reply as was their custom. The chauffeur held the door open allowing Steale to easily slip inside. Once the author was seated, the door was shut with the strong, but muted, thud of luxury.

He settled into the cushions and grabbed a bottled water from the console of refreshments.

The glass divider lowered.

"Mr. Steale, we have plenty of time to make it across the island. Is there anything you'd like to do before heading to the studio?"

Paul thought about it for a moment. "You know—"

"—Devin, sir."

"Devin, let's grab a quick cocktail."

"Any particular place?"

"Not really. But I'm craving a good, stout sake."

The Asian man smiled. The divider began rising.

"How did you know I was Japanese? I know just the place."

"A lucky guess, I suppose. Good. Book promotion interviews are so much better with the edge taken off."

The car moved forward, and he felt it gently pushing against his back. But the cushions were so plush, Steale might as well have been pushed by a cloud.

He opened up his tablet. The *Times* was still up where he left off. It was a dull article about the newest gallery opening. Art in general was a lifelong interest for him, and he found that he had a passion for sculpture.

With his last book on the bestseller list some 10 years earlier, that Hollywood had already optioned this new book was a miracle; a godsend of riches. He would have plenty of money to splurge on new works of art.

The previous year, Paul furnished his apartment with the best Renaissance Italian paintings on the market his stock portfolio allowed. Now, he could afford to outfit his summer home in the Hamptons. It was very much in need of culture.

In the article, the newest force in sculpting was causing quite a stir. The young artist, Shannon McClarty, was currently in jail on suspicion of murder. His artwork was so extraordinary, however, its value was skyrocketing.

Steale planned on making the opening of the gallery and spending heavily on this new phenom.

In school, Steale had earned very low marks—especially in English composition. The author considered it a miracle that he earned money doing something he hated as a kid. When he grew up, Paul wanted to be a baseball player. He was skilled, but losing two years of steady practice, moving from state to state and country to country following his father's diplomatic appointments, cost him his dream. By the time he was ready to play again in organized leagues, Steale was too old for college consideration.

It was the library that salved his wounded dreams. He found himself drawn to the worlds created within pages. His affinity for fantasy and science fiction was boundless. He devoured as many books as he could during this period of his life.

English teacher after English teacher tried to get him interested in established literature, but he vacuumed up the trail of terror from the Gothic poets all the way up to Bradbury and King. Edgar Allen Poe and H.P. Lovecraft, his favorites, were the closest Steale came to classics.

His love was so great and his attention so fixed, that when it came time to devote effort to actual school work, Steale would cram assignments into a few hours in a weekend instead of an entire month.

The results were ugly.

But his imagination was aflame and stayed that way for the rest of his life.

The car slowed, and the divider slid down.

"We're here, sir. I'll be around to open the door once traffic clears."

"Yes, please, don't get hit by an Uber. They're worse than the old taxi drivers."

Before he stepped out, the limo driver replied, "Most of those guys drive their own cars now. So, same difference."

In an instant, the man was out of the car and around to the sidewalk side, popping open the door for Steale.

"Here you are, sir."

Paul strained to pull himself out of the car. He groaned. The weight around his middle section was getting too much. It was time for a diet. Not today. But maybe he would start tomorrow. Stretching his back, the author looked at the Japanese characters flashing neon in the window of the dive bar. They had made it to the lower east side.

"Nice, Devin."

"Thank you, sir. I thought you needed a little taste from my heritage," the black suited young man said while holding the door open for Steale.

"Your heritage include Yakuza?" Steale joked.

Devin smiled but was noncommittal.

The author walked into the bar. It was indeed a dive. Typical of that part of town, but without the usual clientele, the riff raff of Manhattan. Here, it was all Asian—legal and otherwise. Devin spoke some rough Japanese to the bartender. The driver motioned for him to sit at the bar. He joined Steale.

A few more words in Japanese and two shot glasses filled to the brim with a clear liquid were poured in front of them.

"Are you sure about this? You being the driver and all?" Steale asked.

Devin smiled and picked up his shot and raised it to his lips. "Ahh, this?"

He swigged it down, and let out a gasp.

"It's nothing. Try!"

Paul felt the coldness of the shot glass on his lips. He closed his eyes, counted to three and downed it. The alcohol was harsh, burning his throat as it flowed hot down to his stomach.

"Gack!"

Steale tried to inhale and exhale simultaneously.

Devin laughed.

"Suntory vodka puts hair on your chest."

"I wasn't expecting that," Steale said.

"Why? It's not so different than Russian vodka," the driver replied.

"Well, that's true. Gasoline has the same effect. It was the slight peppermint taste that got me."

"Not peppermint. A Japanese herb. Very good for your health."

"I'm sure it is. Until it knocks you out. A few shots of that, and you're feeling quite fine."

Devin seemed to shout at the bartender who shouted back but returned with two bottles of Asahi.

"To wash it down."

They knocked beer necks.

"Cheers," Steale said.

The beer cooled his throat from the burning hard alcohol which had settled and warmed his belly.

"Ready for the interview now, Mr. Steale?"

Paul took another swig of his beer.

"Yes, I think I will be all right."

"Are you ready?" Devin asked.

Something in Devin's tone alarmed Steale, but he stiffened his spine, and did not let it show. He drank his sake swiveling on his seat to face his driver.

"I am. Shall we go?" Steale asked.

Devin stared at him without speaking. Steale looked around the rest of the bar. All of the patrons were staring at him, too.

He turned back to Devin, and the man's face inverted with a sickening rip. The skin settled into a faceless mask.

It said, "We are coming for you, Steale. You have forgotten your bargain."

Paul clawed inside his long coat at the interior chest pocket. Breathing heavily, he pulled out a small pad of paper and a pen. The pain in his chest was overwhelming, and the fear damn near paralyzed him.

The people around the bar—one by one, their faces ripped into the same blank, faceless mask.

Steale tried to write on the pad, but the ink in his pen was dry. He shook it as the faceless people rose from their tables and booths.

They were coming for him.

He scratched again at the pad. The ink had loosened and fallen to the tip. Steale scribbled out the words:

the faceless in the bar disappear.

His heart was racing. He tried to rise from his chair, but he fell against the bar. His chest pounded. Bracing himself and turning around, Steale found the faceless still surrounding him.

His heart spasmed.

And then, in the blink of an eye and whisps of smoke, they were gone.

The bar was empty. No one stood before him. Devin, too, had disappeared.

Steale gasped for air. He dropped to his knees. He pulled out his handkerchief and blotted his forehead which was drenched with sweat.

Growing calmer, he pulled himself back to his feet. He stepped toward the door and swung it ever so slightly open. The limo that had transported him there along with Devin had vanished.

He pushed through the door taking weak steps onto the sidewalk.

The wind off the nearby ocean whipped through the deserted streets of the lower east side and tousled his hair and clothes.

Steale put his cell phone up to his ear.

"Yes, I'd like to request a car, please. Make it fast. I have an interview—" he looked at the face of his phone "—in 12 minutes."

CHAPTER FORTY NINE

The car that Herald hot-wired was the furthest thing from a road trip mainstay. It was a '70s era Ford sedan that belonged in a private detective TV show.

Shannon drove. Dani sat on the bench seat with him. Herald was in the rear seat by himself.

Every bump, every increase of 5 miles per hour, any sudden change in direction, the car would shake and rattle but the jostling was cushioned by the boat-like suspension.

It would have been impossible to sleep without the back and forth, ocean rolling motion, and Dani took advantage sleeping across Shannon's lap as he drove. She needed it.

As far as Shannon knew—from the limited amount of time he had spent with him—James never slept. He kept to himself once they started on the road, mostly silent. He stared out the windows, and it was this fixation that made Shannon nervous. The sculptor wanted to ask him what he was so interested in out there in the moonlight, but he also didn't want to disturb his wife.

She snored when deep asleep, and she was deeply asleep.

Shannon shifted a bit. His right leg was tingling, and luckily, Dani moved her head, relieving the pressure on his leg.

"How long?" James asked in a whisper.

"I don't know. Five hours, maybe."

"Will you be able to drive the whole way?" the librarian asked. Shannon shrugged.

"I don't know. I feel all right. We'll see."

"Do your best. Unless you want her to drive," Herald said.

"And you? I haven't seen you sleep at all."

"I don't sleep, and I don't drive."

"You can hotwire a car, but you can't drive it?" Shannon snickered. "That's weird."

"Weird shouldn't bother you anymore, Shannon."

"Why didn't you ever learn?"

Herald cocked his head, reminiscing.

"I've lived all my life in a city that makes owning a car difficult. Books, they can teach many things except the actual experience of piloting a piece of metal hurtling along at enormous speeds. I know you want some idealized story of me growing up in the school of hard knocks. But I didn't. It was nice for the most part."

Shannon's disbelief became amusement.

"I can teach you if you want. It's just a matter of keeping within the lines and pressing on the gas or the brake."

"I'd prefer to get to the City in one piece. Thank you. I appreciate the offer."

"No worries. The offer stands."

Shannon looked at his cup of coffee in the cup holder. He needed a pick-me-up, but he didn't want to chance spilling even a drop on his sleeping wife. He yawned and felt the pressure growing in his bladder. The little things were starting to add up.

"We might need to make a pit stop soon. So, that would be a good time to switch drivers."

Herald nodded.

"I'll give it some more thought, but don't expect any drastic changes of heart."

"Are we faceless people? Me and Dani? I saw it once. I think. My reflection."

Herald stared at Shannon in the rearview mirror. He thought

hard before speaking.

"It's a matter of knowing all that's knowable. You only know so much. If you open yourself up to the whispers of the world, in the night, out there," he pointed out the window, "you will understand."

Shannon tried to understand what Herald had just told him. He expected some clarity. But, the man's words were still very much opaque.

"What do you expect this Steale to do for us? I keep thinking I should be making my way to Mexico and trying to disappear. I have the Feds after me for sure. Her, too. Escaping prison and fleeing across state lines. Smarter people than me might think you're playing us for fools?"

James shook his head, no.

"Steale is our only chance to make things right. To restore the balance that must be for this world to continue. But we must reach him soon. Before the others do."

"These others. You know them? Right?"

"I do. They are us, too."

"Why would they be so dangerous, then? Can't you talk sense into them?"

"Did I speak sense to you? Is that what you'd call it?"

"You have a point."

The artist remembered what Herald had done in the jail to free him. The snake-like, black tendrils that threw big men around like dolls.

"Besides," James continued, "they feel that the only way to make things right is to start it all over again. And they will kill him to do that."

"If they kill him, what happens?"

"The world ends, and something new takes its place."

"If we save him?"

"We can restore the world as it is supposed to be."

Shannon stared at the blacktop and the stripes in the road flashing by. If this man Steale could give him and Dani a new chance, all of it, the woman, jail, the escape, all of it, was worth it just to find him.

All of it.

"Our lives?"

Herald nodded, yes.

Dani stirred. Shannon glanced down quickly. He met her gaze and quickly smiled at her before returning his eyes to the road. She sat up, still groggy.

"How long have I been out?" she said. "My head hurts."

James looked over. But he waited for Shannon to respond.

"I don't know. A couple hours at least."

"We aren't there, yet?" she asked with a half laugh.

Her arms extended, Dani stretched playfully tapping Shannon's cheek. She yawned again.

"Don't do that. It's catching," Shannon said followed by a huge yawn, himself.

"I can drive, if you want to get some sleep," she said. "Or maybe James—"

James shook his head. It was clear he did not want to revisit that conversation.

"Err," Shannon said, "we've already gone over that. It's not happening. Any driving to do, and it's you and me doing it."

"Got it. James?" she asked.

He was looking out at the blackness beyond the highway, again.

"James?" Dani asked again but this time more softly. "What are you looking at out there?"

Herald shifted on the bench seat. He pulled his face away from the window and met Dani's gaze.

"It's not what I see. It's what I hear."

"What can you hear over this creaky old rust bucket?" Shannon asked.

"If only the squeaks could drown them out," Herald replied.

"Drown who out?" Dani said.

"The whispers of the unformed," Herald replied. "It is terrible in some ways,"

He looked back out at the darkness beyond the dim lights of

the highway.

"When I stare out into the night... out there. I hear them."

"Hear who?" Dani asked.

"The thoughts of things that might be or might never be. They are Steale's unborn children. The ones that lack body, because he hasn't given it to them yet."

"Steale? I don't understand," Dani said.

"He is the author of this world. Given the power to create by the Universe itself. He was given a bargain when he was chosen. A bargain that he has broken. And now, the faceless and the unformed, at the behest of the Universe, are going to make him and all of existence pay the price for that betrayal—unless we can restore the pact."

CHAPTER FIFTY

It took Steale more than ten minutes to get to the studio. With the late unpleasantness having sobered him up, the author felt every weave in and out of rush hour Manhattan traffic from inside his replacement car. It was nauseating and very much like the good old days when he drove a cab to support his writing habit.

But, he got where he needed to go with time to spare.

"Hey! Hey, where you going?" the doorman in front of the network called out to him.

The man stared dumbfounded at Steale who rushed from the idling yellow hybrid now sitting curbside outside the network. Steale continued into the building, opening the glass door for himself. He turned back to respond to the doorman, "Interview. I'm late."

He rushed up to the security desk.

Handing them his ID, he asked, "Is the restroom in the same place?"

One of the suited guards studied his ID while the other man kept his eyes on the security cameras. A few keystrokes on the computer and the guard released his ID back to him.

"Yeah, it's past the elevators on your right, unmarked. We'll call the elevator for you once you're finished in there. Wait for the buzz. Got it, Mr. Steale?"

The author nodded, yes. He rushed off around to the alcove where six elevator doors were stationed with three each on opposite walls. The restroom was exactly where he had been told it was.

The door was locked, but once he twisted the knob, he heard a buzz then the slide of the lock as it opened by remote command. Steale pushed inside.

He stepped to the vanity. His face was dripping with sweat. Grabbing some paper towels, he wet them with cool water and dabbed his face with them.

Normally, he would let the makeup artists deal with his face. His wrinkles and blemishes were scars he wore with pride, rewards for making it through life.

But he needed to calm down. The sound of running water and its coolness on his forehead were helping.

His breathing returned to normal, and he popped open his shirt and used more paper towels to wipe off the sweat trickling down his body.

Sniffing his underarms, he decided that his deodorant was still working. A final wipe here and there, and he buttoned back up. With no further need of the restroom, Steale exited and returned to the elevator alcove.

A momentary wait, and an elevator door popped open. He stepped inside. The guard came over the intercom, "They are expecting you, Mr. Steale. You will be escorted to the green room once you reach the floor."

"Thanks," he said into the empty air around him.

Once the doors whooshed closed, the author felt the elevator rocket upward. It was swift enough to be an E ticket ride. Ding. Ding. Ding. The floors sped by with regularity until the elevator slowed near the 36th floor.

The door slid open after the last ding and a small settling motion between elevator and floor.

Steale was greeted by a smiling young woman clutching a tablet computer.

"Mr. Steale?"

He stepped out next to her into the lobby filled with TV monitors. The entire floor was devoid of the hustle and bustle of people. He expected it to be filled by writers, technicians and talent. Yet, it was only them.

"Yes, I am Paul Steale."

He held out his hand. She shook it lightly taking it by her fingertips, the handshake of an eager, but tepid go-getter.

"Fantastic! I am Ali. I'll be your assistant until the interview with Ms. Winter. Please, follow me to the green room. We have plenty of refreshments waiting."

"How long do we have until my segment taping?"

He matched her brisk strides down the corridor. On one side was a normal appearing high-rise whose offices were empty. To his right, though, was a cavernous, dark studio behind plated glass. A few dark figures moved outside the arcs of the spotlights, likely grips or electricians. The cameras, however, were unmanned and slid around the studio, robotically.

Steale felt his breathing becoming irregular again.

"Any booze in the green room, or is it dry?"

"It's frowned upon, but if you must have some, I can pretty much get you anything."

She opened the door to the green room, which unsurprisingly was not green, but a rather pleasant and comfortable shade of blue. On the coffee table, a small buffet, comprised of a vegetable and fruit platter and pastries. It all looked fresh and untouched. Underneath the large screen TV playing several feeds from the network's lineup, beverages were lined on the hutch.

Steale perused the offerings.

"I'd like some Scotch. I don't care what kind, Ali. Just Scotch," he told the young woman.

A frown, for a split second, curled her face. Her pleasant, but very artificial demeanor returned.

"Right away, Mr. Steale. I will let the producers know of your arrival and return with your drink."

She left him alone.

He grabbed a bottle of water and downed it, and then took another in anticipation of getting more alcohol.

His attention turned to the monitor. His interviewer, Jane Brigham—a middle-aged, white woman who had bounced between networks as a reporter for many years, spoke to a roundish, smiling Indian man whose eyeglasses were rimmed with diamonds, possibly rhinestones.

"—and, Jane, what I'm saying is," the man said in an overly lilting Indian accent that Steale knew was a put-on, "there's so much negativity in the world today that it's easy for a person to get lost in it. People can fight—I hate to use a word that is so violent—let me rephrase that. People can accomplish their desires by embracing the positive possibilities. It's all right there in my book."

Jane smiled, nodded and lifted his book.

"Thank you so much, Vinetra Singh, for bringing your brand of insight to our program. *The Positive Adventure* is available at all major book sellers online and off."

"One last thing, Jane," he said.

"Of course, Vinetra."

"If one has an agreement in place, they must always honor their word. Words create the world, and what are we if we aren't our words?"

The door of the green room burst open. Ali stood in the doorway.

"Oh my God, Mr. Steale, you're almost on!"

"What? I thought I had some time to relax," Steale said. His voice rose in response to her franticness. "What about my booze?"

"I'm so sorry, Mr. Steale, but they just sprung this on me. Jane's unhappy with the current interview. She wants you up and running after this current commercial break—which means we have less than two minutes to get you prepped and in place. Please, Mr. Steale, follow me."

Ali held the door open for him. Steale shook his head disgusted at the latest turn of events.

With a surrendering wave of his hand, he said, "Fine. Lead on." The young woman's gait was no longer simply economical.

Now, she sprinted along the corridor. Steale broke out into a run just to keep up.

"Ohhh, I hope we're not late!"

Ali popped open the glass door that led to the studio.

"Late? Aren't these things put on tape and edited?" Steale asked in between pants.

"We used to do that, but we're competing with Internet shows, and there's a real need for audience interaction," Ali said.

Steale shook his head. "Oh, hell, I don't do live shows, since that disaster I had on CSPAN."

Ali stopped.

"What happened on CSPAN?"

"I don't like to talk about it."

"I'm afraid we should know."

Ali stood in front of him to impede any movement.

"I thought they wanted us on set, stat? Now, I get the third degree? Don't you people do your own due diligence?"

Ali cradled her tablet against her chest.

"I'm the one who they blame if things go wrong. What happened?"

His anger rising, Steale popped open one of the waters he pilfered from the green room. He chugged the water down, messily letting it drip off his cheeks. Crumpling the empty plastic bottle, he threw it into the darkness surrounding the set.

"I don't like talking about it."

Ali stepped back ever so slightly. "Please, tell me."

"The show?"

"They can wait," she said.

"I... I managed to lose my wife live on television for millions to see."

"That's not so bad. I thought you might've shit yourself or something."

Steale frowned.

"She called in and pretended to be a reader wanting to ask me a question."

Ali held a finger to her ear. She was being given orders, and Steale could see that whatever words they were weren't the most pleasant.

"Here I was—newly on the bestsellers list—like some wide-eyed lamb being led to slaughter."

The production assistant giggled. "I already like your ex."

"What? Why do you say that?"

"Because only a really strong woman would choose to humiliate her husband like that. I bet she has a great biting wit —like some Albee heroine."

Steale rolled his eyes.

"She's an actress. You may have seen her on Broadway once or twice. Maybe even a sitcom or two, but she was never good enough to utter Edward's words."

"It can't still hurt. Can it?"

Ali studied him with a measured skepticism written across her face.

"How long ago could it have been? You aren't exactly a young man."

"The compliments keep rolling off that tongue of yours. Let's get on with it. Take me to your damn leader."

The author moved past Ali toward the desk in the center of the studio. The host was absent, perhaps on a powder break. The cameras rolled to different positions autonomously. He wondered where the camera operators were hidden, *probably the control room.*

A disembodied female voice called out from the studio speakers, "Mr. Steale, please, take a seat to the left of Ms. Winter's tall chair. She will be back shortly."

"So are we live, or what?" Steale asked, head craned to the rafters.

No answer.

He sat in the chair as directed.

"We will be back live in three minutes. You look a little sweaty. Do you mind if our makeup person touches you up?"

Steale pulled out some of the paper towels he had taken from

the restroom and wiped himself. "Sure. Whatever you want."
From the darkness, a large black man, carrying a small plastic case, rushed up to the author. With a fey flourish, he immediately brushed Steale's face with a soft, feathered brush. Steale started to sniff in a pre-sneeze.
The man cringed. "I'm so sorry, Mr. Steale."
The sneeze passed.
"Not a problem. Do what you need to. Where is that woman?"
"Who?" the makeup artist asked. "Ms. Winter?"
"She doesn't let you call her by her first name?"
"Ms. Winter?" The man chuckled. "And neither will you if you know what's good for you."
"Is that a challenge?" Steale raised his eyebrow in defiance.
They both could sense movement in the darkness, and the man leaned over, finishing up his work on Steale, and whispered, "Don't. The woman's a first class bitch."
Victoria Winter, all 5'10" of stately, professional womanhood, strode into the light.
"Paul Steale," she extended a hand as she sat in her high chair, "I'm Victoria. Please, address me as such when we go live, and I will introduce you. Then, I will call you Paul. I assume that is your preferred name?"
Steale could not take his eyes off the woman. Though she was nearly his age, she was flawless and could pass for 20 years younger.
She noticed his attention, cocked her head, smiled and then clicked her fingers against the glass table.
"Paul?"
"That's good," Steale said.
She didn't seem to be the bitch he had been warned about.
Over the loudspeakers, "All right folks, settle. Back on air in 20 seconds. Watch the camera lights for the countdown."
Steale leaned over to Winter, "What do you want to speak about first?"
The anchor leaned away from him with a crinkled face.
"When we talk, we talk fresh. I don't tee up topics with guests.

It's about keeping us both engaged. Be on your best game, Steale."

The author pulled back and shrugged his shoulders. *Maybe she is a bitch.*

"Ten seconds."

Steale placed his sweaty hands on his knees, removing them from the glass table. Anxiety grew in his stomach. He wanted nothing to interfere with him getting in and out of the interview unscathed. He put out of his mind the thought that soon hundreds of thousands if not millions of eyes would soon be on him.

"Five… Four… Three… Two… One…"

All the cameras' lights flashed red. They were live broadcasting.

"Welcome back to the *Victoria Winter Show*. In this segment, we are joined by *New York Times* bestselling author Paul Steale. He's here to talk about his latest novel, *The Gamble*, a harrowing tale of revenge and ghosts from America's racial past. Thanks for joining us, Paul."

Automatically, Steale smiled. "Thanks for having me."

"I, of course, want to talk to you about your novel, but there seems to be a connection between one of your previous works and a rather strange and possibly dangerous current event."

"Wha—?"

Before Steale could finish, Winters cut him off and continued, "The curious murder case we've been following out of Chicago has turned into a jailbreak and fugitive situation."

Steale slumped against the back of his chair, staring at Winter incredulously.

"Do you have any thoughts regarding this new situation?"

The author sat mute.

Winter must've counted to three before breaking the dead air, because Steale did.

"I can only assume from your silence that you're unhappy with this news. People will only infer the worst from your silence, Paul."

He prefaced his words with a long, deep sigh. "I don't know what the hell you're talking about, Victoria."

"There's no need for profanity. And surely, you're not ignorant of these events."

With a tinge of sarcasm, Steale responded, "I apologize, but I've come on your program to discuss my book. I am not a reporter or newshound. That's not what I do. There isn't a thing I could say that would illuminate that situation for you."

"It's surprising that you have no insight. Tonight, our police sources have revealed that the fugitive and prison escapee Shannon McClarty claims that the murder he was implicated in was, in his words, 'foretold' in your book, *The Faceless Men*. "

"Oh, come on. You've got to be joking. This is a joke right?"

A wry smile crossed her face.

"No. It's not a joke. I would never consider any murder a joke."

Steale gripped the edge of the glass table with a grip so tight that his fingers were blanching.

"What kind of fool do you take me for?"

"I don't take you for a fool. I'm simply trying to find out what exactly is the importance of your novel. The attorneys representing Dani McClarty issued a statement on her behalf fearing that she's been abducted by her fugitive husband. It states: 'Ms. McClarty attended a meeting at our law offices and was called away from the table by a phone call. We suspect it was her husband Shannon McClarty lying in wait for her outside of our building. He forced her into her rental car and disappeared with her. Shannon McClarty has stated many times to investigators that he was influenced heavily by Paul Steale's novel *The Faceless Men*. He felt it was driving him to commit the crimes of which he is currently accused.' That's pretty compelling, Paul. What say you?"

He snorted. "I don't even understand what that pile of words means. It's incomprehensible. Am I supposed to believe that my 30-some-year-old novel is the catalyst for murder and kidnapping? Give me a break."

"I thought that book was 20 years old."

She looked at him with a raised eyebrow—signaling to the audience a gotcha moment.

"I wrote the original draft while I was in grad school. It wasn't published until 10 years later, and I never read or edited the damn thing in the interim or since."

"Paul, you must acknowledge that facing this accusation head-on will only benefit you."

Again, Steale chuckled. "Benefit me? Or, benefit you? I haven't seen any of this in print. For all I know, you've made the whole damn thing up and are baiting me."

"Why would I do that, sir?"

"Ratings."

"We're already the top-rated show in our time slot."

"And perhaps, an old writer with a middling new book won't keep your viewers tuned in."

Steale regretted calling his current work "middling," but it felt like the flames of the sun were burning in the center of his forehead. He frantically looked around the table for another bottle of water.

Winters pushed away from him with a frightened look. It was apparent to Steale that it was all an act, but probably not to her audience.

"What? I need some water. Water?"

Steale stood up knocking his chair away and onto the floor.

"I'm out. Have fun interviewing nothing."

"Wait! You can't—"

"—Can't?! Well, yes, I can."

He stepped out of the spotlights and into the darkness past the robot cameras. Blinded, Steale stumbled in the direction to where he felt the studio exit was. He kicked at the black linoleum floor, carefully trying to avoid the loose cables and assorted equipment occupying the studio floor. Behind him, he heard Winters go to break.

"We'll be right back to analyze this segment after these messages."

"We're off," the disembodied director said over the

loudspeakers. "Anybody got eyes on that asshole?"

"Go fuck yourself," Steale yelled. He couldn't control himself. "Turn on some damn lights, so I can get out of this miserable shithole!"

He felt a hand on his shoulder, and the author froze.

"This way," Ali whispered.

He turned and saw her shaded grey as the lights from the set caught her dimly. She clasped his hand and guided him through the dark. Her hand was cold.

Very cold.

Steale's eyes adjusted to the blackness just as they approached the stage door.

"Wait a sec," he said. "I need to cover my eyes before you open that."

"Gotcha," she said. "Cover up."

A tug on his hand and a careful step and Steale took his hand away from his eyes. Ali waited for him, but as soon as his eyes adjusted, she pointed him to the elevators.

"I suggest you make yourself scarce. Victoria has a habit of berating bad guests."

Steale shook his head affirmatively.

"Great. It was nice meeting you. Sorry about all this."

"Who do you think you are?!"

Turning to face his accuser, Steale was nose-to-nose with the TV host.

"Look, lady, I'm on my way out of here. That's where I'm going." Winters pushed Ali to the side.

"Hey, hey!" Steale said in her defense.

"Do you think there will be no consequences for what you do?"

Rolling his eyes, Steale said, "Oh, give me a break. I don't have time for lectures today, lady."

"But you do. And you will listen to this one."

Winters put a hand on Steale's shoulder. Instantly, he felt the pressure. It was unexpected—far more powerful than her thin fingers would suggest. With his opposite hand, the author reached over and prised at the woman's grip, but it would not be loosened.

"Get your goddamned hands off me!" His bellow was deep and menacing, but Winters was unfazed.

"This is a different time, Steale. Can't you feel it? Can't you feel your power waning?"

Finally, he threw her off. She hit the glass wall of the studio. The force was enough to crack it.

Steale stepped back, surprised at his own reaction.

Rushing toward Winters, Ali grabbed hold of the woman's shoulder, but, instead, the woman threw her off and into the wall, angrily.

Slowly, Winters straightened.

As she rose, Steale anticipated seeing blood pouring from her wounded head. But there was no wound.

"I'm sor—" he said.

He cut short his words when he fully comprehended the shape of Winters' head. Where a gushing cut in her scalp should have been, instead, there was a flat depression with a single gash, more like a rip, and an ooze of black liquid out from it.

Ali fell back against the wall when she saw Winters. She began to mumble uncontrollably. Dropping her ever-present tablet, the girl raised her hands to her face. Ali scraped at her own skin.

"Stop!" Steale cried.

But he stopped himself from rushing to her aid when he saw the results of her effort.

The girl screamed, "What? What am I?"

Large gouges in Ali's skin curtained by pink, hanging flesh, revealed the black ooze underneath her skin, as well.

Steale barely kept himself standing propping himself against the studio's glass wall.

"Stay away! Stay away! All of you!"

Winters was joined by Ali, erect once again. They blocked Steale's exit from the hallway area into the elevator alcove. They stood expressionless, almost serene.

"Don't you see?" Ali asked him.

"See what?"

"Everything you've ever done. Everything you've ever dreamed. It's all coming to an end."

Winters added, "When we tried to warn you. When we told you of your bargain with the eternal, you would not listen. Now, the cycle ends. A new one begins."

Steale stood with his mouth agape.

"Where have you been when the world bleeds and suffers? Where are you even now?"

"I'm... I'm only a man who writes silly stories for a living."

"Is that really what you think?" Ali asked. "In the face of everything that you've witnessed—just today—you cling to that?"

"It's a fact," he countered.

"You wish not to see. You tell yourself you don't remember. But you were chosen. And you've done what all flesh and blood does. You failed. You failed the world," Winters said.

"Who are you?"

"We are nothing," Ali said. "Because of you."

He pushed through the women toward the elevators. Jamming his finger over and over onto the elevator call button, he was afraid. But the women did not follow him. They simply stared at him with blank, black eyes.

The elevator arrived. The doors slid open. He rushed inside. He was desperate for this current nightmare to end.

Before the doors slid shut, Winters said, "It will end, Paul Steale. It will. Because you failed. But the world will not end before you have been punished for your crimes against us."

CHAPTER FIFTY ONE

Carol fidgeted in her first class seat. The seat next to hers was empty, and she had laid out and sorted the old, ripped-up paperback on it.

She hated flying alone—or rather by herself. She just could not relax. Now that the work of putting the book back together was done, Carol hoped she could lose herself in reading it for the rest of the flight.

The steward passed back into the first class area from coach, pushing the refreshment cart. He noticed Carol trying to get comfortable.

"Miss, would you like a cocktail, perhaps?"

"Oh, thank you, young man. You're a dear," she said, putting an overly sincere smile on, but she did manage to read his name tag.

"How does a mojito sound?"

The very thought of sweet rum relaxed her a bit.

"Oh, please, John."

A scoop of ice and the pop of an aluminum can and John finished her pour.

While the thought of a cocktail from a can would normally put her off, she found the cool liquid calming and refreshing.

"Yum, yum."

"I hate to admit it," John the steward said. "I really like these. Just like candy."

"You are so right, young man. Your taste is impeccable."

"I know. It's a curse."

He pushed the cart into the small alcove just before the cockpit. Carol, her mind finally soothed, sat back into her plush chair. She sipped at her canned mojito and wondered where her daughter had gotten to. From the thousand foot vantage Carol peered down from upon her daughter's troubles, things were amusingly clear. Dani had been very interested in that author in New York City. It was Carol's hunch to return to Manhattan instead of going home to Florida. She would catch up to Dani there.

Where there's smoke, she thought.

Looking at her watch—her cell phone was stowed in her carry-on in the overhead bin and turned off—she had less than 30 minutes before touchdown. One mojito can might not be enough to keep her nerves settled.

Carol looked around the rest of the first class section of the plane. It was mostly all hers. There was one other passenger, and he was fast asleep.

"Psst! John! Psst!" Carol whispered.

She sipped off the last dregs from the aluminum can he gave to her.

"Yoo-hoo!"

Peeking around the curtain that separated the galley from the first class cabin, John said, "Yes ma'am!"

Squeezing the empty can into an aluminum ball, she asked in mock daintiness, "Would you mind sparing another of those oh-so-delicious mojitos?"

He smiled in sympathy with Carol's naughtiness.

"Why of course. If you don't mind sharing the last one with me?"

John held out a plastic cup with ice and snapped open a mojito can and poured.

"Just don't let anyone know."

They both giggled and swallowed their portion of the drink in one gulp.

"Thank you, John," Carol said with a smile. "I'll be able to make the landing without losing it."

He looked at his watch.

"Oh, it's about that time. I better rally the girls."

Moving back into the galley, he activated the intercom.

"Crew begin preparing for landing."

Right after John's announcement, the captain continued, "Ladies and gentleman, we want to thank you for choosing this airline to fly you to beautiful New York City. Our flight crew will begin securing the cabin. We know you have a choice, and we hope you will choose to fly with us again."

John traipsed through the first class cabin towards the more full business class. Carol could hear him loudly order, "We'll be collecting your empty beverages now. You'll need to fold up your seat-back trays, please. Let's raise those seats into their upright position, and snug up those belts, folks."

Carol swallowed the last of the ice in her plastic cup. She could still taste a bit of the sweet, sweet rum.

A rumble crossed the body of plane, and the craft lurched up and down. The sorted paperback next to her flew up and off the seat, scattering the pages all around her.

"Oh, shit," she whispered.

Her plastic cup flew out of her hand. Carol breathed in a small squeal as the plane thudded again.

"Sorry, about that folks," the captain said over the intercom. "There's a little bit of weather going on over the City tonight. Make sure those seat-backs are up, and you are buckled in. Please, stay in your seats until landing. It's going to be a mite jumpy from here to touchdown."

The stewards and stewardesses quickly moved up the aisle to their jump seats near the cockpit.

"Oh, good lord," Carol said under her breath.

She leaned down and tried to pick up the loose pages, but her safety belt was too tight.

Again, the airplane jumped. This time, it was enough to send some of the overhead bins crashing open. Bags spilled out into the aisles. Some landed on top of a few unlucky passengers.

Carol heard them cursing about it in business class. The crew rushed up from their jump seats to help.

A whine shot through the cabin from the left wing. The plane dipped to the right.

Passengers screamed.

"We are experiencing some difficulty with turbulence and a loss of power in one engine. Do not be alarmed. The cabin crew is there to assist you. I will be, as a precaution, dropping the oxygen masks. Place them on yourself before you help any children or elderly. Remain in your seats."

Carol grabbed the mask that dangled in front of her. She slipped it over her face. And breathed deeply.

The sudden rush of cool oxygen into her lungs was soothing. She fell back into her plush seat.

The other occupant of first class had awakened. He looked about the section and locked eyes with Carol. She couldn't determine whether he understood what was happening.

She pointed to the oxygen masks.

He got the message and pulled one on.

Carol felt the thunder rolling through the airplane fuselage before she heard it. Almost all of the overhead cabinets crashed open.

Everyone screamed.

If she hadn't been strapped in tightly, Carol would've spilled out into the aisle herself.

Craning her neck carefully, she looked into the economy class past the curtains. People were splayed out everywhere amid the debris of their strewn luggage.

It was then that reality dawned on her that there might not be a landing at all.

Her stomach knotted. Her chest grew tight. Even though the cool oxygen splashed her face, Carol suddenly could not draw a breath.

She began babbling, "... please... God... don't let me die like this... my daughter... please..."

The plane tilted into a nose dive. Carol was driven into the back of her seat.

"... Jesus... oh... Jesus..."

Time slowed to a crawl. Carol watched as one of the loose aluminum cans from the beverage push cart floated past her as slowly as a paper boat might sail down a lazy creek.

She raised her hands to her face. But Carol was too slow—even in the current time dilation—to protect against more cans flying through the air.

One can hit her square in the forehead. Another hit her in the chest. Blood trickled down onto her oxygen mask from her split scalp.

Carol Straus knew she was going to die. The pain rushing through her body no longer mattered. It was all coming to an end.

Until the pages of the paperback swarmed her body.

They spun up around her and covered her like the wrappings of a mummy.

All light faded from her eyes, and an inky black undulating fluid flowed around her. The pages were the black nothing.

Carol felt herself reach out into the never-ending blackness.

Her body was feverishly hot. Only the oxygen flowing from the oxygen mask was cool.

Then, a silence as black as the fluid around her muted the screams of the passengers and whine of the failing engines.

Carol pulled her hands back and felt her face. The mask was still on. Deaf and blind, she found a strange calmness. She grabbed at the mask until it fell from her mouth. She gasped and breathed in the blackness.

"Carol Strauss, do you want to live?"

The voice reverberated around her like the trembling of the airplane fuselage. She tried to speak, but the inky darkness choked her mute. All she could do was scream in her mind, "Let me live!"

"You will live for a time, but there is a price."

CHAPTER FIFTY TWO

Across the river, still in New Jersey, Dani and Shannon watched the waiting City. Even at three in the morning, it was lit up bright as ever and pulsed with a heartbeat made up of all the souls on the island.

"Pretty," Dani said.

"It'll look better when the sun rises through the buildings," Herald said. He had silently joined them. "We only have a few hours. I can sense… changes."

"What is that supposed to mean?" Shannon asked.

Herald opened the door of the car and jumped into the back seat.

"Let's go," he said. It was bordering on an order.

Shannon moved towards the driver's side, but Dani stopped him.

She whispered into his ear, "We could let him go alone. We can give him the car, and go hitch a ride on the freeway. Go out west. We don't have to do this."

Shannon thought for a moment. Indecision roiled behind his eyes.

"He can't drive," he said, resigned.

"We don't have to do this," Dani said again.

"What makes you think we have a choice? The book didn't give us a choice."

"Why waste your freedom?" she asked.

He smiled and shrugged. Since Herald had freed him, Shannon hadn't thought of anything but what the little librarian told him they needed to do.

"Freedom? We got some old book that knows everything we do or will do. That doesn't sound like freedom to me. That doesn't sound like something we can run away from."

Dani made sure to look into his eyes. She found resoluteness there.

"Dani," Herald said from inside the car, "I can hear you. Even without ears."

"Well, I'm sorry, James," she said. "Am I supposed to blindly follow you?"

The librarian leaned over and poked his head out the window.

"Blind? You've been given an insight hardly anyone in this world has. I'm trying to save the world, for one, and the other, I'm doing this for you, for all of us. If you hadn't come and asked for my help at the library, I would've been perfectly content to let everything end knowing that I would return again, someday. Recycled."

Herald chuckled.

"Don't tell me you don't have any desire to remain among the living, in this life," she said. Her anger was rising.

"Hey, now, let's not get carried away," Shannon said. "I believe in this, Dani. I don't really know why. But, I do."

Shannon tried using his big smile and embrace to defuse her frustration.

"We can all get along and get along. We have a great big city to visit."

Dani pulled away from him, stomping toward the passenger side door.

"Okay, I'm ready. Ready to give it all up. Let's go."

She slammed the door shut, and Shannon jumped in, too. Instead of slamming his door in retaliation, he gently shut his.

"I say that our latest argument is over. Let's get into the city before the sun rises, please," Herald said. "We need to get to him. Convince him to do what is right. Before they kill him and restart the cycle."

Shannon revved the engine.

"All right, boss. The bridge is less than a mile away. We'll be in the city in 15 minutes."

Flooring the accelerator pedal, Shannon sent the car spinning onto the road from the turn off.

"Can we get there in one piece, Shannon?" Dani said.

She slipped her seatbelt over her shoulder.

"Yes, Shannon. It is imperative that we do not encounter law enforcement. I saved you once, but I don't believe I have the strength to do it again. My ability to do... things is waning."

Herald sat back into his seat and likewise buckled up.

"You got it, boss."

Dani cringed at the word: "boss."

Shannon straightened out the car and headed toward the bridge gunning for the on ramp. Flood lights from the large concrete bases shone up at it. The structure gleamed bright white against the black sky above it and dark water below it.

"Stop calling me that," Herald said. "Despite my seniority at the library, I'm no one's boss, and I don't aspire to be one."

"At least, we agree on that," Dani said.

Shannon sent the car up the on ramp for the bridge. The wheels whined when they touched the different grooving of the bridge's pavement.

Dani craned her neck and tilted her head up under the windshield. She peered up at the lattice work for the bridge.

"It's pretty," she said.

Reaching over to her and pulling her back into her seat, Shannon said, "Not as beautiful as you, babe, and I want to keep it that way."

"The bridge's empty," she said.

"He's right," Herald said. "We have to be safe from here on out. The unformed are growing powerful around Steale, and they will not want us to get to him before they do. They will do whatever it takes to make that so."

Dani swiveled around to face Herald.

"Will they kill us?"

The librarian breathed deeply.

"I think so. Yes."

Shannon drummed his fingers on the steering wheel.

"Can't you talk to the unformed?" Shannon said.

"Once, they might have listened, but I am formed and taken sides. Like you. I am no different to them now. They will kill me and you just the same. Our desires no longer converge. We are at odds."

"Why?" Dani asked.

Herald closed his eyes and held his breath.

Finally, he sighed and said, "They desire to live, and Steale has not given them that life. They are starved on the edge of existence."

"And just how would Steale give life to them? They are living. Right?" Shannon said.

"He is *the* creative force. He plucks them from the darkness and pulls them into the light. He did that for you. He did that for me."

"We're just people. How do we reason with God?" Dani said.

"He isn't that. But still difficult, at any rate. We make the unformed that are here and their faceless allies expose themselves. Then, we strike the unformed down. So he remembers."

"Strike them down?" Shannon said, surprised. "With what? You said, you can't work your magic any more. We don't have any weapons. Would guns even work on them?"

Herald slunk back into the backseat. The faux leather squealed with his weight. He stared forward, thinking.

It was clear, however. He had no answers to give.

"Look, man, we need things to fight back with," Shannon tried once more.

In the rearview, Shannon saw Herald slump in despair.

"Dani, help him," Shannon said.

"What?" she asked.

"Look. Something's wrong."

Dani unsnapped her seatbelt and leaned over the bench seat into the rear cabin.

"Hey, James? You okay?"

"What's wrong with him?"

She reached out. Shaking him by the shoulder, Dani jostled him. But Herald fell over, fully, in the back seat.

"Oh, my God," she said.

"What?" Shannon looked over his shoulder. "Is he dead?"

The car swerved with his inattentive over-steer.

"Watch the damn road, Shannon!"

"What do you want me to do? I can't pull over on the bridge! If he needs a doctor, we got no choice but forward. Tell me what we need to do!"

Almost entirely in the backseat, having crawled over the bench seat, Dani pushed Herald back up to a sitting position. She shook him.

"James, wake up. Wake up!"

"Assuming that he's not dead?!"

"Shut up, Shannon. He's breathing."

"Good. That's good news," Shannon said.

He slapped the steering wheel.

"Shaking him isn't waking him. What should I do?"

"Do we have any water? You could throw that on him," he said.

"I'm not going to do that," Dani answered.

"He could be dying! Throw some water on him."

"And a splash of water will save him?!" she screamed.

"I don't know! Do something!"

Dani grabbed the side of Herald's head. With her other hand, she slapped him, hard.

"James, I want you to wake the hell up!"

The librarian mumbled a bit but remained unconscious.

Shannon struggled to pull a bottle of water up from under his seat. It was rolling around underneath his section. He managed to get his fingers on the bottle. He lifted it up and passed it to Dani.

"Here," Shannon said. "Splash this on him."

"The whole thing?"

"Anything! Just do it! C'mon, Dani."

Dani shook her head but had no other options. She snapped open the bottle and tried to sprinkle the water into her hand, but the car was rocking too much.

"Shit," she said.

Giving up, Dani flicked the open bottle at Herald. A large stream of water flowed out and splashed over the librarian's face. Herald choked on the water.

"He's alive?!" Shannon said.

"Pretty sure."

"He's coughing! Don't let him choke on his tongue or something!" Shannon screamed.

He took his eye off the road, looking over at Herald in the back seat. But with that, they swerved violently out of their lane.

"Shannon!" Dani yelled. "That's twice now. Don't kill us!"

Shannon recovered control of the car. Luckily, he hadn't crossed over into oncoming traffic of which there was little but still enough to make a head-on collision a deadly possibility.

"Sorry, about that. It's just... We need him."

Shannon forced himself to calm.

"Really?" Dani said, annoyed.

"I'm still here," James said, scaring them both.

"Jesus, man!" Shannon yelled.

"How are you feeling?" Dani asked. "You passed out. We thought we lost you for a minute there."

"Did I throw up?"

James pulled at his wet collar.

"No, I tried to wake you up with this. Sorry."

Dani held up the half-empty bottle for him to see.

"What the hell is going on back there?" Shannon said. "We can't lose you, James. We do, and we're done."

"I know..." he said. "I reached out to the unformed, and they took me. Wouldn't let me back."

Dani pulled herself over the bench and back into her seat. She snapped her seatbelt back on.

"Are they that powerful?" Shannon asked.

"They can do anything they want as long as they are of a single mind to do it," Herald answered.

"Did you learn anything?" Dani said.

"No. Not really. It was all a mass of confusion. Swirling and grabbing. But elated at the same time. Joyous at a new beginning on the horizon. They almost made me want to stay with them. To be there at the new birth. I fear, their joy means the decision has already been made."

"No, no, no," Shannon said. "What does that mean?"

James stretched out against the backseat. He rested his head against the top of the cushion at the join of the seat and the rear window shelving.

"I am of the unformed. More than you either of you. Ashes to ashes as they say. I'm afraid that at some point I will no longer be able to resist them. I will lose who I am."

"What do we do if that happens?" Dani said.

She feared the answer, but knew it instinctively.

"Kill me if I become violent. Bury me if I die."

"Oh, that's great. Fantastic. We bury you. What happens when all that black goo comes after us again, and you're in the ground?"

Herald chuckled.

"I may be that goo that comes after you. At that point, it's only a matter of time for the big crunch to snap existence into a singularity, and the big bang to unleash it all over again."

"You were right, Dani. We should've left," Shannon said.

"How?" she replied. It was her turn to equivocate. "We might have gotten only a few extra days by the sound of this. You're a fighter. Always have been."

"I'd take those days. Take them and cherish you. I only know how to be a man. A fighter? I didn't really fight the unformed in my cell. I fought nothing. I barely made it. This supernatural shit... "

Herald leaned forward listening. Dani drank in her husband's confession.

"Tell us," Herald said. "What saved you?"

"I... I... don't really know. These shades, they must've come from the dark. Forming in shadows. Like men. Like the thugs in that jail. But they weren't men... I was asleep. But they woke me up. Hitting me. Throwing me around the cell. I tried screaming for the guards. They wrapped these black, liquid hands around my mouth. Suffocating me. The more I hit them, the more they became solid. I was done for. Until the sun rose. It was the sunlight that struck through them. The light defeated them. Not me."

Herald sat back. His mind churned, and then he spoke.

"They started as shadows and ended as shadows. They never took full form like us, because Steale hadn't willed it... We were willed into being. But, we all live at the mercy of fate," Herald said softly. "The problem is Steale. He had the task of continuing Creation, and he failed or forgot. He stopped writing. Started again, but it was too late. The anger in the unformed was too strong. It awakened the Creator."

"If we kill him, will this end?" Dani asked.

"If we kill him, everything ends. That's what they want. To survive, Steale must go on. We must remind him of his bargain. If he does not act in accordance to it, then everything begins again."

Shannon gunned the accelerator. All three of them were rocked back into their seats.

"Let's find the man, then. I don't understand any of it. But, I mean, it's better to head into the apocalypse than away from it. Right?" Shannon said.

He looked over at Dani, and in the meeting of their eyes, she could see he was as much trying to convince himself of the truth of his words as he was them.

She knew, then, they were but gnats, or less, flying into the winds a hurricane.

CHAPTER FIFTY THREE

Steale sat in front of the fireplace in the salon of his apartment. A half-empty bottle of Macallan whiskey sat on the table next to his chair. The cap was off. His snifter was empty. He was drinking straight out of the bottle now. There was no need for niceties.

His dogs were sleeping in the corner of the room. They knew to leave him well-enough alone when he was drinking.

Amaretta, his ex-wife, had threatened earlier to drop off their only daughter, but Steale refused her. With the world coming apart, he couldn't bear to have the girl in his care. He wouldn't know what to do if she were to be used as a pawn against him.

The dogs could fend for themselves when the time came. His daughter could not and was best left under her mother's wing. One of the dogs got up from its pillow and brushed under Steale's free hand begging for a pat. The author barely noticed, but out of reflex curled his fingers on the animal's head. The dog whimpered and lay down next to the chair.

"It's okay," Steale said. "There's nothing out there. Nothing that doesn't start with me."

He knew he was lying. There was a time when that would have been true. He had been the author of everything. He had been able to conjure up anything out of his imagination, but Steale feared that that was no longer possible. He hadn't tested it with his notepad since the interview.

He was afraid to.

When he arrived home, he lit the fireplace, but kept the electric lights off. Light from real fire affected the clay—as he liked to call them—made them weak if they were still unformed.

"Settle down," he said to the other whimpering dog. It was still laying at the corner of the fireplace. "Get over here with us."

The black and white terrier bitch did as she was told. She settled next to the Labrador retriever.

"This is what we're going to do," the author grabbed the bottle off the table and took a swig. "We're gonna take that wood and light it on fire when they come. And they'll knock down the big door, but we're going to be ready. I'll light those sticks, and you fight them red in tooth and claw."

The dogs perked up. Their ears twitched, discerning a distant sound.

"Hear something?" Steale asked the dogs. He sat up in the chair from his slump. "Where is it? Find it."

The dogs looked at him, scared, as if to say that they did not want to go.

"Do it. Go on," he insisted.

The Labrador responded. He rose and reluctantly moved out from under Steale's arm.

"Go on. Find them. They can't hurt you. They won't hurt you, boy."

Steale pulled out his pad and wrote that down. He showed the scribbles to the dogs.

"See?"

The female stood up and followed as Steale wished.

"Do it," he commanded again.

With the male leading the smaller female, the dogs galloped into the darkened outer apartment. Steale sat at his seat edge waiting for them to return. Minutes passed and the wood in the fireplace popped many times over, the most ancient of timepieces.

The dogs had disappeared.

The author walked to the edge of the room where the darkness was deepest. He looked out into it. It turned and churned like a living thing.

It was a living thing.

He whistled for the animals.

Nothing.

"C'mere, dogs. Get on back here," he said, ending with another wolf-whistle. "Where are you?"

He stepped to the very edge of the black. A faint bark. He whistled again. The dogs barked, but they seemed far, far away. Steale closed his eyes and stepped into the shadow. It coalesced around him like a blanket, but it did not suffocate him. At the edge of his hearing were the whispers. Each voice called to him.

"You forgot. You betrayed us. Arrogant. Doomed this world."

He opened his eyes and the black flew into them. Steale tried to shut them, but the streams, columns of onyx, were too heavy into his pupils. They were solid.

"Don't fight. You can't fight the spark," the voices said.

His eyes burned hot as coals. Tears streamed down his cheeks. He screamed and cried. His knees buckled. He choked. The black was in him now. He fell to his knees.

"You aren't dying. We are. Because of you."

He choked out, "I don't understand."

"You possessed the gift. One you let die. And now, all of this will end."

"Why?"

"You are flesh and blood and imperfect. You could create. But you didn't."

Steale yelled, "Make me understand!"

"You breathed life into the lifeless. And then you stopped. The cycle will begin again. And destroy this world and everything in it."

He closed his eyes once all of the darkness found home within him. His head felt light, and a pounding pressure traveled from his lungs to his belly. Steale retched, but voided nothing.

"I... will... not... allow... it!" Steale managed.

He fell onto his back. He counted the beats of his heart into the hundreds.

Then, all fear fell away. He stood up.

The two dogs appeared from the hallway, still dark but devoid of the living blackness. They licked his hands.

He walked back to his chair. It was still warm.

The two dogs—Doberman Pinschers—sat next to him, one on either side of the chair like the dogs of ancient Egypt sitting next to the pharaoh's throne.

Steale reached down and patted both of their heads. He looked at each one in turn. Somewhere it registered with him that these jet black dogs were not as before.

It didn't matter.

Everything was different now.

CHAPTER FIFTY FOUR

They ditched the car at the bottom of Manhattan. The sea air blew in around them and blew down the empty streets. Herald summoned a rideshare to take them to his apartment.

"The app says the car is a block away. We say we're going to share the fare. Let's not raise any eyebrows," the librarian said.

"What does it matter?" Shannon asked.

He pulled his jacket tighter around himself. Shannon was cold. Dani leaned against him warming him as much as she could.

"The world's ending. Why do we need cover stories?" Dani said.

"Because you might be recognized. And I won't be able to do anything about that," Herald said. He watched the rideshare's progress on his phone. "Something's changed. Different. It's just at the edge of my knowing. Maybe with Steale, himself."

"Isn't that good?" Dani asked.

"I don't know. I'm as confused as you are at this point."

"Why doesn't Steale just destroy everything?" Shannon said. "He could do that. Just wish it all away?"

"He might," the librarian said. "That could already be underway."

A small hybrid turned the corner and flashed its lights.

"The car's here," Herald said. "My apartment should be safe. For now. We can freshen up there, and I can prepare."

With the car stopped, the driver unlocked the doors once Herald's app indicated the fare payment was accepted.

"Are we fighting god, little g or big G?" Dani said.

"We walk in the middle plane. Beneath the divine. We are but shadows cast by that divine light."

"More shadows," Shannon said. "How about we get some damn light for once."

Dani peered up into Shannon's eyes. He was still fighting with something. She wrapped her arms around him holding him tightly. At first, he didn't reciprocate, but finally relented and held fast to her.

"You and me, Shannon. We're together. We've come this far. Let's finish it."

Herald raised a finger to his lips to shush them.

Dani and Shannon piled into the back of the small car while Herald sat in the front passenger seat. He smiled cordially to the driver.

"We're all going together. Please, as quickly as possible. Thank you," Herald said to the driver.

"Yes," the man said with a hint of a Middle Eastern accent. "We go down avenue. Very fast this time right now. Buckle up, please!"

They all stared out at the city in silence once the car was underway. Dani watched as Shannon's face was alternately illuminated by streetlights and then wiped away in the shadows.

The ride, though quick, was uneventful save for the cluster of NYPD cars at Times Square. They seemed to be out in force.

Shannon piped up, "Fun in the Big Apple this morning?"

Now, Shannon's face pulsated red and blue as their car approached gaggle of police vehicles. Dani had an unexpected urge to hold him again. To wrap her arms around him and never let him go.

"Always out," the driver said. "Cops is everywhere. Times Square so bad now."

"Any problems uptown?" Herald asked.

"No, I don't see."

"Good," Herald said. He looked back over his seat at Shannon and Dani. "So far, so good."

Dani's attention turned to him, and only registered the strange acceleration of their car at the very edge of her senses. Herald, wide-eyed, whipped back around, but time was frozen. In a painful slow motion that held her captive, she helplessly watched as their car sped into the back end of a stopped cop car.

She felt the car crumple. They all did.

With a firmly clasped shoulder belt, Dani watched as her husband, who hadn't put his belt on, flew face first into the back of the passenger seat where Herald was firmly belted in. She reached out for him, but she was not fast enough nor strong enough to protect him from the force of the impact.

Herald, in the front seat, was engulfed by an airbag.

The world spun.

Their car bounced off one stopped car after another and was spinning into other lanes. The hybrid slammed into a few parked civilian cars before squealing to a stop in the middle of oncoming traffic.

They had traveled nearly a full block after the initial accident. The shops and restaurants lining the streets were still dark, and the street was silent save for the liquids flowing in streams out of their wrecked car.

Dani, hyperventilating, was the first to regain her faculties. Shannon was slumped over against the passenger door. Blood oozed from his face. Grabbing him, she pulled him upright. He began to cough and spit blood.

Through the open hole where a glass window once was, she saw the distant flashing lights of emergency vehicles. If there were any cops there, she couldn't make them out.

"Herald, wake up. We need to get out of here!" she screamed. "I need help with Shannon! They're coming!"

The librarian pulled himself free of the airbag, coughing, too. He looked over his shoulder into the back seat. Dani managed to pull Shannon over the seats, prostrate. She was already out of the car. The driver, however, was unconscious or worse.

"Hurry! Look, they're almost here," she said.

Herald turned and saw new flashing lights headed their way. He pressed against his passenger door. It was too crumpled to open.

"Good Lord. It's stuck. You're going to have to leave me."

"What's stuck?!"

"The door. It won't budge!"

"Crawl out the window. I can't carry Shannon alone. I need you." Dani struggled to pull Shannon out through the open rear passenger side door. "He's too heavy!"

Sirens grew louder.

Herald struggled with his gut but managed to crawl through the division of the bucket seats. He plopped onto the rear seat as Dani pulled Shannon from the car, and he managed to keep Shannon's head from hitting the pavement.

"Ahh," Shannon moaned through spouts of blood. "Dani..."

"Hurry, James. They're nearly here! We need to get down that alley. Now!"

Out of the car, Herald held Shannon by the man's arms.

"Let's go!" he said.

Struggling, they managed to get a handle on the artist's dead weight and were able to make the alley in time to avoid the arrival of the ambulance. Several policemen were approaching on foot, but Dani, Shannon and Herald were hidden the darkest parts of the alley and were out of view of the street.

Shannon came awake, "We... Go... Down..."

They propped him up against the brick wall of a bordering building.

"Keep him quiet," Herald told Dani. "I'm going to reconnoiter the situation. We still need to get to my place."

"How am I supposed to stop him from making noise? Suffocate him?" Dani asked.

"You'll figure it out," he said.

"He needs a hospital!" Dani called out through clenched teeth.

Herald walked around the corner exiting the alleyway leaving her to deal with her dying husband. Shannon continued to mumble louder and louder.

"Hey, Shannon," Dani said in a strong whisper. "You need to be quiet, please."

He let out a moan. With no other solutions, Dani did what first came to mind. She pressed a palm to his face to cover his mouth. She felt like she was killing him.

"Stop it, Shannon," she sobbed.

He came fully awake and looked at her in perplexed silence for a moment. But then, Shannon tried to pull her hand away, but his strength was gone.

"Dani?" he said behind her hand.

"Shhh! We had an accident."

"James?" Shannon said while his eyes scanned the dark alley.

"I don't know."

Shannon started to struggle against her.

"Calm down, Shannon. Until he comes back, we are staying right here," Dani said. "Don't move, please. We'll figure out how to get you help."

Dani, succumbing to her guilt, let go of him. She was crying.

Pushing away from her, Shannon tried to stand. Sharp pains stabbed at his ribs, he leaned against the nearby dumpster.

"I need some—"

"Shannon, you have to wait," Dani said.

She tried to steady him, but he held her at arm's length.

"My chest. I can barely breathe."

With each inhale, the pain forced him to stop short of a full breath.

Dani's guilt dissipated, and she felt panic rise within her.

"Sit, Shannon. Please, if you don't relax, you'll hyperventilate. Please," Dani said.

Shannon fell back against the brick wall losing his grip on the dumpster. He slid to the ground. His limbs were limp. Dani knelt beside him.

"Shannon, please."

Herald entered the alley.

"Get him up. I have a taxi waiting for us. But we have to move quickly. The cops are talking to our driver. Presumably about where we happen to have gone. They will come looking for us."

"Help me," she said.

Dani tried to lift Shannon, but he groaned and could not lift himself. His breathing was shallow. Bursts of inhalation. He was hyperventilating now.

"Hurry," Herald hissed. "They are coming. If he can't move on his own, leave him!"

"Are you serious?"

Dani was stung by Herald's order. Her emotions welled up in her eyes. *How could she leave Shannon?*

"Leave him. Or we risk losing everything!"

Dani watched Shannon gasping for air, powerless to do anything for him.

"I'm so sorry, Shannon. I have to go. I have to save us. Don't panic. Just breathe. When they find you, let them take you to the hospital. I will come for you after. I will find you."

The librarian grabbed her by the hand. He pulled her up.

"There's no time," Herald said.

"Goddamn it! I can't leave him!" she said.

"If you don't, then everything you love will be destroyed and lost forever. Including him!" he said.

"And if he dies, here, without me?!"

Dani pulled away from Herald and turned back to Shannon.

"How can you be so cruel?" she spat.

"Cruel? What is cruel is not doing what is necessary when it is necessary, so that others—many, many others—might live!" Herald answered.

"Leave me," Shannon managed to choke out.

His lungs were almost fully collapsed, and they could hear it in his gulps.

A spray of blood erupted from his mouth.

"Go... Dani. It's okay... It's okay." His words were but bloody gasps.

Shannon's body went limp. His eyes closed.

Dani cried, but Herald yanked her from her sorrow. He dragged her out of the alley and into the cab that was waiting for them down the street, away from the accident. He shoved her inside and slammed the door shut.

"You know the address. Let's go!" the librarian yelled.

"I'll never forgive you," she said to him.

"Let's survive the night, and then tell me you won't," he replied. "You might actually be able to live up to it."

The cab sped down the empty street. Dani turned around and watched the scene recede into the darkness through the rear window. She watched until the flashing lights faded from her tearing eyes.

CHAPTER FIFTY FIVE

Carol came to.

Even in the darkness of unconsciousness, she heard the yelling and screaming. What brought her to full consciousness was the wetness on her feet.

There was a heat coming from her left, and she felt warm rushes of air crawl across her face.

She pulled the oxygen mask off her face and instantly began choking. The smoke and heat stung her throat and burned in her lungs. Crumpling over, she found that the air below the smoke was breathable.

Carol opened her eyes. It was chaos.

Water covered the floor of the airplane. Cushions, luggage, cans floated in the churning black, rising water. The man who had been in first class with her was gone.

She could hear others. People were struggling just like she was. Carol pulled herself free from the seatbelt and dropped onto the floor and into the water.

She crawled into the aisle. Flames were licking up the side of the fuselage opposite her. Near the back of the plane, some passengers had gathered.

Carol called out, "Wait! Wait!"

But what came out was more of a choke.

She cleared her throat and tried again, "Wait!"

Some of those gathered heard her. They turned to look for her.

Carol pushed through the remnants of the curtain that divided first class from coach. It had been burnt rather badly, but now only smoked being half-wet.

The water level had risen fast enough that instead of crawling she was nearly swimming—and swimming against a rush of water.

"Here," a man's deep voice rang out.

Carol felt strong hands gripping her by her arms. She was dragged toward the emergency exit.

"Get her out on the wing!"

Carol gagged from the billowing smoke. More hands pulled her through the open emergency exit.

On the wing, Carol could see her fellow survivors illuminated by the orange glow of fire from inside the fuselage. Out of the several hundred people onboard, maybe 20 people were gathered on the tilting wing. It was rising up into the air slowly as the plane dove into the black waters.

Through the smoke, she could see the lights of Manhattan.

They were in the river.

"Listen up, people. We can't stay here. This thing's sinking, and it will drown us if we let it." The voice was strong and commanding. "We're going to have to swim. It's not far. But the water is very cold."

"We can wait for the rescue boats!"

"No, if we get caught near the sinking plane, it will pull us under." The voice was closer to Carol this time.

"What are we waiting for?" Carol asked, her voice raspy from smoke inhalation.

The voice continued, "Everyone, let's go before this wing shifts any more!"

The smoke cleared, and Carol saw the others, just black silhouettes, jumping into the water one after the other. She hated cold water like a cat, but she hated the idea of drowning in the undertow of a plane more.

At the edge of the wing, the last to dive into the roiling river waters, Carol heard the fuselage groan. Already half wet and shivering, Carol braced herself for the cold water.

A deep breath, and Carol fell forward off the wing.

The river swallowed her eagerly.

It was inky black to her open eyes. It was undulating. Before she rose to catch another breath, she felt something brush against her leg. It wasn't a random touch or some floating detritus in the river. She jerked away and pushed herself upward reaching for the air.

Erupting through the surface of the water, Carol gasped, filling her lungs. She looked over her shoulder while treading water. The aircraft had curled with the wing swinging over opposite its original, normal position relative to the ground. If she didn't start swimming, the other wing might sweep up and lift her into the air.

Carol gasped once more, then began her struggle towards the lights bobbing off in the distance. She could see the black heads of her fellow survivors as they, too, struggled against the river's current.

The cold water tightened around her muscles, but Carol, wanting to live, pulled her arms and legs free of any growing paralysis. She splashed forward headed to the bright, smeared lights of the shore.

Ahead of her, the black heads bobbed up and down with every stroke.

Behind her, a mighty groan sent shockwaves through the dark river. She looked over her shoulder, but the horror of the plane tail in the air before submerging, panicked her into paddling faster.

Carol worked hard against the heavy current. It was pulling her away from shore and out to sea.

"Hang on," the strong voice called out to her. He grabbed her. "If you start to pull me under, I'll let go, and let you drown. Got it?"

Carol shook her head. *Yes.*

"Say it."

Carol gulped in water and then spat it out, "I won't pull you under."

"Let's go."

The strong arm pulled her. They moved in the water, together, with power.

By the time all the survivors stood on the grass leading to the water's edge, the flashing lights of the firetrucks and assorted emergency vehicles overwhelmed the small park where they had landed.

The red, flashing lights strobed her group of survivors. The voice as it turned out belonged to their pilot, a tall, heavyset Asian man.

"Thanks," Carol said to the man. "I'm alive because of you."

She could see him nod a modest approval against the lights of the sleeping city.

"All those people back there. I wish I could've saved them, too," he said.

"What happened?" Carol asked.

"We lost power. Engines died. Can't explain it."

He lowered his head.

"You the captain?" a firefighter shouted at him.

"Captain Eli Katsua, yes."

"Come with me. The rest of you, stay where you are until our crews treat you."

The pilot and the fire captain disappeared into the mass of uniformed people descending upon them. Before she could regain her bearings, Carol was wrapped inside a heavy blanket.

"You can remove your clothes," the female EMT who draped the blanket around her said. "We have emergency clothes, so you won't be naked. Do you have any wounds? Have you sustained any injuries that caused you to black out?"

Carol slipped her wet pants off. Her blouse was next.

"Yes. I think so. I don't remember anything after the plane started to dive mid-air."

"Okay, I'm going to have to ask you into my rig. I'm going to give you a quick visual examination. Is that alright?"

The older woman acquiesced and followed the squat, stocky woman toward the end of her parked ambulance. The EMT opened the rear doors and motioned for Carol to step inside.

"Sit on the gurney, please. I'll grab you some scrubs I have packed away."

The woman followed Carol up into the large vehicle.

"What about the blanket? Drop it?" Carol asked.

She looked at the nametag above the woman's badge. It read, **Sgt. Sceals**.

"Ms. Sceals?"

The young woman nodded.

"Don't do anything until I close the doors. We need to provide you with some privacy."

Sceals reached out towards the open doors and pulled them shut.

"My partner may come back with another survivor or two, but he knows to knock first."

"Survivor? Is that what we're being called?" Carol asked.

"That's what you are. You're pretty lucky. The manifest was 248, and there's only what, 24 of you?"

Carol sighed. "That's all that made it? I was hoping for more."

"The plane sank fast. Faster than anybody expected," Sceal said. "Okay, if you don't mind laying down. Do you feel any pain anywhere?"

The EMT opened up several cabinets. She retrieved the scrubs and slung her stethoscope around her neck.

"No, I'm just cold."

"May as well start to get changed into the scrubs," the EMT said. It was more of a command.

Carol laid the blanket to the side and quickly put the light green pants and blouse on. It felt good to be in dry clothes.

Sceal held out her stethoscope ready to touch Carol's chest.

"Need to do a routine set of readings. It's cold, so be prepared."

She pressed the stethoscope against the older woman's upper chest. It was indeed cold even to her, who had just been in a freezing river.

Carol breathed deeply knowing the course of such things.

"Good." Sceal moved the stethoscope. "Again."

Carol complied. She closed her eyes with this deep breath.

At the end of which, she was back in the water bobbing up and down and choking on river water. The fire of the plane warmed the back of her head. Had she imagined being saved?

There was no one else in the water. There was no one she could cling to for her life. There was a weight pulling at her legs.

Trying to drag her under.

Dragging her under.

Carol sank.

She kicked her legs and freed herself.

At the surface, she looked over her shoulder. She watched the last of the plane disappear below the waterline. She felt the pull again, but she kicked and swung her arms wildly. Carol made for the shore.

Through the lapping black water, she could see the empty park above the river. But her arms were so heavy. Her legs were useless weights, now. Carol could no longer keep her head above water. The struggle had made her so very, very tired.

The black came for her like it had on the plane when it erupted from the pages of the book. She didn't have to fight any longer. She simply let it envelop her in its cold but comforting embrace.

Where are the ambulances and fire trucks and police cars? Where is the nice EMT Sceal?

"You will do my bidding."

The words moved through the pitch blackness like electricity. It wasn't sound. She didn't hear it in her ears. She felt it on her skin.

"You are mine. As you always have been. You will do my bidding."

The voice was so very right. She drank it in as she had the darkness. It burned her insides but the burning felt good.

Cleansing.

And then the black was gone.

Sceal, the EMT, removed her stethoscope from Carol's back. Carol opened her eyes. She let that last breath she was holding, out.

"You sure you don't feel any aches or pains? Sometimes, adrenaline masks injuries. If not, I will send you to the hospital as low priority. You won't get a bed right away. The nearest hospitals are already experiencing heavy use. A full moon on a Friday night."

The EMT put the scope away and palpated Carol's limbs.

"Tell me if any of this hurts."

"I was drowning," Carol said. "I wanted to. It felt right."

The woman looked at Carol with a tinge of concern.

"It's a common thing for survivors to have guilt."

"I'm not feeling guilty. That would be silly, and very unlike me... I think I was supposed to die. But I was saved. Because I have something to do."

Sceal leaned back away from Carol.

"I will send you in as priority. Okay?"

"I'm not suicidal. If anything, I'd like to have a stiff drink. That will cure me. If you have any booze, hand it over," Carol said with a giggle.

"That will have to wait until a doctor checks you out further. I'm going to clear you for transport," Sceal said.

"Good," Carol said. "Let's get this show on the road, then. I'm ready to see some damn doctors, so I can wrap my lips around a Mai Tai straw."

Sceal opened up the back of the ambulance and hopped down off.

"The non-crit transport ambulance is this way. You'll be on it shortly."

Carol smiled not only because she could taste the sweet cocktail already, but because she felt liberated.

"The rum better be sweet! Take me to my carriage!"

Sceal walked Carol through the maze of emergency vehicles, workers and a few of the victims who had also survived. Near the thoroughfare off the park, several smaller ambulances were parked.

Some of her fellow survivors were already being loaded into

them.

"Looks like the gang's all back together!" Carol said, strutting like a vaudeville stripper.

The others turned to look at her, also similarly dressed in dry scrubs. Their reactions were a mix of confusion and amusement. Her rescuer, the pilot, smiled.

"Glad you made it back to us," he said.

"Okay, folks, you are all happily deemed non-critical," the fire chief said. He was clearly the responder in charge. "Please, start moving into the vehicle nearest you for transfer to the hospital."

Carol chose the smallest of the ambulances. She was joined by the pilot.

"They take care of you?" Katsua asked.

"If by giving me a nice cocktail, you mean, my dear captain? No. They did not," Carol answered dryly.

"Well, maybe after we get released, we can catch an early bird special somewhere. Bloody Marys on me."

Carol's laugh filled the ambulance.

"I know it's strange to be joyous after our plane wreck, but I feel damn good."

CHAPTER FIFTY SIX

Shannon's blood looked black in the streetlights. His blood was black reflecting the night, and it was black with every beat of the red strobes from the ambulance.

He could feel himself slipping away.

Slipping into that black.

Icy tendrils of cold ink crawled up his legs. They curled up and around his skin. Anastomosing into new veins and arteries. Growing like a chrysalis around his body to silence his flame, forever.

Shannon closed his eyes which were only slits except when a flashlight was shone into them. It wasn't that he was tired of hearing the blue-uniformed paramedics talk in grunting efficiency. He was happy that they were there. He wasn't alone and wouldn't be when the darkness snuffed him out.

The artist was simply tired.

Somewhere, floating on the periphery of his consciousness, Shannon understood why Dani left him. He might have even agreed with her reasons, but her leaving him to die was the only other feeling that broke through his weariness.

If only to feel her hold his hand while he slipped out of this world. The one person he wanted by his side at a time like this had run away when he needed her the most.

The tendrils reached his belly, but the paramedics seemed not to notice.

What at first were cold, the black, writhing vines became white hot against his skin.

Shannon tried to cry out but only coughed up more blood. He felt a finger probe his throat, but he hadn't any energy for his gag reflex to do its automatic work.

"Airway clear! Hang on, buddy. Don't move!" It was the voice of one of the EMTs. "We're gonna get you to the hospital. Just keep breathing."

The stinging hot tendrils wrapped around his chest. Shannon tried to inhale, but the tendrils forced the air from his lungs until his heart stopped beating.

Into the black.

His heart started again.

He was floating.

Shannon opened his eyes. He was being lifted into the ambulance. His body seized. He had no control of the thrashing.

"Shit, he's coding."

Shannon tried to sip the air. But none would come.

"We've got you. Hang on."

Shannon could feel cold lips pressed onto his face around his mouth, then pressure. Air squeezed into his lungs. He heard the swooshing of air filling a balloon over and over and his shirt ripping. His seizure stopped.

The oxygen was good.

Two cold, wet pads were pressed onto his chest. Then, a constant beep in rhyme with his now stabilized heartbeat.

Shannon tried to lift his arm, but a much stronger grip held it in place. Straps were pulled tightly around both his wrists and then his ankles.

"Don't move. Keep breathing. Concentrate on breathing."

He felt the tendrils retreating. Their oily blackness moved below his diaphragm. Any tightness in his breathing was gone.

"I'm going to give you a shot. It's going to pinch a bit."

He winced at the prick in the big muscle of his leg. Tears formed and fell from the outer corner of his eyes. Immediately, Shannon's heartbeat quickened. The cold tendrils faded entirely from his body.

He choked on the air force fed him, but Shannon was breathing again, and he was glad to be.

Opening his eyes, Shannon watched the paramedic lift the clear plastic resuscitator from his face. The plastic lips were stained with his blood.

He tried to talk, but he could barely force a sound from his throat.

"Where... Dani?"

"No, buddy, don't try to talk," the young black man in his paramedic uniform said to him. "Save your energy. We're four minutes out from the hospital. We need to get you there still breathing. They have the best docs waiting to make you right."

Shannon nodded and closed his mouth.

"Don't answer me, but tomorrow, when you're out of the woods, I want to know how the heck you got all the way in that alley? Were you thrown out of the car? That was at least 100 feet."

His eyes closed easily. Shannon remembered the accident. It came to him in bursts.

Then, he remembered in full.

His heartache for Dani was gone. It turned cold. Shannon saw her leaving him in the alley.

In the trash.

When he had called out to her, she didn't even turn to face him. Dani left him.

To die.

A calm descended over his body. Shannon heard it in the beeping heart monitor. It was so apparent that the paramedic looked at the machine, surprised.

Hate made Shannon open eyes in slits. It clenched his jaw.

Shannon summoned the black. He cried out for it in his mind.

He felt it, at first fit-full, then with purpose move up his legs once more. When it crossed his diaphragm, his breathing grew stronger, not weaker this time.

The black tentacles curled in and around the folds of his brain.

Each touched a memory firing them alive in. Any recollection of Dani became a red hot ember that burned. His eyes closed, and the black filled them.

From the void, Shannon heard the strongest voice he had ever heard in his life. It resonated through his body echoing out from his mind.

"Sculptor, you will sculpt. For me. Do you accept?"

Shannon, small in the inky void, panicked. He didn't understand.

"Accept me!"

The voice was louder and hurt his ears even though it came from the void and not the real world.

"You will create again. But for *me*!"

"Yes," he said. It was a whimper, but no less an answer.

Shannon's eyes opened, but not on his command. His body and mind coursed with power not his own. He was not himself. He was something more. But he accepted it with all his heart. Shannon let it pour through him.

The paramedic removed the oxygen mask from Shannon's face.

"Damn. I've never seen someone stabilize like this. You don't need this anymore."

"There's nothing wrong with me," Shannon said.

The EMT was stunned. He pulled out his stethoscope and listened to Shannon's breathing. "Your breathing is clear. When we found you, you had a collapsed lung. Probably a couple of broken ribs puncturing a lobe. Now, nothing."

Shannon smiled and did his best to shrug despite the straps tying him to the gurney.

"I'm a strong guy."

The paramedic removed the stethoscope earpieces from his ears and tossed the whole of it onto a counter.

"We still need to have you looked over by a doctor. Maybe we've misdiagnosed you. I'm stumped."

The paramedic banged on the wall.

"Pete, how soon we hit the ER?"

A voice called back, Pete said, "Less than a minute. We can't go any faster."

"No need. You can slow down."

"Aww, shit. We lost another one?"

"Nope. He's... better."

"What?"

"You heard me."

"You heard the man. I'm better," Shannon said full-throatedly.

"It's some kind of miracle."

The paramedic smiled at Shannon, weakly. There was a hint of suspicion in it.

Shannon settled back onto the gurney, loosening the tension in the straps. He didn't want to make the man more nervous than he already was.

From the cab, Pete called out, "Heading into the bay. Get ready for the orderlies, Ernie. Heading to ER 2."

"Got it. Swinging the doors."

Shannon felt the ambulance stop. His gurney swayed back and forth, but its wheels were locked preventing him and it from sliding against the back doors.

With two bangs on the door, the paramedic released the locks. They immediately swung open. Ernie jumped out and both paramedics hoisted the gurney out of the ambulance. They dropped the extending wheels before setting the gurney onto the ground.

"ER 2!"

They quickly slid the gurney, and Shannon, past the sliding doors which were fast opening.

"Possible pneumothorax. Broken ribs!"

Shannon laid still and said nothing. Amused, he waited and watched the events unfold from his supine position. The ceiling tiles and bank lights flashed over him while the paramedics pushed him along.

A quick turn, and they were in the ER.

The pounding of the paramedics feet and brushing movement of their uniforms was replaced by many voices loudly shouting and electronic beeps from every corner.

Around Shannon, a group of nurses and orderlies appeared.

"Okay, let's move him."

With a heave, they all lifted Shannon onto the receiving table. Watching through barely open eyes, he toyed with the idea of getting up and walking out as if nothing had ever happened. If he let them continue, it would be a giant waste of time, for him, for them. A passing fancy, he decided to let them perform as usual.

It was cruel. But it was the easiest thing to do.

"He's all yours," Ernie the paramedic said.

He heard the paramedic team push their gurney out of the ER. More probing by prying fingers, stethoscopes, flashing of lights in his eyes were becoming tiresome.

"Good breath sounds. Heart rhythm okay. Pupils reactive."

That was Shannon's cue to rise.

He faux coughed.

"What's going on?" he asked.

"No, stay down. We're examining you, sir. You were in a very bad car accident," the lead physician told him.

It was she who was holding the latest cold stethoscope.

He forced himself up against their protests and stepped down onto the floor.

"I'm okay," he said easily.

The assembled doctors and nurses were stunned that he could resist their efforts to push him back down onto the table.

Shannon smiled affably and parried their moves to restrain him.

"Security!" one of the nurses yelled.

"Don't," Shannon said. "I'm going to get up and move to that bed. I'll let one of you examine me. But no more. You have other people here who need your help much more than I do. Do you understand?"

Two large men in security uniforms rushed into the ER.

"He needs to be restrained," the attending said.

They moved on Shannon who was standing beside the

examination table with his arms out in warning.

"Don't touch me."

The men ignored him. They tried to grab both of Shannon's arms, but Shannon, instead, grabbed them by their throats. He held them at arm's length as they scratched at his forearms. He squeezed, slowly. A cruel, horrible smile crossed his lips. Shannon had a thought of crushing their windpipes. It was a familiar feeling, a feeling that he knew was always in him.

Several of the men in the emergency room tried to free the security officers, but Shannon's grip was steel. He shrugged them off easily sending them flying into equipment.

"Let go!" someone screamed.

Shannon, tired of the whole thing, flung both men against the far wall. They crumpled to the floor.

The others in the room cowered.

"Come here," Shannon said, pointing to a young nurse.

"Me?"

Fear was written across her face.

"Yes, come here," Shannon said. There was kindness in his voice, contrasting his previous violence.

She looked side to side for any guidance from her fellow medics. They gave none. Reluctantly, she stepped forward.

"Come," he said.

Shannon beckoned and held his arms open in invitation.

"Come here," he said gently. "I'm not going to hurt you. Come."

She stepped inside his embrace.

Shannon wrapped her up and held her tight. He held her unblinking eyes on his. Their breathing synchronized.

He felt the darkness, the black welling up from inside him. He felt it cross into his arms—saw it move through his veins like snakes. The inky darkness shot out from his skin and pierced the young woman.

She let out a gasp and for a moment tried to pull away from the tendrils. Several people shouted and some screamed. They were of no consequence.

Her eyeballs went black.

It was done.

Shannon released her.

"Now, go on. Show the others."

The nurse did as he ordered. She moved to those cowering behind the table. They tried to back away until there was no longer any more room for them to move. A few rushed out of the emergency room.

Their time would come.

Shannon watched the nurse touch each person. First the medical staff and then the patients—awake and unconscious.

All were his now.

Completely.

"My friends, be fruitful and multiply."

He surveyed his work.

It was good.

Shannon walked out into the hallway. He could see more ambulances arriving. The duty nurses were nowhere to be seen. Behind him, the ER staff, assembled like an army, waited for his next command.

"Multiply!" he said.

They fanned out as they normally would greeting the new incoming patients. Nothing seemed amiss.

Standing in the middle of the hallway, Shannon observed. People ran every which way doing their lifesaving best. Some were wheeled around him. His ER staff did as he ordered, though.

He closed his eyes. With every touch of the newcomers, with a mere brush from his converted, Shannon felt his number grow.

Filling him with power.

Closing his eyes, he celebrated his victory.

A familiar voice pierced his silent exultation. He reached out with his mind, but the voice did not originate from the black. It came from the world.

Opening his eyes, he found Carol Strauss, his mother-in-law, standing haughtily in front of him. She regarded him with a furrowed brow and cocked head, a familiar disdain.

"Well, well, well. Look who the cat dragged in," Carol said. "Aren't you supposed to be on the lam?"

"I suppose I still am."

"This doesn't look much like the lam to me," she said. "Where's my daughter?"

Shannon reached out with his mind. He cried out for her in the void of the unformed. Dani wasn't there.

"I don't know. I'd like to find her, myself," Shannon said.

"Oh, sorry, I've been so rude. Captain, this is my son-in-law Shannon. He's a famous escaped prisoner. Shannon, this is the captain who saved my life, by plunging me into the Hudson first."

The big man offered his hand to Shannon.

"Nice to meet you."

Shannon took it. He felt white hot black spider webs shoot across his flesh and into the pilot. Shannon turned his attention to Carol. Withdrawing his hand from the black-eyed captain, he reached out and touched her shoulder. The tendrils shot out of his hand toward her flesh, but he was jolted. The tendrils rushed back into him, rejected.

"Oh, honey, that crap won't work on me," she said. "I've got a job to do."

Carol laughed.

"I need a drink, though."

Shannon touched her again with both hands. But, the black receded into him.

"Told ya so," Carol quipped with a wink.

"Where's Dani?" Shannon said tersely.

"Do I look like I would know that? I asked first."

She brushed aside him.

"Look, I'm serious about that drink. If you want to find my daughter, I'm willing to help. But not until after I get a nice, refreshing snort of booze. Got it?"

CHAPTER FIFTY
SEVEN

Dani thought of Shannon slumped against the dumpster. Dying.

"We can't go back," Herald said.

"I know. What are we even doing here?"

"I think," the little librarian said matter-of-factly, "we're going to save our world."

They stood outside across the street from Steale's building and away from the watching security cameras. They waited until the taxi cab disappeared into the Manhattan night.

At Herald's apartment maybe thirty minutes before, Dani waited in the taxi while the librarian went inside. She declined to join him preferring instead to dwell upon how she betrayed the only man she really loved.

"Maybe it's for the best. Maybe this world should die," Dani said.

Herald scoffed, "I don't want to go back into the black. Being nothing. I want to remain here. In this world. I still have things to do. Books to read."

"I should have died. Why wasn't it me who died?" Dani lamented.

"You just might if you don't get your mind right. I can't do this alone. I need your help," Herald said.

"What can we do?" she asked. "All this running around is silly."

"We have to get to Steale. We need to talk to him. Reason with him."

Dani laughed a little too loudly.

"Let's not end up attracting unwanted attention, please," he said.

"I've seen him. I've talked to him. Steale's only a man. What you're talking about... What we're fighting against, is the domain of gods."

"No, he isn't a man. He only looks like one. He probably thinks he is one. But it's just a facade. Like the one I have, and you have but have forgotten about. He was the first of the living things in this Universe. It was his mind that created all this."

A cold breeze shot down the corridor between buildings. It rustled the leaves of the trees in the park behind them.

"Why would God need a man to create any of this?" Dani asked.

"The mind of the Creator is beyond me. But, if I were to posit a reason, it would be the imperfections in living things. Even the great masters left flaws in their art. But those flaws make it beautiful all the same. Maybe God just wants to be entertained by a master's art?"

Dani wrapped her arms around her chest. Even with a sweater, the cold was bitter.

"At any rate, we need to convince Steale to continue making this world and all the others. He has stopped for many, many years and the unformed grew restless. Too restless. Until renewing the cycle was all that was left for them. Almost a petty revenge."

"Will Steale understand?"

"I don't know," Herald said. "He's been lost to his own fantasy for a long time."

Herald pointed toward Steale's building and the window separating the lobby from the outside. The doorman was comfortably behind the locked, glass doors with the security guards sitting at the front desk.

"We have to get in there. Any ideas?"

"Me?! I'm no cat-burglar," Dani quipped.

Herald looked down at his feet and scratched his head. It looked to Dani as if he was struggling with himself. After a few moments of kicking at the sidewalk, he raised his head.

"I can revert to my original form. I will be completely amorphous. I won't like it, but I'll do it. It will also take time for me to reform. You will be on your own during that period. You alone will need to do what needs to be done."

"Me?"

"There will only be you. It could be for a short time, or it could be for forever... But I can get into the building and disable all the security. Then, you walk in and head to the seventh floor. His number is 13. I will enter the elevator with you. I will open his door. What happens then is dependent on how good you are at convincing an elemental creature to do its job. To do that —"

Herald looked at her. His discomfort was apparent. Raising his arm, he showed her the black undulating matter just below his skin.

"It's happening before I wanted it to. Sorry."

"What do I tell him?!" she asked.

"I... Will... Be—ack!"

The librarian's skin ripped apart starting with his face. He turned inside out. What was left of him was a shade. A black pulsing shadow.

Dani's stomach churned. It was a disturbing display to see a flesh and blood man inverting, but she did not turn away.

Instead, she stared at Herald's shade. It was at once there and not. It rippled like a black sheet in the breeze. She reached out. But she did not touch it. Before her finger met its surface, it bolted away and across the street.

Before she followed, Dani looked both ways. She felt the need to be cautious. There were only a few cars on the streets at this time of morning. It was safe, and she crossed.

Herald's shade waited for her. It nestled up against the dark side of the building—away from the light and the windows. Dani could see it, but barely. She wondered if the doorman and guards would. There were cameras pointed every which way around the entrance. If they did see it crossing, their behavior betrayed no concern. The guards continued to sit at their consoles studying the screens like they had since she and Herald began studying them.

As soon as Dani touched foot on the sidewalk, the shade glided toward the window. It shimmered through the glass like the ripples of a pebble dropped into a pond.

From the moment Herald's shade appeared to them, it was clear that the men inside the lobby did not understand what was happening. One security guard tried to get to his feet while the other grabbed his walkie-talkie. Before either completed their action, the shade expanded like smoke engulfing them, and the doorman and then the entire lobby.

The lobby became a glass container filled with smoke.

When the shade condensed, it was a writhing ball of void leaving the men seated in their chairs, slumped over, staring straight forward with dead eyes.

Herald tried reforming into himself and was only partially successful. An arm. A leg. Part of his head protruded from the floating dark sphere. All were enough to allow him to open the door for Dani.

She quickly moved inside. The men's staring eyes stopped her.

"I didn't kill them. If that's what you're thinking," Herald's voice emanated from the shimmering dark cloud. "They are... comatose."

"Oh," Dani said.

She moved away from them not quite believing Herald.

The shade glided to the elevator and pressed the call button.

"Hurry. Quickly," the shade said.

His head had disappeared again back into the inky cloud.

The elevator chime sounded. Its door slid open. Dani rushed inside, and the shade followed. She could not help but slide into the corner of the elevator as far away from it as possible.

A tendril shot out of the cloud. It activated the button for Steale's floor, floor seven.

The shade began to shudder and undulate more rapidly. The Herald cloud let out a long moan. It became the shape of a man. And just as his skin appeared to rip apart when he was unforming, his skin encircled the shade in reverse fashion joining at the seam.

"I'm sorry about that," he said. "It takes time to gather the energy to come back together."

Dani's fear faded upon seeing Herald once more as himself.

"Welcome back," she said.

"Yes. Yes. Believe me. I don't like doing it. I very much prefer my human form. It feels right," he said.

"What's it like being that other thing?"

He thought for a moment while the elevator continued to rise.

"I lose myself. I'm just a whisper inside a vast sea of darkness. Somehow, I am able to see and affect the world. Like I just did. I can't really explain it."

"I'm sorry," Dani said.

"Don't be. It was good that I did revert to my unform. I heard a new voice. A very strong voice in the darkness."

"Whose voice?" she asked.

The doors of the elevator slid open to the seventh floor. Dani moved forward.

"It was Shannon's voice."

She stopped.

"What?"

"Come," Herald said.

He put a hand in the small of her back. The librarian pushed her out of the elevator.

"I shouldn't have told you."

"Explain to me exactly what you mean, James."

"Let's take care of Steale first, please. We have to remain focused."

"We have to remain focused?" Dani raised her voice. She was loud enough for Herald to try to shush her. "Explain to me exactly what you heard. Because, we left my husband dying in the damn trash. Remember?"

"Need I remind you that if you wake the neighbors, and they call the police, that we will lose the opportunity to save everything?"

"I'm not so sure I'm interested in saving this world."

Overcome with fatigue, Herald leaned on his forearm against the wall of the hallway. The doors of the elevator closed with a pleasant chime that freed him from his pain.

"I'm waiting," Dani said.

"He's alive."

The world rippled like a cloth in the wind. Dani felt it. The nausea it induced made her retch, but Herald was sent to the hallway floor by its magnitude.

"What was that?" Dani asked.

She helped him to his feet.

"Your husband. He sent a warning. He's coming," Herald said.

It took a moment for his breathing to normalize.

"Sent a warning? Shannon?"

"That was a show of force. Something he knew I would feel. And apparently, you did, too. Quickly."

Herald let Dani prop him up while they searched for number 13. He felt lighter and weaker against her shoulder than she had ever noticed before.

"Why? Why send him? What does that mean? I thought Steale was the problem?" Dani's mind was racing. "If he's coming, he's coming for me."

"Steale *was* the source of the Universe," Herald said. "Maybe not anymore."

"Who? Who is sending Shannon?"

Dani let her fear go. She resigned herself to confronting Shannon again. Very much alive. Very much angry at her and quite possibly homicidal.

"Who?" she implored.

"I have my suspicions... Your mother is with him," James said in a breathy whisper.

They stopped. Not only because they had found apartment 13, but because Dani could not understand Herald's last revelation.

"My mother?" Dani said. "I guess I shouldn't be surprised. What does that mean?"

"I don't know. Except perhaps that we should expect the unexpected."

James shifted his weight and allowed Dani to move out from under him. He held himself against the apartment's door jamb. His breathing was steady but measured. Dani knew what was coming next would not be pleasant for him. Closing his eyes, Herald placed a hand on the door just below the numbers.

"What do we do now? Knock?" she asked.

"That's always the way to maintain the element of surprise," Herald said. He tried to smile underlining his attempt at humor, but that faded quickly.

Wincing in pain, Herald forced his fingers to become black and liquid. The pain grew in intensity and erupted in a grimace across his face. But, his unformed fingers coursed through the wood of the door.

Dani watched them undulate then recede into fingers again.

"He's here. He's drunk. I can open the door, and we can wait until he awakens. Or, we can wake him ourselves. That's the best course of action in my estimation. It gives us a chance before Shannon arrives."

"How long do we have before he gets here?" she asked.

"Ten minutes. Maybe less."

"What are we waiting for? Do your black magic."

Ignoring the pain, Herald's fingertips turned black, again, and squeezed through the door's solid matter. They heard the deadbolt snap open and the lock chain fall from its slide holder. Done, the librarian pulled his hand away from the door. It was a human hand again.

"Ready?" James asked.

"Not really," she said. "But, let's go."

Before Herald could, Dani grabbed the door knob, twisted it and pushed the door open. Hot, almost scalding hot, air rushed out toward them from inside. It smelled of smoke from a wood fire.

Dani gave Herald a questioning glance.

"He's asleep. I sensed nothing else."

Dani peered inside, and then, after mustering her bravery, stepped carefully across the threshold. She expected something to reach out and grab her from the hot, smoky darkness. But, nothing happened.

Herald followed stepping closely behind her. He shut the door and dead bolted it making sure to reattach the chain.

"It won't hold out long against Shannon's power, but seconds may be important." He whispered, "He's in there."

James pointed out into the dark room past the foyer.

"Shannon's power?" Dani said.

"Oh, yes."

"Wonderful."

Occasionally breaking the darkness, Dani could see the light of flames dancing off the room. She trod lightly, and nearing the room, she heard dual growls and stopped.

Barely controlling her fright, Dani whispered, "I thought you said there was nothing else here."

"It's just him. That's all I could see," James stammered. "There was nothing else!"

Her heart racing, Dani leaned in and scanned inside the room. A large mirror hung over the fireplace. It caught her eye. In it, she could see the lone chair was occupied by the author. Steale, asleep, sat slumped over in it. At the sides of his chair, four unblinking eyes glinted by the shimmering firelight.

"Dogs," she whispered.

"Oh, I see them now."

Bristling and undulating, the dogs' fur alarmed Dani. She pointed.

"What's wrong with them?" she asked.

Herald followed her finger. He shook his head in recognition.

"They are unformed. Caught midway."

"Can you disappear them?"

At the suggestion, James concentrated. His eyes became black pools. But before long, he broke off as if stung.

"They are his. And his alone."

"What do you mean?"

"Steale has made them. His ownership of their creation is ultimate. I can do nothing to them."

The animals growled.

Dani took a small step forward testing their obvious hostility.

The dog closest to them rose on its haunches. It sniffed at her and eyed her with suspicion, unblinking. It bared its glistening teeth to add more peril to its warning.

Dani took a deep breath. She let her fear fall away. She knew what she had to try.

Dropping to one knee, Dani held out her hand curled at the wrist—just as she would meeting any new dog. She hoped that these animals obeyed the rules of this world, the one that Steale created, and acted like normal dogs would.

"What are you doing?" Herald asked. Now, his panic was out of control. "Get up! It will kill you."

She held fast.

Suspicious of Dani, the dog stood slowly. It sniffed the air pointing its snout at the woman. The other Doberman, noticing the actions of its twin, lifted itself up on its forelegs, curious.

"It's okay," Dani said in her best baby voice. "C'mere, boy. I'm a nice person. You'll really like me."

"And if it doesn't?" Herald said through a clenched jaw.

"Let's hope it's quick."

The black dog took one slow step toward Dani's hand. It continued to sniff the air. Wary of her, its black eyes darted from her hand to her face and back again.

"You can do it. Good dog. That's a good dog."

Dani felt its hot breath on her hand before she felt the dog's cold, wet nose on her fingers. It snorted, breathing in her scent, tasting it, judging her. The dog considered her for what was an almost interminable moment. She was sure she was going to feel its sharp incisors tearing into her hand.

Instead, the warm stickiness on her fingers was the animal's wet tongue lapping her skin.

Herald sighed in relief.

"They like me," Dani said.

Both dogs sidled up against her hoping for a scratch, a pet, any affection. Allowing herself to smile for the first time that morning, Dani obliged the animals. It was the first normal thing she had done in days. It was a simple action that comforted her as much as them.

James reached out to the black dogs, too. The dogs didn't mind his reluctant strokes, either. They were quite loving to them both.

"Are these dogs him?" Dani asked. "Are we dealing with him?"

Herald considered the idea.

"If they are him, then so am I. So are you. Truth is, this world is a reflection of him."

"Is he a god?"

"No. A tool of God, perhaps."

Their conversation was cut short. Another wave curled the fabric of reality. Dani dropped to her knees. James wavered between his human and shade forms, his bones surrounded by a smokey outline. The dogs cowered and seemed to fade out of existence then back again. The fire in the fireplace pulsated, alight and not.

"I do know, we will soon be dealing with the devil," James said after retching and pulling himself up from the floor.

The dogs whimpered and returned to Steale's side.

"Shannon?" Dani asked.

Herald shook his head, yes.

"That was him."

"Is Shannon with us?" she said.

Herald looked at her sadly.

"I don't believe so."

Dani stood.

"Wake him. If he's controlling this, he's our only chance to stop Shannon from doing whatever it is he's doing."

"I'm not sure that's a good idea," James said. "Honestly, I don't know what to do."

The librarian was more frightened than Dani had ever seen him.

"I don't think I can keep myself together for very much longer." Dani grabbed his shoulders.

"Stay with me. I can't do this alone. You said so yourself."

James started to blubber, "I-I-I-will-try!"

Dani released Herald. He was shaking, almost in a seizure.

She turned to Steale. Dani knelt down next to the sleeping author. His head laid across his shoulder. A small stream of drool pooled and then dropped from his lips onto a dark, wet patch on his shirt. Slow and steady, his chest rose and fell. His sleep was peaceful in the face of the apocalypse.

She took Steale's limp head in her hands. Holding it upright, Dani studied him for signs of life.

The whole room shook again. The building bowed with the power of another wave. With a crack, the mirror above the fireplace split in two, but its frame held it from crashing down on top of them. The dogs whined, almost entirely fading out of existence. Furniture shifted. Artwork, glasses and books were knocked from the shelves. The things that could break, broke and scattered across the floor.

Dani shielded Steale from any falling items and was lucky to have not been hit. Herald, writhing in agony, was not so lucky. He was pelted and slashed by debris.

"I think the whole world felt that one," Herald said. "He's here. We are out of time."

"Damn you, Steale. Wake up!"

Dani shook him by the shoulders, but the man remained unconscious.

"It's not working! He won't wake."

"Strike him. Beat him," Herald said. "As hard as you possibly can! Oh no..."

The librarian held up a hand. It bubbled and ruptured. Herald's body was dissolving. The left side of his head drooped horribly.

"James?! What's happening to you?"

"Wake him, Dani! Hurry!"

A black tendril erupted from Herald's pulsating chest. It probed the air, a horrible, undulating snake. What was left of his melting face looked in terror at the tendril. He squealed trying to talk, but he emitted only the sounds of a wounded, dying animal.

He grabbed at the tendril with his melting hands. The serpent turned and snapped away his arms. It circled around the librarian until it squeezed him into black liquid that spilled across the floor.

Dani and the dogs backed away from the black, bubbling liquid. What was once her friend was an oozing puddle. She watched it congeal, reforming into the black serpentine tendril.

The tendril uncurled and returned its dead-eyed sights on her. With all her strength, she reached down and heaved Steale out of the chair.

The serpent reared to strike. It opened its jaws revealing two rows of long, sharp fangs that Dani was sure could both deliver poison and rip flesh.

The Dobermans circled the snake opposite each other. They issued low guttural warning growls.

The snake hissed its own warning.

Both dogs launched into an attack!

The animals were a swirl of teeth and black matter.

Dani dragged Steale into the next room away from the fighting creatures. It was the author's library. In its center was an antique oak writing desk. Despite the earthquake like waves, the shelves on the walls were still lined with books. She slammed the doors shut and pushed over the free-standing cabinet to block the doors from opening.

Boom!

Space and time were rocked more violently than ever before. The wrinkle in the fabric of reality rippled through everything. Dani was knocked onto the floor by the force of it, missing the corner of the large oak desk, but just barely. She rolled over onto her back. Steale was on the floor opposite her.

Steale was, himself, rolling onto his side.

The dogs were still barking in the other room. They were growing louder and more vicious.

"Jesus Christ," Steale whispered.

"Steale?" Dani said. "Get up! You need to help me!"

Coughing, the author regarded her with alarm and curiosity, unasked questions moved across his face. Then, he gave them voice.

"Who the fuck are you? What the hell are you doing in my house?"

Dani was frantic, and she tried to tamp down on it. She knew she wasn't helping her cause acting crazy even though the situation was insane on its face.

"My husband is here. Shannon... Shannon McClarty... You created him. You wrote him in your book."

Steale studied Dani's face carefully. Recognition grew in his eyes.

"It's you! Get out of my fucking house. Get the hell out! Get out, or I will call the cops!"

An explosion rocked the apartment. Localized, it wasn't a tear in reality and left Dani and Steale unharmed. Debris, however, impacted the closed library doors in successive pops and thuds.

Steale backed up against his oak desk, frightened.

"The dogs?" Dani said. "Do you hear the dogs?"

There was no more barking.

"What the hell is happening? Where's my phone?" Steale said.

The author searched his desk.

"The cops can't help us. You're the only help we have," Dani said.

"What the hell are you talking about?"

Dani hung her head. She wished Herald was there with her. He could've explained things. Now, the fate of the world rested with her. It was a task she felt entirely inadequate for.

"I don't understand it, myself. But you are why this is all

happening," she said, finally.

"This is some bullshit."

In a rage, Steale scattered the items on his desk.

Bang!

The doors to the library rocked against a powerful blow. Steale and Dani turned toward them, fear in their eyes. Distracted from her own fright, she was surprised that the author of their reality could be so scared.

"Dani, honey, I'm home!" Shannon's voice was sharp and clear even through the thick library doors. "I know you're in there."

Dani, wheeling around from the doors, locked eyes with Steale.

"Herald said you needed to remember your work. To remember who you are. What you are meant to do."

"What work?"

She grabbed him by the collar.

"Remember, damn it! Write it!"

Steale stared at Dani. In his eyes, she was a strange, desperate, insane woman. Yet, there was something in what she was saying.

"This is your world. You're the author of it. Finish creating your world. If you don't, my husband—out there—will remake it. Killing us all!"

The library doors creaked against the overturned cabinet that Dani used as a blockade.

"Dani dear, will you please open up. I'm appalled by the mess out here," Carol Strauss, Dani's mother, purred from behind the blocked doors. "This really could be a nice place if someone cleaned up around here."

"Mom?"

"Yes, dear, open up. Mommy's home. Let's not bicker. Come give your loving mother a big hug."

Her mother's voice was so inviting. Dani very much wanted to open the door.

To see Carol.

To be with Shannon once again.

Dani moved to the cabinet, but Steale caught her. His face was blank with confusion.

"Wait," he whispered. "Don't."

"I wanted to see them," she said. There was weakness in her voice and shame. "Oh my God. What am I doing?"

"Help me understand," Steale said.

She whispered, "Write it down. Your ending."

"What do you mean my ending?" Steale asked.

"This is your book. What is happening this very minute, is your book. *The Faceless Men* is happening right now. Go past the end pages. Write a new ending. Save us. Save all of us."

Steale smiled and laughed.

"A book is a book. Nothing more."

"If you believe that, you've killed us."

The author studied her face. Her earnestness was stone. It was convincing.

"You left me to die! We could've escaped. But you chose him!" Shannon screamed through the closed doors.

Thunder!

Reality stretched and distorted in another wave of destruction. Dani flew against the shelving. She pulled herself upright.

In front of her, the wave had stopped at Steale. He held a hand up. It was inches from his flesh and surrounded him, but did not touch him. It rippled then dissipated.

The author looked at Dani, his mouth agape.

"I told you," Dani said. "Find that book!"

Steale shook his head, yes. He rushed to the bookshelves on the far wall. His finger flicked along hundreds of spines.

"Where is it?!" he asked. "Where is it?!"

Fear rose in Dani. Her mother and husband had grown very silent on the other side of the doors. *Had Shannon figured out that Steale stopped his attack?*

She pressed herself against the door, listening with one ear. Silence.

"Mom, you still there?" she called out meekly.

Softly, her mother said, "I'm here, little girl. Let Mama in, and we can talk about everything. We can make this right."

"Where's Shannon?" Dani asked.

"Him? Oh, he's such a bad boy. I wouldn't worry your pretty head about him. The worst husband I could have wished for you."

Steale pulled out a book at the very end of the rows and rows of books.

"Found it!" he whispered to Dani.

She smiled and nodded to Steale.

Placing it on his desk, he quickly flitted through pages to the end of the book. He motioned for her to join him.

"Here… Here we go," he whispered. His finger traced the words on the page. "Your mom just tell you she wished a better husband for you?"

"Yes," Dani replied. "Something like that."

"This is where we are!"

Steale began to read, but to Dani's eyes the words on the page appeared only after he read them.

> " 'Shannon, his eyes filled with hatred, returned from the living room. There, he found a screwdriver and hammer. One swing, and the bottom hinge of the door pushed free.' "

Bang!

They heard the impact of Shannon's swing and the rod of the door hinge fall onto the floor with a metal ping.

"No, don't read it! Write what you want. They can't control this world. You can," Dani pleaded with Steale.

The author was overcome with confusion.

"This is what I wrote. I can't change it."

Bang!

Another rod was free with a ping.

"I don't know how to do this," he said. Steale searched the pages at the end of the novel.

*" 'They watched as he peeled the door from its hinges—'
"*

Dani and Steale turned to see the door on the right side of the library entrance fall. Shannon pushed it away.

"We made it, baby," Shannon screamed.

He kicked the downed cabinet out of his way. It shattered against Steale's desk with the force of Shannon's strength. Steale fell back into his desk chair.

Dodging the shattered furniture, Dani rushed to Shannon.

"Please, Shannon, no!"

He looked at Dani with pity in his eyes.

"When death came for me, you were the last thing I held on to. Will I be the last thing you think about, Dani?"

The sculptor, without a shred of attachment, pushed his wife away, discarding her like a shard chipped off a stone. He walked around Steale's desk.

"Shannon, please, don't do this!" Dani pleaded.

"I know you," the writer said to Shannon.

Steale raised himself up from his chair. The men stood opposing each other. The older man, who once was strong, was weak against the power and youth of the other.

Carol peered out from behind the remaining door and gleefully waved at her daughter. She held up a full cocktail glass, sipped from it and raised her eyebrows playfully.

"This is going to be fun," Carol said, winking at Dani.

Shannon held his arms out wide.

"It's time," he said.

"What do you want from me?" the author asked.

Shannon wrapped his arms around the man in a powerful, but not unkind embrace.

"A beginning."

Steale dropped the novel onto the floor. It's pages fanned out, open to the world.

A blinding white hot light exploded from the pages.
Dani screamed, but it was lost to eternity.

EPILOGUE

The sculptor pounded against the rock with his hammer and chisel. The blazing hot suns had sapped his strength for the day. He had been working since morning.

He paused and drank the cool water from the cup that he kept in the shade.

The animal brushed against his leg. It's fur tickled him.

She was a curious and clever animal and gave him much amusement.

Her growl meant she was thirsty. She was always thirsty.

He poured water into her bowl, and she lapped it up happily.

"Drink, Carol," he said.

He liked that name for her.

The little feathered herald of the evening flitted down under his canopy. It sang a pleasant song.

He rewarded his little friend with a cool drink, as well.

Returning to his work, he looked down at the face that was slowly appearing from the stone, he wanted to continue.

The softness of the forming lips and the sad beauty of her eyes reminded him of... He could not quite remember.

She was the most beautiful creature he had ever seen. She stirred something inside him.

He didn't just want to continue. He was compelled to continue.

His longing for true companionship had grown too great as to be almost unbearable. The creatures he created thus far were beautiful and filled the world with wonderment.

But, they were not enough.

Steel hammer to chisel, he would birth her into this world.

He would breathe life into her, the face in the stone, like he had done to so many others.

Yet, she would be his and his alone.

THANK YOU

We appreciate all our readers and strive to give them the highest quality reading entertainment.
Please, visit xynobooks.com for more exciting new releases coming soon.

ABOUT THE AUTHOR

Russ Barnes

Having worked for decades in Hollywood, doing just about every job there is in that town, he writes novels in his spare time.

Follow him at @russbarnes33 on Twitter.

PAPERBACK

a novel

Russ Barnes

www.ingramcontent.com/pod-product-compliance
Lightning Source LLC
Chambersburg PA
CBHW070736180626
46818CB00007B/2874